No Reason

Laurence Ference

Copyright © 2023 Laurence Ference
All rights reserved
First Edition

PAGE PUBLISHING
Conneaut Lake, PA

First originally published by Page Publishing 2023

ISBN 979-8-88960-501-0 (pbk)
ISBN 979-8-88960-509-6 (digital)

Printed in the United States of America

To my wife Joann and my three adult children—Stephen, Scott and Karen.

Life has, and will always offer twists and turns, but may the paths you choose be as clear to follow as tracks in the newly fallen snow!

Chapter 1

It began as most all other workdays. Up at 6:30 a.m., wash and dress, consume two pieces of toast, and swallow a glass of orange juice. Then brush the teeth and race out the door, only to endure the almost-hour-long drive to work, shooting for an arrival by 8:00 a.m. There were of course days when that didn't all come together. Maybe an accident on I-84 in Connecticut, heavy fog, or in winter, almost any amount of snowfall might bring traveling to a crawl or complete halt. But on this particular day, it all worked.

The date was September 11, 2001, a nondescript Tuesday. It was just another day—it followed a routine Monday that might have been used to drive into New York City as a favor to a part-time employer who wanted a ride to the city. But having an aversion to city life in general, the thinking was to merely go to work as usual and pass up the chance to see the sights—the Empire State Building, Statue of Liberty, and the Twin Towers, along with streets littered with garbage where people lived one on top of another—and somehow seemed to enjoy it.

With work beginning at eight o'clock, the first order of business was to pour a cup of coffee. The next item of business was to pour through the mountain of paperwork that accumulated each day on the desk. It wasn't that it was disorganized; it was more like organized chaos. If anyone else tried to find a particular piece of paper on the desk or in the office for that matter, good luck. But the president of the company knew that any time he needed information on whatever he was looking for, it could be found usually within a minute or two by me. As long as that kept happening, there was no need to file, organize, and mandate having a clean desk by nightfall.

At about eight fifty on that Tuesday, the mail room guy came into the office with a quizzical look on his face. Shorty was a big dude, close to six feet four, and built like a linebacker. He had an almost constant smile, a dry sense of humor, and was quite a personality, complete with his rusty-red hair he kept in a crew cut.

"Hey, good morning. You want to come in the mail room for a minute? I have the TV on in there, and there is a news flash about a small plane hitting one of the Twin Towers in New York. Want to come see?" Shorty asked.

Not knowing if this was some elaborate prank set up by Shorty or a real news item, we both walked into the mail room. The TV was mounted up, out of the way of shelves and a desk, so we looked up into what appeared to be video of smoke coming from one of the Twin Towers. After watching TV for about a minute, it was apparent that the plane was not "small" but quite large in fact.

"Shorty, that's not a small plane. It's big, like a commercial jetliner."

"Yeah, I guess you're right," he replied.

"But how does a large jet accidentally fly into one of the Towers in New York?" I asked.

And at that point, another plane could be seen flying into the South Tower. It was United Flight 175 that crashed at 9:03 a.m.

"Oh my god. That is no accident. We are being attacked," I stated.

Shorty agreed.

The remainder of the day got progressively worse as everyone in the office took turns watching the TV and became more horrified as to what had happened and what was in fact happening. At about 10:45 a.m., gasps could be heard throughout the building as both Twin Towers began to collapse. News coverage showed people jumping from heights no one could possibly survive rather than be burned or crushed. And people on the streets had almost nowhere to go, no good hiding place to get out of all the debris, dust and filth raining down on them. That was not to mention the first responders who all were trying to go against the tide of humanity coming at them in order to help save lives, even as they put their own lives in jeopardy.

Shorty was not his smiling self the remainder of the day. Everyone at work walked the halls in somber silence, wanting to disbelieve what they had witnessed. And then there were reports of another plane crashing into the Pentagon and still another plane that somehow didn't make its commandeered destination and crashed into a cornfield somewhere in Pennsylvania. As it turned out, there were many, many heroes on that plane who refused to let hijackers keep control of the situation. There is no telling how many lives they saved at a cost of each and everyone's lives on that ill-fated flight.

So all flights in the United States were cancelled, Wall Street closed, each and every police department, the FBI, CIA, Border Patrol, sheriff's departments, and security guards were on high alert. The public became more vigilant, home protection came to the forefront of many, and gun and ammunition sales soared. Even if it was just a perception, people had to feel like they could protect themselves should some other unspeakable thing happen in their city, town, or on their street.

Across the country, citizens felt violated. How could people from another country, another culture, take the lives of innocent men, women, and children? It wasn't like anyone who was caught up in the destruction and mayhem had personally done something to warrant such an attack; instead it was indiscriminate. No one person had gone out of their way to humiliate or incite an action that would change their lives, or their country, or the world, forever. There was no "one-on-one" retribution, no "eye for an eye" for some wrongdoing. At least that would be something explainable. But this made no sense. What would happen next?

The world as we knew it changed that day. You could no longer board a plane last minute without being searched, your baggage x-rayed and searched, searched again, and have satisfactory and up-to-date identification. Security in all public places was enhanced and more and more security cameras were being installed—where they had never been before.

But as with everything else, people have short memories—or some do—and life soon went back to everyday living and existing. Up in the morning, eat a quick breakfast, out the door, go to work, go back home, eat, watch the news, and go to bed. And do it all over again, and again and...

Chapter 2

Amid the day-to-day routine of work, I had finally managed to purchase another house for myself after living in a very small (and illegal) apartment after my divorce. It was exciting having my own place once again, a yard, gardens, a garage, and a certain peacefulness. It had taken almost six years to do it after being raked over the coals by my ex-wife. Of course, I had been partially to blame as I hadn't contested the divorce in court even though she had been the one unfaithful. I had wanted my three children to feel as little of the painful process as possible, so I took whatever was thrown at me by my ex-wife's lawyer and dealt with it the best I could.

But now I was back on track! I had a house again. Sure, it needed some updating and work, but that was to be expected. So now the routine was to get up in the morning, eat my quick breakfast, drive the hour-long route to work, go to my part-time job after work, and be home by about midnight. Then I would make dinner followed by a couple hours of work sawing, hammering, fitting, or working on whatever I had planned for the house. As long as I got about three hours sleep, I was good to go again and again.

Wednesday, November 7 was a day I had been looking forward. I was due for my yearly review and felt I should be getting a needed reward for my good work and effort over the past year—and over the past fourteen years with the company.

The morning had gone smoothly, and soon after lunch, the vice president called me into his office for our meeting. I was somewhat surprised to see Cathy, our HR person, sitting in his office as I entered as I had not ever remembered having her there at any previous review. As I sat down, I sensed something was not quite right.

No Reason

Cathy was fidgeting next to me, and Dan had a noticeable smirk on his face.

Cathy and I had always gotten along well. In fact, there were times when she would pull me aside and ask for my advice and input on matters within the company as she knew I had also done some human resources work in my past. She knew she could trust me to keep everything confidential, and I was only too happy to help.

It was not like her to not make eye contact with me and appear nervous.

Dan, on the other hand, had been with the company "forever." Well-known throughout the industry, he saw himself as being better than everyone else—no matter what the program, competition, or subject might be. He was in most cases knowledgeable and effective in what he did, but his arrogance toward those he worked with did him no good. He also fancied himself a "ladies' man," though he was prematurely balding and almost but not quite pudgy. He had a good command of the language and made sure he used it to best effect when he wanted to impress—especially a good-looking lady. Dan was married to some "old money," and his wife took care of Dan like a little boy. She was seldom around his workplace, however, and almost never on a trip with him, so he could be uninhibited in his actions with other women.

On this day, Dan was all but giving himself away with his smirk. He got right to the point. "We are letting you go effective immediately," he said matter-of-factly.

"What?" I replied in disbelief. "Why? Please tell me what the problem is."

"We are rearranging some positions here, and we are eliminating yours."

I knew that was a lie and that they had no other person to do what I had been doing for the past fourteen years.

"Dan, that can't be true. What is the reason for letting me go?"

"No reason. I don't have to tell you anymore." He smirked. "We want you to pack up your things and leave as soon as possible." He sat back in his chair and glared at me.

Cathy nervously chimed in with, "C'mon, let's go to your office, and I will give you the paperwork I need you to have."

I stared at her in disbelief. My immediate thought was *Dan, you ass, you had to have known for quite some time you were going to do this to me, and you purposefully waited until after I went through with the purchase of my house before you pulled this! How am I going to afford the mortgage?*

Back in my office, Cathy looked upset and was trying to hold it together and explain the paperwork she was giving me. I half listened.

"Cathy, what the hell just happened? I can't believe this—after fourteen years? Cathy, this is my 9/11. You know what this does to me? Dan just literally flew a plane into my house and my life—and my children's lives!"

All she could manage to do was look down and away. She sniffled back her runny nose and teary eyes.

Still in disbelief, I began packing the few items I had in the office that were mine and that I wished to keep. I quickly found that my computer was locked and that I could not even send an email to anyone.

"Really, Cathy? After fourteen years of service to this company, you think I am going to blow it out of the water using my computer? If I can't email anyone in the building, I am going to take a walk and thank everyone here and say my goodbyes." I glared at Cathy and added, "And I don't need an escort!"

Everyone without exception was aghast at my being let go. There were solemn handshakes and hugs from the guys and tears and hugs from the women I had worked with so closely over the last number of years. Only the president of the company, Bill, had of course known about this for some time, and he "hoped I would be all right." I assured him that I wasn't fazed in the least and that I was already good with it! I lied, but I wasn't going to let him or Dan see how devastating this was to me.

But I did try to clarify the situation when I asked Bill why I was being let go. His answer, however, was little better than Dan's earlier response of "No reason," saying that "It was Dan's decision." What a great help that was!

No Reason

On my hour-long ride home, I reflected on my time at work, especially over the past year. Had I done anything wrong? Not that I could think of other than always show up for work and take care of all the programs of which I had been in charge. I was kind of known in the industry as "the answer man," as all of the phone calls and inquiries whether straightforward or weird were usually sent my way to answer. I was well-liked throughout the industry and began to think, *Maybe too well-liked,* as Bill was going to be retiring soon and possibly Dan wanted to solidify his hold on becoming the next president.

Then there was Laura! Dan, for a number of years, had her consult with us on various programs and events. I had felt that he had always had his roving eye on her, and I know that he had recently found out that when we could—as she lived across the country—that we had dated a few times and enjoyed each other's company. Could there really be jealousy coming from this married man? I began to think that "no reason" was looking like a lot of reasons—all about egos, manipulation, greed, and power!

Wouldn't it have been wiser to at least part ways on better terms rather than with a smirk and no explanation? How hard would it have been to feign regret and come up with some far-fetched reason for terminating my employment?

I began to think, *There are a lot of ways to get revenge, to make Dan's life hell, or worse, and to make him and whatever family he has suffer as he was making me and my family suffer.*

I had one thing in my favor, time. I was a patient person.

Chapter 3

Over the next few days and weeks, as industry executives and acquaintances called me at my home, I was told more than once that I had been "railroaded," and after many discussions, I came away with the feeling that they were right. Two themes seemed prevalent. The first was that Dan wanted to be sure he eliminated all possible competition to be the next president of the company, and because I had over the years run many extremely successful programs and events, he saw me as a threat. The second scenario was that indeed, I had crossed the line when I had dated Laura a few times and that she was "his possession." He both wanted and needed control, and he effectively "killed two birds with one stone." I also heard numerous stories on the escapades of Dan when he was traveling for business of which I had no previous knowledge.

There were many reports of inappropriate behavior, especially with women—many from within the industry. My contacts told me that because of his prestige in the industry that no one outwardly complained about his behavior, but many people talked behind closed doors of his domineering demeanor toward the opposite sex. And it didn't stop with women. He was not above bullying and insulting other men in the industry, especially it seemed if they were younger and trying to "move up the ladder" in their company. Rumor had it that in fact Dan had suggested that a few aspiring young talented men be dismissed or held back in their careers because of Dan's ego and even more so because of his greed for more power and lust for young women.

I was getting the picture that I was not the first person he had derailed from a good career, and he seemed to enjoy it. It worked for him. Five months later, Bill retired, and Dan was ushered into the president's chair by the board of directors of the company.

Through the grapevine, I found that spending in the company rose dramatically, especially for Dan when traveling or working on one of his programs. In addition, quite a few more young, good-looking ladies were hired—an amazing coincidence. These were women with little to no previous experience within the industry or with no experience whatsoever. But as eye candy, they served Dan's purposes and who knew what else?

It was difficult to give up most all contacts with the industry I had been a part of for over twenty years. I had worked for three different companies, made many friends across the country, and missed the people, work, and the money. But I had made the decision not to seek employment back in the industry and managed to make my part-time job into full time and barely scraped by paying the mortgage, alimony, and taking care of my children as I thought they should. It meant literally getting by on twenty to thirty dollars' worth of food each week and making sure I combined trips anywhere I went in order to save on gas.

Alone most of the time except when at work, I had a huge amount of time to think, plan, and plot. I still found it amazingly difficult to believe that I had been so unceremoniously let go—and for what? I would have been more than happy to keep going along in the job I had and do whatever was asked of me. I had no thoughts of getting serious with Laura or anyone else at that time, so there shouldn't have been any problems with anyone thinking I shouldn't be dating on occasion. I had lots of time to think of how all this affected my children, my ability to take care of them, and their future. The more I thought, the angrier I became.

Wild thoughts raced through my head depending on my mood. I now understood why some people did crazy things after getting fired, or splitting up with a loved one, or after breaking off a long relationship. But many times, their retribution was not just aimed at a particular person; it became much more indiscriminate and hurtful or even deadly to many.

In the news, reports were too numerous on how someone who had lost their job later went back to their former employer only to start shooting randomly at those still employed or who broke into their former girlfriend's apartment only to stab her and her new boyfriend, or a family, or friends partying or... The horrific news just didn't seem to stop. In fact, it sensationalized it and almost encouraged random acts of violence in our society.

My thoughts were different, more focused. I certainly did not want to injure or even put anyone in harm's way that didn't deserve it. I had to be clear in my mind as to the extent I was willing to go to seek my revenge. I had been tossed out like the garbage for "no reason" and had been literally left out in the cold to sink or swim while trying to keep my family from drowning. I fought. I sacrificed. I planned. I thought about the consequences, and I decided. There was no rush, no hastiness. My plan was going to be perfect, both in timing and in execution.

Chapter 4

Dan was a golfer—not much of one, but he played at it. Knowing where he golfed and when would be easy to find out, but the openness and foursomes style of play would not do for what I had in mind. Besides, I didn't even own a golf club with which to crack him over the head. There were far more intriguing and certain ways for Dan to have an accident.

Sporting Clays is a great shotgun sport that is essentially "golf with a shotgun." It is comprised of many different and unique presentations of simulating the flights of ducks, pheasants, woodcock, or grouse, as well as the occasional bunny rabbit or faster jackrabbit. Trails through woods and meadows lead shooters to various stations to confront their clay targets. At the call of "pull," each shooter, in turn, looks for their target to either cross in front of them, "spring" up from the ground, take off going away from them, float toward the shooter, or bounce along the ground. Each presentation differs from the last, even when shooting the same "bird," as wind, sunlight, or variations in the terrain all affect what the target does and how it needs to be shot. Great fun—and difficult!

So I decided. Justice would be dealt at a private gun club in Connecticut that Dan frequented quite often. I had also shot the course there many times knowing locations of each station and knowing more importantly how to approach a certain station without being seen by anyone. I had grown up in the area and knew the woods from my many days afield bird and deer hunting. Knowing just how to isolate Dan from his shooting partners would be the trick—but one that I worked out.

Dan, I knew, liked going out to shoot in the first squad if possible as that gave him more time to relax later in the comfort of the clubhouse, drink, and elaborate on stories that never seemed to end. His pride and ego was all going to help my plan.

It had been over five years since I was fired. It was summer. Leaves were in full display on trees and warmth was in the air. It would be difficult to see through the woods this time of year, except where paths had been cleared and shooting "windows" opened up for the competition.

I was in lightweight camo. It almost perfectly matched my surroundings in the woods. Station seven was a difficult presentation that simulated ducks landing in a pond. The trap which threw the clay targets that would cross and settle over the pond was located about one hundred yards from where the shooters would call for the target. This necessitated a remote button that would be pushed at the shooter's call of "pull" to activate the arm on the machine and release the target.

All had gone well for Dan and his three fellow shooters through six stations. I had been in the woods at station seven prior to the opening of the competition, waiting as the club staff had been loading the traps with targets. As the attendant finished loading the targets and moved on to station eight, I quietly moved down to the trap and gently pushed it off its location so that when the first shooter at the station called for their target, the trap would be flinging the clay bird into a tree some ten yards away.

Dan's group approached. They were all talking about the last station and how they did and were now turning their attention to this somewhat long presentation. It happened that Dan picked up the control button so that everyone could look at the presentation of the target before the first shooter made their call. He hit the button, but they saw nothing. He hit it again, but again, no bird flew by to settle into the pond.

It was decided that two of the shooters were going to see what the problem was with the trap. As I had hoped, Dan stayed behind with the remote accompanied by the one young female in the group. She was obviously a novice in the sport but obviously one Dan would love to teach of just how to shoot the wily "setting ducks."

— No Reason —

So while the two men attempted to fix the trap one hundred yards away, Dan and the young lady cajoled and touched. Then they confirmed my suspicions with kissing and fondling each other. It was a classic Dan move.

"Dan, try the button!" was the faint call from across the pond.

"What?" responded Dan.

"Try the trap," it could hardly be heard.

So as with everything in the shooting sports, safety is first and foremost. Not being able to hear what the two men were saying, Dan asked his "girlfriend" if she wouldn't mind going about halfway down to the men, so she could listen to what they were saying and relay the message.

Of course, she obliged and left through the path in the woods, leaving Dan standing alone with the remote in his hand and an erection in his pants.

Approaching Dan silently from behind, he never heard me until I was but a few yards from him in the small clearing. He turned and looked at me, but I could tell it was not yet registering with him as to who I was.

"Yes," said Dan, "are you here to fix the trap?"

"No, Dan. You don't remember me, do you?"

And the light bulb went on. "What are you doing here? Get out, you're trespassing!"

"Oh, I've come to finish our little talk we had over five years ago in your office. I've been patient, very patient, in seeking you out. I haven't only experienced the wrath of your unwarranted dismissal of me, but you had no conscience about what it would do to my family, the fact that I had just purchased a house, and had been struggling to keep everything going in the right direction. Had you talked to me like a real man, I'm sure we could have come to an agreement that would have benefitted us both. Instead, you issued your triumphant statement on why you were letting me go. 'No reason.'"

"Push the button," filtered through the woods on a melodic female voice.

"There's just two things I have to say now, and we don't have a lot of time to do it in, Dan."

He glanced at his shotgun leaning on the handcrafted rest made from natural wood from the surrounding trees. It was to the right of the other three shotguns and closest to me.

"Do you think you can really get to your gun, load it, and shoot me before I pull the trigger on mine?" I approached the gun rest and picked up his shotgun, a Beretta over and under.

Breaking the gun open, I placed one red Winchester shell in the top chamber and closed the gun. I had been sure to bring a selection of shells with me to be confident that I would have the same ammo Dan had been shooting on the day. I had green shells from Remington, maroon shells from Federal, and just to be sure to cover almost all the bases depending on who Dan might be shooting with, I had shells from Fiocchi which were violet. I had been able to see Dan's ammo pouch, which was loaded with red shells.

"You should be happy that I have given you over a five-year reprieve, Dan. After all, you never even made an attempt to help me, only wanted to ruin me. Now it's come back to haunt you. And for what? For no reason!"

The melodic female voice once again urged Dan to try the trap, and he did indeed. I could see the clay target flying across the pond and starting to settle. I pulled the trigger on his Beretta with my gloved hand and placed the barrel of the gun on the ground facing Dan. I retreated into the woods, blending in with the woodlands in a matter of seconds. There was momentary silence.

"What are you doing!" yelled the two men and young lady.

I could hear fear and consternation in their voices as the trio kept yelling at Dan to not shoot. After all, they were all downrange, and he shouldn't have been shooting at the target yet. It had only been a test. It wasn't safe!

Less than a minute later, I heard her scream and keep screaming. The sight of Dan's head almost blown off by his own gun was too much for this novice to handle. I could hear the two men trying to console her and, at the same time, pull her away from the gruesome scene.

Then I was gone, out of sight, out of earshot, and almost out of the woods and in my car.

— No Reason —

It wasn't long before I was back on I-84 headed toward the east. I was careful to stay within all of the speed limits so as not to afford any police an opportunity or reason to stop me on my way home. My entire round trip took less than four hours, and because of my living on a back road with very few neighbors, I was not missed by anyone. It had been a good day.

Of course, the next day, I read a report on the Internet of a possible suicide or shooting accident in Connecticut at a prominent gun range. State and local police were investigating the death of a local businessman who either committed suicide or accidentally shot himself with his own shotgun. No foul play was suspected as there were three "eyewitnesses" near the scene all attesting to the fact that Dan had been alone for a short time but that the three companions were nearby and would certainly have heard if anyone else had been involved.

It was a tragedy no matter what, but one that would likely be written off as an "accident" rather than put the family through any hassles that accompany the stigma of a suicide.

Weeks later, after all police investigations were completed, it was ruled that Dan had somehow tripped and fired his shotgun by accident—for there was no other reason to be found.

Chapter 5

It was mid-November and deer season had finally arrived. Hunting had been a passion all of my life, and I was especially fond of deer hunting. It was a quiet time, one that I relished being in the woods alone with only nature's animals in close proximity. There were other hunters, of course, but I managed to stay a safe distance from most of them. Only upon occasion did one stumble across my path. For the most part, when I didn't want to be seen, I wasn't. Why, I had even had a hunter one year pass in front of me on a deer trail only six yards from where I sat motionless, and he never saw me!

I thought, *How is he ever going to see a deer?*

But the animals living in the woods and fields were another story. I loved having a chickadee land on a branch but two feet from my face and hop and dance singing its name, *Chickadee-dee-dee-dee, chickadee-dee-dee-dee.* And hearing the rustle of leaves always put me on guard, waiting for a buck to emerge when in fact it was merely two gray squirrels cavorting on the ground looking for nuts and acorns and then seeing them race up a tree in what looked like a game of "catch me if you can." And chipmunks are amazing creatures. They can be as silent as the wind, or they can chirp loudly, but sitting on an old stone wall waiting on a hoped-for ten-pointer to show up could actually get you run over by one of these striped animals as they scurry in and out of the stones on the wall. What peaceful solitude.

On this opening day of the season, my goal was twofold. I wanted to put some meat on the table, but I also wanted to "visit" my old boss, Bill, from the quiet and cover of the woods. I knew just where he lived in Ridgefield, off the beaten path. He had more than a couple of acres which included his lawn, fields, and woods that surrounded his house. The terrain was of rolling hills, just right for getting close to the back of the property.

As I slowly and methodically still hunted my way toward Bill's home, I was ever vigilant for deer sign. I had been patient in seeking my revenge with Dan, and I could afford to be even more so with Bill. I moved almost silently through the trees, glancing down every few steps to be sure that I wouldn't snap a branch lying on the forest floor or kick a loose rock, of which there are many in Connecticut.

My efforts were rewarded when I came upon a good-sized deer under an apple tree. It had its back to me and head down, chewing on fallen fruit. I froze and waited. When it finally picked its head up to look around and listen, I saw that it was antlerless. Although legal, it being the first day of hunting season, I wanted to try for a buck, so I was more than content to hold my ground and merely observe the deer continue to feed. It wandered off and disappeared into the forest after about half an hour of peaceful watching on my part. It was already a great day!

Slowly picking my way through the woods once again, I soon came upon the silhouette of a large house. As I moved closer, details of the home became noticeable. I was on a small hillside overlooking about an acre of lawn, looking at large windows in the rear of the house. I could not be seen from the house as I remained a good ten yards in the woods and in shadows. But I could see clearly into the house. Again, there was no hurry. I waited.

Some two hours passed with no movement from within the house. I was, however, enjoying the peacefulness, calm, and quiet of the forest and its creatures. Chipmunks scurried over the dry leaves looking for food or possibly playing—it was hard to tell the difference. Small woodland birds of various colors flitted in and around trees, singing their individual songs. And somewhere near I could hear the machine gun-like sound of a pileated woodpecker drilling for insects in an old tree. And then there were minutes of utter silence as well. Great therapy.

Finally, I saw movement within the house. Through my Leupold Scope, I could see all that I needed. I found that my favorite setting for my scope was around eleven times as that seemed to give me the magnification I was looking for yet also gave me the ability to acquire my target easily and quickly. I estimated that the house was just under one hundred yards from my concealment.

Soon, there was movement once again within the house. I shouldered my Marlin .30-06 with which I had taken many deer at much greater distances than this and verified that the person now sitting at a desk near the window was indeed Bill. As he had done during my employment, he was writing longhand on a pad on the desk. He was old school, preferring to write on paper rather than compose on a computer. Only when he finished writing to his satisfaction did he normally then transfer his words to the computer.

The surrounding forest remained silent. Peering through the scope, I placed the crosshairs on Bill's head. It was an easy shot—nothing in the way, no wind or sun glare to worry about, and no rush. I released the safety. The first digit of my trigger finger began to squeeze the trigger until the sound was almost deafening in the still woods. The "click" of the firing pin hitting air sounded like an explosion in the quiet. I was satisfied. Knowing that I could have, maybe should have but didn't and wouldn't, had further made my day. Songbirds began to chirp once again. Bill, oblivious, kept on writing. I turned and filtered back into the woods again looking for a nice buck with at least an eight-point rack. I carefully loaded my rifle with three 150-grain Remington Ballistic Tip bullets, only one of which I hoped to need, and began my slow hunt through the forest once more, aware of every slight sound, and watching for any almost imperceptible movement.

Chapter 6

What is it with people in positions of authority that they don't realize or remember where they came from? Does ego, the feeling of power, and domination get in the way of being a down-to-earth human being with feelings for others? Does money and material things alter their thinking so much that they must deny others of any semblance of humanity? Why must those on top keep kicking to make sure no one reaches the same level they have attained, even though they may not have truly achieved that fortune? In many cases, the old saying "timing is everything" applies. Being in the right place at the right time, meeting the right person by happenstance, or even merely filling a void that no one else is filling at that time can mean the difference between someone who is truly qualified to manage a company and more importantly manage people or having someone who is totally self-centered, egotistical, and a power-hungry dictator lord over employees, their families, and other's well-being.

Our current societal state is sad. No longer can we talk about people in an honest, forthright manner because we may "offend" them. What ever happened to being up front with people? Why must we hide our feelings and observations about people, programs, or events for the sake of being nice? No one wants to live in reality anymore. Yet we have "reality shows" on TV that in truth aren't reality at all. We bring up our children to believe that there are no winners and losers. No one keeps score at their ball games anymore, and we let them play their video games ad nauseam as it keeps them busy and out of our way and promotes the thinking that there really are no consequences in life. People don't really get blown up or killed in video games. Is this teaching our society about reality? We have successfully taken the honesty out of our everyday lives. We have replaced it with superficial and artificial games that mean nothing to really be able to survive in the real world. All that we need in life seems to be at our fingertips for at the push of a button, our phones can tell us the answers. Or for even larger-than-life answers, we can always sit at our computers and laptops and see even larger pictures, videos, and assorted answers to our queries. Why think anymore? Common sense and logic seem not to be valued any longer—we only need be fast with our fingers and have a fully charged phone!

What happens when reality really does set in? Let's just say there is no electricity for a month. What happens? People run out of food within three days. Cars are useless as no one can pump gas. Trucks loaded with food cannot get to cities, towns, or anywhere. People begin to starve. They fight. They riot. They kill each other. They don't help one another as would be a far wiser endeavor. No. It's just like our working world, where everyone is out for themselves and has to be better than everyone else. Claw your way to the top—or get clawed. But we digress.

Chapter 7

Three hunting seasons flew by in the blink of the proverbial eye. Over those years, I kept working, keeping a low profile, volunteering to help coach some baseball, doing a little fishing, and trying to do a lot of hunting. I also found a lady with whom I could be myself and with whom I could have a great time. This was something of a novelty as between trying to meet women at a bar, in the supermarket, or online, meeting anyone worth even talking to was a trick. Either these women were superficial, so into themselves that they have trouble dealing with everyday life, or in the case of online dating, used a twenty-year-old photo of themselves and supplied stories about themselves that were so far from the truth that it was laughable. Not that guys didn't do the same thing I suppose—but really?

She had one son, in his early twenties. They were their own little support group. Dillon helped his mother with everything, and Liz continued to support her son as he navigated getting through college in the evenings while working a part-time job during the day. Her ex-husband had left the state after their divorce four years prior to our meeting and had basically severed all ties with his son—or Liz.

"What's Dillon doing today?" I asked after driving to Liz's apartment, walking in the front door, and giving Liz a heartfelt kiss.

Usually, he was around on a Sunday, but I hadn't seen his car in the parking lot out front.

"He apparently has a new girlfriend. But I just found out about her this week. He's been keeping her a secret for well over two months."

"Wow, that's not normally what Dillon is about," I responded.

"No. And that's what concerns me a little. Normally, he is up front about everything he does or wants to do and has never hidden his relationships from me. But…I guess there comes a time and place for everything, including leading a more private life."

"That may be true, but it still seems odd that he didn't even give you a hint about her until now. On the other hand, maybe it will give us a little more private time together."

Liz smiled and looked thoughtful. "Would that be a good thing?" she teased.

I smiled and offered one of my typically snide remarks, "Only if you want it to be."

We had planned to visit a local gun range, so I could instruct Liz about gun safety and have her practice with one or two of my handguns, beginning with a small Charter Arms .22 Pathfinder I had. Depending how she did with that, I might introduce her to my Smith & Wesson 9 mm, my everyday carry gun. Slow and easy was my teaching philosophy over the twenty-five or so years I had been a certified NRA rifle and pistol instructor. I had seen too many so-called experts get their kicks introducing females to shooting by starting with a .357 Magnum or something even bigger! I knew of no faster way to turn a new shooter off than by letting them experience the recoil of such a firearm.

I had witnessed macho-type guys roar with laughter after one of their girlfriends shot such a gun for the first time and almost lost all control of the firearm. After that, it was very difficult to get the unsuspecting female to even try shooting again, let alone allow her to become proficient at it.

And actually, it had been my experience that females, once taught correctly, would most normally be better at shooting than males. I believe this to be for a number of reasons. First females have no "macho" thoughts to overcome. They admit to not knowing about guns and shooting, and they actually pay attention to instruction. Not to mention they seem to have better hand-eye coordination than guys. Ever see a man try to thread a needle?

So off to the gun range we went, with our conversation focusing on the finer points of gun safety, including loading, unloading, aiming, proper grip, squeezing the trigger, with a little bit of instruction on breathing and body control thrown in. And after hearing

Liz more than once answer my gun safety questions accurately and without hesitation, we arrived at the range ready to put theory into practice.

I unlocked the car's trunk and picked out the two handgun cases holding the guns. I had Liz pick up the four boxes of ammo we might shoot that day, depending on how she would do and how she felt about shooting that much in one day. Of course, I was ready to step in and fire a few rounds downrange for some fun—and to possibly show off just a bit.

I had Liz read all the signs posted at the range and told her that every range was a little different and to always err on the side of caution—ask questions of range personnel and not take anything for granted. We signed in at their front desk and paid for our time in advance, also purchasing a couple of paper targets. From there we waited about ten minutes until the range official announced a "cease fire" on the line and ordered everyone shooting to unload their firearms and make them "safe." It wasn't until the range official walked up and down the firing line visually inspecting each gun on the tables that anyone was allowed to go downrange to change or check their targets.

Even though I had gone over these aspects of range safety and more with Liz, she was nevertheless impressed with the protocol set forth.

"This is amazing," she said. "If more people who don't know a darn thing about guns saw this and understood the safety procedures in place for shooters, they might have a different take on guns, their use, the fun, and the safety."

We walked over to our shooting bench and placed the ammunition and two pistol cases on top. We then walked downrange and placed our target frame in its place and taped one of the targets to it. We did the same with the other target, placing it ten yards further away. We walked back to the shooting bench and waited for all of the shooters to return from being downrange and waited for the range master's call that the range was "hot" and that we could now uncase, pick up, and load our firearms.

I proceeded to make sure that both our hearing and eye protection were in place and began loading the little .22 Pathfinder, making sure that Liz could see just how I was doing that. I then showed her how to safely unload the gun and, with cylinder open, handed her the gun to load. She did so without hesitation and looked to me when she was ready to fire downrange.

"Remember, there is almost no recoil from a .22, so don't worry about that," I instructed. "Concentrate on maintaining a solid grip, holding steady, aiming, and squeezing the trigger."

And with that, Liz took her first shot and hit her target at about three o'clock about two inches off of the bull's-eye.

"Not bad for your first shot! Now take your time and see if you can't bring your group into the center of the target," I said.

After shooting a couple full cylinders with the .22, Liz couldn't stop smiling. She had effectively brought her group into the bull's-eye of the target and was beginning to pick up a bit of speed.

"What fun!" she exclaimed. "Who knew you could get so much satisfaction from putting holes in paper seven yards away?"

"Yep, it's almost instant gratification. Keep on practicing on this target until you are thoroughly comfortable with it and then try shooting the one out at seventeen yards."

After another twelve rounds, Liz announced she was going to shoot at the farther target. I smiled with anticipation.

I was already very proud of how fast Liz had picked all this up and of how well she was doing and doing it all safely. I also laughed just a bit after she took her next six shots at the farther target and didn't do quite so well. Her group was much larger, and she was taking more time, trying to be deliberate with each shot. That was both good and bad as she was concentrating more, but by taking more time, she was also holding the gun in her outstretched arms longer and becoming more tired. All part of a huge learning curve.

I later proceeded to show her my 9 mm and how to load the clip, insert it into the gun, and pull back the slide and let it go in order to chamber the first round. She only had a bit of a problem pulling the slide back as it was stiff for someone as small as she was.

Nevertheless, she did manage to do it and proceeded to address the closer target.

Liz handled the increased recoil reasonably well and tightened her grip on the gun. Although not quite as accurate as when she shot the little .22, Liz would have still "ruined an attacker's day" had she needed to. After a half dozen clips from the S&W, I knew Liz was tiring and asked if she wanted to quit.

Her response, "Well, I don't want to, but I think I probably should at this point. I am getting a little tired, but at the same time, it feels awfully good!"

I couldn't wipe the huge grin from her face if I tried.

So it was my time to show off just a bit. I loaded my carry gun and put eight rounds in the bull's-eye at seven yards in quick fashion. Since I was on a roll, I reloaded and pushed my luck a bit, firing fairly rapidly at the target at seventeen yards. Five of my shots were center shots while the other three were scattered a little.

Liz was still impressed. I was happy. It was a good day.

Chapter 8

Just two weeks later, Dillon informed Liz that he was going to be a father! Shocked as she was, Liz held it together and feigned excitement and joy over this announcement.

"Are you okay with this, Dillon? And how is Maggie taking it? I didn't know you two were that serious. When do you think I can meet her?" Liz couldn't help blurting out all her questions at once.

"Yes, Mom, I'm fine. It will of course mean big changes to my life and probably all of our lives, but we are both willing to make the best of this. We didn't plan it—it just happened. I would like to have you meet Maggie this coming Sunday over lunch, out."

"Yes, that would work," replied Liz.

"And since you seem to be pretty serious with your beau, it would be great for him to join us, so we could all be together for a bit," Dillon added.

"That would be great. I'll let him know."

Later that evening, Liz informed me over the phone of Dillon's news and his invitation for lunch. I could tell it wasn't the way Liz had imagined first meeting Maggie, but I could tell she felt better about it because I was hopefully going to be there by her side.

I teased, "Why should I be there? She's not my family."

But the pregnant pause on the other end of the phone soon gave me to know that my joking about pregnancy and meeting with Maggie and Dillon wasn't really appreciated, so I immediately reassured Liz I would be happy to have lunch with them. There was a noticeable sigh of relief.

Sunday morning at about eleven, I rolled into Liz's parking lot. Upon knocking and entering her apartment, I was greeted by a somewhat nervous Liz—not her normal self.

"Are you ready for this?" I asked.

"As much as I can be. It will be good to put a face with a name finally. And hopefully we will immediately fall in love with her, and there will be a fairy-tale ending to all of this."

Wow, I thought, *that would be amazing.* "Well," I said instead, "let's hope that they both are living in reality and have a good handle on all of this. It wouldn't be good for them to be living in a fantasy about how this all might turn out—or what it could turn into!"

Liz gave a heavy sigh and agreed, "We can only hope."

It was twelve thirty—Liz and I were right on time for lunch. Not seeing Dillon's car in the parking lot told us that either they had not yet arrived, or they had taken Maggie's car, which neither of us knew the make or model.

We were greeted at the door by the hostess and offered seats at a table that overlooked the water. We both chose to wait to order a drink until the soon-to-be parents arrived. By one thirty, we were both thirsty and hungry. Liz could not reach Dillon on his phone. We ordered.

Just before two o'clock, Liz's phone rang. It was Dillon apologizing, saying that Maggie wasn't feeling well and that she just wasn't up to meeting us. There was no further explanation. Liz was visibly upset. After questioning her on what Dillon had said exactly, Liz revealed that she thought it very out of the ordinary that Dillon wouldn't have called earlier and given a better explanation for the apparent problem. I could only agree.

We sat. We ate slowly. We talked minimally—but we mostly wondered. *What had indeed caused the delay in our meeting Maggie? Why was Dillon so secretive about Maggie in the first place, and what exactly had happened today?* All questions going through our minds, or at least mine. Liz most likely had many more questions.

Later that evening, Dillon finally showed up at Liz's apartment. He was obviously tired and really didn't want to talk—especially with us, after what had happened earlier in the day. Liz, however, wanted none of that.

"So, young man, how is Maggie feeling, and what happened today that you couldn't even call me for a couple of hours when we were both waiting to have lunch with you and Maggie?"

"Do we have to talk about it now?" Dillon asked as he began walking away.

"If there is a problem or something I can help with, this would be a good time to let me know," Liz responded, stopping Dillon in his tracks.

He knew from the forthright question and tone in her voice that this was serious and that he would have to answer sooner rather than later.

"Mom, she just wasn't feeling well and was kind of out of it. We were waiting to see if she was going to feel better, but she wasn't. So I'm sorry I didn't call you earlier, but we really did want to have lunch with you and have everybody meet. It won't happen again, and we will set up another meeting really soon. Promise."

Liz, sensing Dillon's tiredness and half-baked excuse, decided to let him off the hook and allowed him to retreat to his room.

"I don't like the change I am seeing in Dillon," Liz whispered to me. "It's not like him to evade speaking the truth and to make excuses."

"I guess we will have to wait to see what happens and how this plays out in the next week or so. Let's see if we, or at least you, are invited for a lunch or meeting again. It could all be absolutely nothing, and we both might be making more of this than need be. Or there may in fact be trouble with this fairy tale, and we may have to lend our support to Dillon in any way we can."

Liz smiled. "Thank you for being you and wanting to help Dillon—and me." She gave me a soft kiss on the cheek. "Let's sit on the couch for a bit and watch some TV," Liz added.

She obviously didn't want me to leave yet and needed some time to allow her mind to be at ease with all that had happened or didn't happen.

We sat and were mindless together in front of the TV screen.

Chapter 9

As it happened, the next two weeks were a blur, both for me and for Liz, and apparently for Dillon as well because there was no follow-up on having lunch with or meeting Maggie. Liz seemed a bit perturbed on more than a couple of our late-night chats over the phone but, at the same time, didn't want to push Dillon too hard. I, however, began thinking that I should try to investigate the situation and see what I could find out about Maggie and for that matter Dillon with regard to their relationship and what would bind them together in a few short months.

So on a cloudy, misty evening, I sat in my car waiting for Dillon's Ford Taurus to emerge from the parking lot at Liz's apartment. I was not easy to pick out amongst the long line of parked cars on the side of the road as my black Jeep was half hidden and certainly one of hundreds like it in that part of Connecticut. My plan was to follow Dillon at a distance to see what he was up to and hopefully lead me to where Maggie lived. I had no other way of finding out her whereabouts other than asking directly, which I did not want to do. It might have simplified matters if Liz had found out Maggie's last name, but that hadn't happened either.

Finally, after almost an hour of waiting, Dillon took a left out of the parking lot. I began following at a distance. For twenty minutes, I followed Dillon through intersections, over bridges spanning the interstate, waited at traffic lights, and managed to keep him in sight until in New Haven, I got caught at a light that Dillon had gone through at yellow only to stop me at red. My fingers nervously tapped on the steering wheel while I waited and waited. Then making sure I didn't leave any rubber, I sped off to see if I could catch up to him.

I had lost Dillon! But I was now in a residential neighborhood of New Haven, so I began to travel each intersecting road in the hopes of spotting the Taurus. Three streets later, success found my efforts as I passed by Dillon's car parked in a small driveway of what looked like a two-family house. Lights were on only in the upstairs apartment, indicating that that was where Maggie lived. I noted the address and soon found an advantageous parking spot where I could observe the house and any comings and goings of Dillon, Maggie, or other people. Again, I waited.

It was a quiet neighborhood, except for the large dog (by the sound of it) that kept strangers away from its home by barking every five minutes or so. For over two hours, I listened to this watchdog until finally Dillon departed the property, alone in his car.

Having found out what I had wanted, I too was ready to leave a few minutes later when two men walked down the sidewalk and turned into the two-family driveway. They proceeded up the side stairway that Dillon had just used earlier. I was very interested.

After waiting at Maggie's door for about half a minute, the door opened, and the two men entered. I was intrigued. What were these two doing there almost immediately after Dillon had left? I didn't know, but it only took about two minutes before the two left the apartment. I could see them better now walking down the stairs facing me with the stairway light on above them. One man was Black with a knit hat over his head and dark-black leather jacket and black pants. Not too tall, maybe five feet ten, and of slight build. The other was White, a bit taller and larger. His blue jeans were covered partially by a long dark overcoat which swung back and forth as he walked, it not being buttoned.

The duo walked back the way they had come, soon disappearing into the mist and the night. I waited another five minutes and pulled out onto the street, rolling slowly past the apartment.

This just might get interesting, I thought.

Chapter 10

My first reaction was to tell Liz what I had seen. Common sense prevailed, however, as Liz would see it as a total invasion of privacy. After all, I wasn't a real part of this soon-to-be family, just an interested observer. Besides, at this point, what did I really know? Not much!

I did know where Maggie lived—and that was a good thing. But as far as who the two men were that arrived shortly after Dillon had left Maggie's apartment, for all I knew, they could have been Jehovah's Witnesses who gave their spiel to Maggie and were then ushered away. Instead, I would have to set up surveillance again to see if I could find out more.

Armed with a meatball, sausage, and onion pizza from my favorite pizza joint, I once again parked in an advantageous spot near Maggie's apartment where I could observe—but not be conspicuous. It was two nights later than my first stakeout, and this time I came prepared for the long haul. I wanted to see how much activity there was in and around Maggie's apartment and was willing to stay until at least her lights went out. Maybe a bit longer.

It didn't take long for things to start happening. Dillon drove up at 6:00 p.m. and entered Maggie's apartment. Although one of her windows was open a bit, I was too far away to hear any of their conversation, but after about five minutes, I could hear that the decibel level coming from the apartment had increased noticeably. I no longer considered this normal conversation.

About ten minutes later, Dillon exited the apartment with an exclamation of slamming the door. He appeared to be very unhappy with whatever had happened between him and Maggie as he literally flew down the stairs and jumped into his car. A small part of the road was repaved with a bit of rubber.

A half hour later, a shiny new black Audi parked in front of Maggie's. Totally out of place for this area. I watched and waited. A minute or two later, a young woman emerged from the apartment—I assumed it was Maggie. She opened the rear passenger side door and climbed in. The Audi departed, and although it had tinted windows, I could make out the silhouettes of three people—the driver and two in the back seat, one of which was obviously the woman I believed to be Maggie. I sat tight.

My patience was rewarded about fifteen minutes later when the Audi again pulled up to the apartment. After a brief stop on the road, the young woman exited the car and entered the second-story apartment while the car drove away. Lights went on, and I was back in surveillance mode.

I waited—but not for too long. Soon after, my two friends showed up once again. Same look, same direction, same timing. They stayed only a few minutes and left the same way they had come.

About a half hour later, it was like a parade had begun! One by one, and sometimes two and three people, began to knock on Maggie's door, enter, and leave after only a minute or two. Most were walkers, but every now and then, a car would drive up, park, remain long enough only to allow the occupants to enter Maggie's for a brief time, and then leave. By 11:00 p.m., there were no more visitors, and shortly thereafter her lights were turned out. Nevertheless, I remained vigilant until midnight when the local police drove by. I lay in my Jeep out of sight as they drove past and waited until they turned the corner before I drove away.

I had learned a lot that evening. Although I couldn't know for sure what was happening, I had a pretty good gut feeling. It didn't bode well for Dillon, Maggie, or their baby—or for Liz. More information was needed.

Chapter 11

The following weekend, I stopped to pick up Liz and go out for a bite to eat. As I had not seen or talked with Dillon for quite some time, I was pleasantly surprised to see him at home with his mother.

"How are you doing, Dillon?"

"Not too bad, and yourself?" he replied.

"I'm well," I stated. "How is your girlfriend doing? And I hope all is well with her pregnancy."

"She's okay and so is the baby."

"Good, good. By the way, I've been meaning to ask what she does for a living."

Dillon looked a bit sheepish at my asking only to reply, "Well, right now she is not working and most likely won't get a job until after the baby is born."

I decided to push just a bit further, asking, "Well then, how does she support herself? Does she have money, or does she have some kind of income from some other source?" I could tell I had reached the edge of what I could or should ask at this point.

But still, Dillon replied, "I think she is getting some unemployment, and she has a little side business going on that she makes a few bucks at."

"Oh, great! What's the side business?"

"She does some kind of consulting for some people" was the hastily put-together response to my question. "Anyway, I have to run some errands and am going to see Maggie. It was good to see you again." And Dillon was gone.

After greeting Liz with a kiss, she acknowledged that I had gotten about the same information out of Dillon as she had so far. I could see the concern in her face and knew she was not yet happy about this chapter in Dillon's life.

"It does seem that Dillon is being a bit evasive about this relationship and what exactly is going on," I stated. "And I'm very concerned about you and what it is doing to you on the inside."

"Well, thanks, but I'm sure this will all work out, and we will all get back to a more normal routine. I actually did speak with Dillon today about finally meeting Maggie, and he said he would try to set something up in the next week. It would make me feel a lot better if I could just meet her. And I hope we can both meet her in fact."

My mind raced to keep ahead of my mouth. I didn't want to say something I shouldn't, and I didn't want to let on that I knew more about Maggie than Liz did. Or at least I thought I knew more, but what did I really know? I didn't know yet!

Our "bite to eat" turned out to be more of a "silence is golden" routine. Liz uttered mostly one- or two-word answers to any questions I asked about the last few days and became even more quiet upon bringing up the subject of Dillon, Maggie, and the baby. I could tell that that was all Liz was thinking about but obviously didn't want to go as far as verbalizing about it. Liz was trying to get it all figured out in her head before she would allow herself to get into a deep conversation about it with me—or anyone else for that matter.

So we mostly sat in silence across from each other. I watched as she dipped her french fries in ketchup and mindlessly chewed her cheeseburger so well that I thought her enzymes in her stomach wouldn't have much to do to break down her meal.

The drive back to Liz's place remained quiet. It was only upon parking the car that Liz thanked me for dinner and apologized for being so pensive.

"I'm really sorry I wasn't very communicative tonight, but I was thinking about Dillon. I really hope we can meet Maggie soon, and I will feel much better, I'm sure. Right now I am exhausted from worry and just want to go in and go to bed."

So with that said, we gave each other a peck on the cheek, and I watched Liz enter her apartment and close the door behind her. Another exciting night!

Chapter 12

Work seemed to just keep happening. The routine of getting up each morning, eating a quick breakfast, going to work at a job that each day became more unfulfilling, going home, and collapsing either from physical or mental anguish or from pure boredom was becoming more the norm than I ever wanted. I was starting to consider my options. And there were many.

Would just changing jobs do the trick? Or had Liz and I become so humdrum together that there was little to no excitement in the relationship, or had Dillon's situation merely interfered with our time together, and would it eventually recover and get better? Should I venture into starting my own business and pour myself into that for at least five years in order to make it viable and a success? None of these options really struck me as one I should go for. There were no guarantees that any one of these paths wouldn't lead me to where I was already going. So why not just stay on track and not rock any boats and keep doing the same things day in and day out?

As easy as it would be to keep doing what I was doing every day, the more I thought about it, the more unsettled I became. No, none of my options were going to be the right ones for my future. Instead, I was becoming more aware that I needed a real change, one that would include leaving my job, leaving the people and friends I knew, and leaving Connecticut. It was something to consider. I needed to think of the pros and cons to such a move, what it would mean to me, to others, to my family. And where would I most like to be? Europe or Asia didn't strike me as an option—I had yet to ever "cross the pond" and that it seemed would be too radical a move. Neither did South America or Mexico intrigue me at all. I had visited Mexico briefly but really didn't find life there to my liking. I had encountered lots of impoverished people who quite frankly had trouble putting food on the table, but who apparently still gave a good portion of what they did have to their local church as some of the churches I had seen were ornate facilities that stood out from the remainder of the surrounding towns.

As far as moving within the United States, while I certainly hadn't seen it all, there were parts of it to which I might consider moving. Tucson was nice—not too large a city, and in about fifteen minutes, you could be in the mountains and beautiful desert regions. But it did get hot, "dry heat" or not. Although in my past, I had done quite a bit of business and traveling in Florida, and there were parts I really liked, I did not want to end up where 90 percent of the seniors from the northeast ended up.

I liked the changes of season. If I were to make this life-altering decision, I would have to remain in New England. That being said, there were only three possibilities left in my mind. Maine, New Hampshire, or Vermont.

Maine offers the choice of seashore or mountains—lots of land, not too many people. In fact, there are so many acres of woodlands in Maine I am sure man has not yet trampled on them all.

New Hampshire has no sales tax and lots of mountains. To me it seems to be busier than either Maine or Vermont—just a perception.

Vermont, the state I had spent the most time in other than Connecticut and New York when I was in school for four years, has great mountains, only six hundred thousand–some odd people, makes the most maple syrup in the country, and seems to encourage artisans of all backgrounds to make Vermont a one-of-a-kind state.

I decided I was going to take some time off and travel through all three states to see if one stood out from the others for me. Even if in the end I didn't want to move, it would be a good thing for me to decompress and take it easy for ten days or so. I needed it and I deserved it.

Chapter 13

The following weekend, it had been arranged, finally the meeting between Liz and Maggie. As the initial cancelled meeting was to have been, this would again be a lunch at a local restaurant. Liz informed me of this over the phone, and I could tell she was both relieved and nervous at the same time.

And as I had anticipated, Liz then asked the question, "Will you come and meet Maggie with me, please?"

I had really wanted to remain apart from this whole encounter at this point, but I could tell by the tone in Liz's voice that I had to comply. I accepted the invitation. This might prove extremely interesting given the things I believed I already thought I knew. I also knew that I would have to be very careful in what I said as well as how I acted. I made an instant decision that it would be best for me to listen a lot and speak minimally.

Sunday came quickly, and as once before, I picked Liz up and drove to the restaurant once again to await the arrival of Dillon and Maggie. It was to be a one o'clock meeting, and Liz and I arrived about five minutes early. We were escorted to a nice table overlooking the water, and we waited. Liz, I could tell, was again nervous, and I was trying not to show some of my amusement in this whole meeting.

A few minutes after one, Dillon walked in with Maggie in his arm. After quick introductions, we all sat and began our conversation as we all scanned the menu.

Liz began, "It is so nice to finally meet you, Maggie. I know Dillon has been anxious for us to meet and get to know one another."

"Yes, I'm sorry our original lunch date didn't work out, but I was a little under the weather and just wasn't up to meeting anyone.

I seem to be doing much better now and am comfortable with the growing baby."

"It does take a little getting used to," added Liz. "That's all in the past now, and what we are looking at now is the future."

The waitress arrived and asked if we were ready to order. Liz and I were ready, and Dillon and Maggie said they would be by the time we ordered our food. When all four of us had ordered, Liz continued trying to coax information out of Maggie.

"From what Dillon has told me, you have lived in the area all of your life and have family in the area as well."

"Yes," replied Maggie, "my parents still live here in New Haven, and they are very excited about me having a baby. We will have to have you all meet sometime soon."

"That would be great," Liz replied.

As Dillon was remaining almost silent and no one else seemed to want to broach the subject in spite of my plan to listen and not talk too much, I couldn't help but ask, "So, Maggie, what do you do, or what have you done in the past as far as work goes?"

Maggie glanced at Dillon, and Dillon glanced back at Maggie before Maggie responded with "I have had mostly odd jobs working in various retail stores in the area, but right now I am not working—just trying to manage while pregnant. I left my last job and have been collecting unemployment now for a few months and am getting by. My parents have been a big help too."

"That's good," I responded, "and have you been doing anything to supplement your income on the side or trying to get into any other work for the future?" I knew I was bordering on asking too much too soon, and I saw Dillon shoot me a look that I know wasn't good.

Nevertheless, Maggie answered, "No, I really haven't been looking to do anything like that at this point. I've just been trying to lay low and stay under the radar, so to speak."

Interesting, I thought, *directly opposite of what Dillon had previously mentioned about Maggie having a consulting business on the side.* I now wondered how much "Mommy and Daddy" did help or in fact how much her night visitors helped in making ends meet.

No Reason

I decided to only speak when spoken to for the remainder of the meal. We all chitchatted nicely, and there were no other revelations through our luncheon.

Liz seemed to feel good about the meeting, being fairly relieved that Maggie wasn't related to the Wicked Witch of the West. I, on the other hand, had become even more apprehensive about this relationship and about Maggie's dealings. Possibly Maggie was more like Cruella de Vil! I didn't let on to Liz.

Chapter 14

Two uneventful weeks followed our lunch out with Dillon and Maggie. I purposely had minimal contact with Liz as I wanted her to hash out in her mind what was about to happen to her, her son, and her son's girlfriend and maybe future wife. Then I just needed time to clear my head and decide what it was I wanted to do.

I decided to take ten days to explore. I phoned Liz to let her know I would be driving through Maine, New Hampshire, and Vermont to "sightsee" but that I would keep in touch by phone. She wasn't thrilled with my announcement, thinking out loud that it might be nice if I postponed my trip for a while, so she could go with me. That wasn't the point—but I couldn't tell her that!

"Welcome to Maine," read the sign on I-95. My thought was to travel north on the interstate and take various excursions off the highway, sometimes going east toward the shore, and when I felt the urge, travel west, inland to the mountains. Although I like the shore, I was never sure I could live there all the time. But I was willing to try to find that ideal little coastal village that would welcome me and make me feel so at home that I would want to stay.

On the other hand, the mountains always attracted me. They were always a bit quieter than the shore, less people, less tourists, fewer roads, more isolation, and more nature—except possibly for the fish and lobster off the Maine coast. But the mountain's moose, deer, bear, and all other creatures of the woods have always had a special place in my heart. In fact, the Maine woods near Brownsville was where I encountered my first moose while deer hunting years before.

I had been with a party of eight hunters set up in an old hunting cabin off on some logging road. There was a small lake nearby. Nights were so dark that you took your life into your own hands by going to the outhouse after dark as it was so black you couldn't see your own hand right in front of you. Yet when the night was clear, the number of stars in the sky was amazing, far out-surpassing the number of stars one could see surrounded by light pollution.

Anyway, it was day four of our six-day hunt—no hunting in Maine on Sundays—when I met up with one of the other hunters in our camp. We were standing at the point of a ridge, talking softly and trying to plot a strategy for seeing some deer, when all of a sudden we heard what we thought were a herd of deer running through the woods toward the point of the ridge. We raised our rifles in expectation, but seconds later, a large female moose bounded toward us and abruptly applied its brakes but a scant seven yards from where we stood. She looked at us, tilted her head, kept looking at us with that stupid-looking face, which she had up until the time when her calf that was following slammed into her rear end because "Momma" had stopped too fast!

Gathering themselves, the mother kept her gaze on us for probably fifteen seconds or so. We were both laughing at this point, but we kept our guns ready just in case she decided to charge. Instead, she took a hard left turn as we watched her avoid trees and branches while running and seemingly, in an instant, vanished! Baby moose, who was all legs and stood about five feet tall, decided to perform the same exit as "Momma" had done, but when it tried to take the hard left, its back feet went out from under it, and it fell sideways to the ground. We were roaring with laughter! The calf got up, pointed itself in the right direction, and soon vanished as well. An experience that I truly never will forget.

So traveling at no urgent pace, I visited Portland, Yarmouth, Augusta, Bangor, Old Town, Millinocket, and Houlton along I-95. In between, toward the shore, I hit Rockport, Bar Harbor, and Bucks Harbor. Inland I checked out Skowhegan, Dexter, the Baxter State Park area, as well as briefly went all the way up to Caribou. Gorgeous country, not much to do, great place to retire or to disappear. Next stop, New Hampshire.

Chapter 15

Portsmouth, New Hampshire, proved to be a great coastal town—not too big, some really good restaurants, wonderful shops, and really awesome possibilities for fishing and boating. Traveling north, I had wanted to check out the Conway and North Conway area, both being very close to the Maine border. But after driving through and doing some walking around town, it just seemed a bit too commercial for my liking. I really wanted a down-to-earth small village to reside in that not only was close enough to employment and conveniences but that also had some great cultural influences as well. Of course, traveling through the White Mountains was gorgeous and more my cup of tea, so I made a note that I might want to consider it after exhausting other options.

Both Manchester and Concord were too large for my liking while the Sunapee area seemed really nice and offered at least employment opportunities associated with tourism if nothing else. But nothing I had seen yet "bowled me over" with enough excitement to make me want to make a lifestyle change. But one thing I did keep in mind, although a little tongue in cheek was the fact that New Hampshire has great state-run liquor stores! It features no sales tax, leading to low prices, easy access from main highways, large stores, and an incredible selection of wine and liquor.

New Hampshire's "sister" state is Vermont, almost an upside-down mirror image of each other. Whereas New Hampshire geographically starts out wider in the south and narrows as you travel north, Vermont's southern region is narrow and widens the closer you get to Canada. The Green Mountains in Vermont are at least the equal of New Hampshire's White Mountains, both extremely picturesque and serene in their own right.

— No Reason —

I entered Vermont on I-89 through Lebanon, New Hampshire—right on the border. Traveling north and west, I first checked out the Currier and Ives setting of Woodstock in Central Vermont. Now this was certainly a town I could live in, or near, as I had no trouble in finding convenient and quaint stores, good cafés and restaurants, and really nice people. While Woodstock is known for its tourism, towns near Woodstock are a little less busy having a bit more of a laid-back atmosphere. Being just about a half-hour drive from New Hampshire was also a plus and being centrally located in the state offered a reasonable drive back down to Connecticut to visit Liz or whoever.

Driving west on Route 4, I soon came to the Killington area. A great mountain and with Killington and Pico ski areas right next to each other, a skiers' paradise. Lots happening there and in the surrounding area with a great many restaurants and shops all geared for skiers and tourists. A great place to visit but maybe a bit too busy for my liking.

Rutland, on the western side of the Green Mountains, was a commercial bonanza. Chain restaurants, car dealers, big box stores, and more all lined the streets. I moved north toward Brandon and Middlebury. Both of these towns and the surrounding areas reminded me of Woodstock and neighboring towns. Somewhat quaint and quiet yet with enough happening that you didn't have to search for something to do, a place to eat good food or to find a decent cultural experience. And again, both were within an easy drive of my old stomping grounds in Connecticut.

Going north one more time up Route 7, I hit Shelburne, Burlington, and the Essex Junction region. Certainly beautiful along Lake Champlain. Again, just a little too bustling for my liking. One advantage this area did have was that it boasted a bit warmer climate in the winter than did most of Vermont, saw less snow most years, and is now able to grow more cold hardy grapes for local wineries in the area.

I called Liz to inform her that I would soon be back in the nutmeg state and to see how she and Dillon was doing. After having such a relaxing trip, I should have known better than to ask.

"I'm at my wits' end with Dillon and his relationship with Maggie. He is having trouble. I can't seem to help, and I don't know how to fix it," Liz blurted out.

"When I get back, let's get together and see what we can work out. If necessary, Dillon can join us, so he can explain the problem and see if we can't offer some advice that might help."

My calm voice over the phone seemed to relieve Liz a little, even if only for a short time. I, on the other hand, now had a lot more to think about than just where, if anywhere, I thought I might like to live now or in the future. I hoped this was just a bump in the road for Dillon—and Liz—but with what I thought I already knew, I was afraid it might be a major roadblock in this relationship.

A couple hours later, I read, "Welcome to Massachusetts," and another hour past that, "Welcome to Connecticut." I was officially back in the rat race.

Chapter 16

"I'm back" was my greeting to Liz over the phone that evening.

With that said, I in turn was greeted with sobbing! Not quite what I had expected or wanted; nevertheless this was reality. Liz was beside herself. I could hardly get a coherent sentence out of her and knew she was in panic mode.

"Liz, please, calm down so we can talk. Take a couple of deep breaths and try to relax a bit and then we can talk."

But Liz just kept sobbing and could barely catch her breath.

"I will be over in just a bit. Don't go anywhere or do anything, Liz. Let's see what we can figure out together. Okay? Liz, okay?"

Finally, after some heavy breathing and a succession of sobs, Liz answered with a faint okay.

Shortly thereafter, I pulled into the parking lot at Liz's apartment. I hurried to her door and found it locked, so I knocked lightly and waited. After waiting a short while, I knocked again, a bit harder this time. With no response coming from the apartment, I began to get excited. I knocked vigorously this time and shouted for Liz. Finally, I heard movement from within, and a few seconds later, Liz unlocked the door.

"Didn't you hear me knock?" I asked.

But I instantly knew my question didn't matter. Liz was falling apart. She was shaking as she cried and could hardly speak.

"Liz, calm…calm…settle…relax," I urged quietly and calmly.

I held her until she stopped heaving and caught her breath. Rubbing Liz's back while holding her seemed to help quiet the frantic state she was in.

Finally, there was a heavy sigh and silence.

"Oh, Dillon's in such a mess," Liz whispered. "He told me this morning that Maggie had told him to get out of her apartment and that she wanted nothing to do with him anymore. He said she told him that he would only need to give her money to support the baby after it was born and that other than that, he wouldn't need to ever come by or see the baby."

Liz added, "Dillon is devastated and doesn't know what to do, and I don't know how to help him or what I should do either."

"The first thing we all need to do is to calm down and think logically about what just happened. We need to talk with Dillon and find out exactly what transpired, who did and said what and why. We need answers before we can go forward. Do you know where Dillon is right now?" I asked.

"No" was the exasperated reply.

"Then we wait until he comes home or until you hear from him. Either way, we need to make sure Dillon understands that we are on his side and here to help him in any way we can. Got it?"

"Sure," Liz murmured.

We waited.

I made Liz some tea and sat with her. We continued to wait. We both fell asleep on her couch, Liz being exhausted from crying and worrying and me from my trip and my trying to help Liz through this crisis.

At 5:00 a.m., Dillon finally returned home. As he entered the apartment, I could feel Liz taking a deep breath and holding it. There was silence as Dillon's eyes met Liz's, and he stood motionless for a time. Finally, he walked over to a chair and collapsed in it, still not uttering a word and with Liz nor I saying anything to begin a conversation. For myself, I was determined not to start asking questions before either Liz or Dillon began talking.

After sitting in silence for a good five minutes, Dillon spoke to break the ice. "I'm sorry I worried you so much, Mom, and I'm sorry for bringing this all to you. But I don't know what to do—or even what not to do at this point."

Liz replied with a typical response, "That's okay, dear, we will work it out. Can you tell us what happened, and hopefully we can figure out what to do."

No Reason

"So here's the deal," Dillon began with a sigh. "When I met Maggie, we seemed to hit it off really well, and we were good together. But I realize now that I really didn't know her at all. We had fun. We talked. I thought we were falling in love, but it really was just sex. I am ashamed to admit it, but that's all it was. Then when she told me she was pregnant, I wanted to do the right thing. But again, all this time I was kidding myself. The more I was with her and the more I found out about her, the more ashamed I became because of who and what she is. I still can't believe I let this happen for so long." Dillon began to tear up, and it was increasingly hard for him to speak.

I got up and got him a glass of water in hopes that he could compose himself enough to finish what he had started.

Liz, in her motherly way, said, "Dillon, just take your time. Tell us what you need to. There is no rush, we are not going anywhere."

After a few sips, Dillon began again. "I was ready to step up and be a dad for our baby. Hell, I still am, but I can no longer even think of being married to Maggie or of her even being my girlfriend. I can't believe all this," he blurted.

Finally, I thought it was time for me to speak and try to put some calm logic into the situation.

"Dillon, if I may, I think your mother and I are in agreement that we both want to help you. We both need to understand the entire situation, and we both are going to stand by you no matter what. So…when you feel ready, you need to continue on. You need not feel ashamed about anything that happened in the past. What we need to focus on is what we can make happen in the future."

I could tell the short break in Dillon speaking to us helped settle his nerves a bit and that my reassurance of our backing him was, too, a step in the right direction.

Dillon began again. "Shortly after I found that Maggie was pregnant, I also came to the realization that she had done nothing but lie to me since we met. And I was stupid enough to take it at face value and believed her. What an idiot!"

Once again, I could tell that Dillon was breaking down and beginning to wander in his explanation. Though I didn't want to say too much, I felt I had to keep him on track as Liz seemed to only be able to wait and listen for Dillon's next statement.

"Dillon, once again, keep calm, collect your thoughts, and breath. Then once again slowly explain what you want to tell us. We're listening, take your time."

"Thanks," Dillon uttered. After another deep breath, he continued, "Bottom line is, she is a drug dealer! And worse yet, she uses too! I thought when I found out that I could change her and make her stop using, which she claims to have done now that she is pregnant, but even if that is true, she is still dealing in drugs. Oh my god! How could I have been so blind?"

"Dillon, calm, calm," I reminded. "Just tell your mother and I what you need to tell us and let everything else go."

With that, Liz got up and walked over to Dillon, fell into his lap, and hugged her child as if he had never been hugged before. Liz seemed to have composed herself and to have risen above the turbulence in Dillon's statements.

"Please just continue so we can all think this through," urged Liz.

"Well, I finally confronted Maggie about all this," Dillon stated. "She said she had not used drugs since getting pregnant, but I don't believe her. But she also said that she was going to and had to continue to sell drugs in order to take care of herself. She also said that she couldn't stop selling because her suppliers would not look kindly on her stopping."

"So in our increasingly panicked discussion, I suggested we go to the police and let them know about all of this. That's when things went crazy. Maggie was shouting that she couldn't and wouldn't. That if that ever happened, she would be killed. She told me to get out of her life, that she would contact me after the baby was born and let me know how much money I had to give her every month to support the baby. And that I was never to come around again. She further stated that if I were to ever go to the police, her suppliers would make sure that the baby had no father!"

Liz looked at me. I looked at Dillon, and he began to sob.

Since Liz was saying nothing, I felt that I needed to step in again. "Dillon, let's all take a step back from this for a day or so, collect our thoughts, and talk about what the options are after we have all settled down. We can't do anything rash, and we need to look into all the aspects of what is happening. So we can make the best decision possible for you and for your baby."

Dillon agreed almost silently. Liz kissed Dillon, and I held them both, already knowing full well that the best decision might not be an easy one.

Chapter 17

Relaxing back on my own couch with a Harpoon beer I picked up while in Vermont, I began to go over options for my future as well as make a plan for dealing with Dillon's problems in order to help both Dillon and Liz. It was a jumble of thoughts.

What a time to begin thinking of selling my house and moving, I thought. How would that play out with Liz and with all that was happening—or that was yet to happen?

Obviously, Dillon's desire to go to the police was not a smart way to go—at least at this point. It seemed to me that the authorities would have no alternative but to begin an investigation that could ultimately backfire on Dillon and his future baby, not to mention Maggie. While certainly not condoning the selling or use of drugs, having an irate and threatened drug dealer lurking in the area would not be the safest and wisest choice to make at the moment. I needed more information in order to begin making a solid plan of approach to the problem. The beer tasted good. I would be patient and see what transpired in the near future.

The "near future" came and went. From what I understood in talking with Liz, Dillon tried to speak with Maggie in order to calm things down and make sure she wasn't still insisting that Dillon would not be able to see his baby—only pay for it. That wasn't happening though. Apparently, their conversations were short and anything but sweet, and Maggie had abruptly hung up on Dillon, refusing to reconsider her stance. Dillon was devastated according to Liz, and Liz, I could tell, was at her wits' end.

I decided that the least I could do for them both was to once again stake out Maggie's apartment to see if anything new could be uncovered. I decided on barbecue for my surveillance dinner and ordered smoked brisket to go with a side of fries. After picking up my order, I found a spot that would be advantageous to watching the apartment. The long night began.

As before, various people began stopping by Maggie's apartment, no one staying for longer than about two minutes. Among the visitors were my original "friends," the Black man with his White counterpart, still wearing their long coats and coming and going from the same direction as before. Through eleven o'clock that evening, when Maggie's lights went out, no new revelations were revealed that would help anyone, especially Dillon.

The next day, however, was a different story. After work and after picking up the newspaper, I saw a photo of two people I recognized. The two men were dressed in long dark coats, and both had been found dead in an alley about a mile from Maggie's apartment. Apparent cause of death was a drug overdose. There were pending autopsies and a police investigation.

The next night, I went to set up for surveillance once again but decided to abort that thought when I found police cruisers combing the area about every ten minutes. I did not want to be associated with anything that was happening or that had already happened in that neighborhood. My decision proved to be a good one as shortly after I pulled out of my parking spot, two officers were walking the streets talking with everyone they met, including people parked in their cars.

I decided to lay low for a few days and let things calm down around Maggie's street. I did ride by the apartment each evening after work though, just to keep tabs on things. A week later, I decided that the police had other things to worry about, other deaths, other muggings, robberies, and other drug busts on which to work. I parked my Jeep on the street and began eating a homemade roast beef sandwich. The watch began once again.

Soon, cars began stopping by Maggie's apartment as well as walkers who all visited Maggie for just quick stays and moved on. The only visitors who were not there were the two deceased individuals who I assume either remained in the morgue or had been buried by now.

The following night, I was once again at it, thinking to myself that I had become obsessed with my surveillance while honestly learning little more for my efforts. To my surprise, no one was showing up at Maggie's this night until the black Audi I had seen before drove up the street, stopping briefly in front of Maggie's. Almost immediately, Maggie descended the stairs and got into the Audi. It pulled away into the darkness only to reappear as it had before, about fifteen minutes later, stopping only a few extra seconds to let Maggie out of the car as her belly seemed to be slowing her down at this point.

The lights went on, and within half an hour, a procession of individuals began showing up as observed earlier. It appeared that the system worked quite well—no one any longer concerned that two young men had died from the drugs they had purchased from Maggie. Nor did Maggie seem like anything out of the ordinary had happened as she continued business as usual. I made a mental note of my observations.

Chapter 18

With random surveillance checks over the next two weeks, I found little new information on the dealings of Maggie or of the system that seemed to be working with her "friends" in the black Audi. However, this finally changed in the proverbial wink of an eye!

On a misty, damp Tuesday evening, which otherwise felt like any other night I had chosen to watch Maggie's apartment, the unexpected happened. As I observed and gnawed on a Macoun apple, to my amazement and chagrin, Dillon approached Maggie's apartment and ascended the stairs. I watched and tried to listen to anything I might be able to hear.

Dillon knocked on Maggie's door and, after a brief moment, entered the apartment as the door opened fully to allow him to enter. It didn't take long before I could hear the conversation become rather heated and loud—I could not tell what was being said, but knew it wasn't very friendly. I could do nothing as still no one knew I had for months now been staking out Maggie's apartment in order to try to help this situation come to a fruitful end.

Then my worst fear appeared. The black Audi pulled up and began to wait—longer than I had ever seen it stationary at one time. Finally, after about three minutes, Maggie burst from her door and maneuvered down the steps toward the Audi. To my horror, Dillon followed!

This could not be good, I thought as I tried to come up with a plan to mitigate the situation that might unfold. I couldn't act fast enough.

Maggie tried opening the rear door to the Audi in order to get in and depart, but Dillon had caught up with her and stupidly was trying to keep her from getting into the car. It was brief and happened way too fast, but the driver's door opened, and I saw the glimmer from the streetlight of a stainless steel handgun being pointed at Dillon over the roof of the car. Thankfully, Dillon immediately retreated with his hands in the air, running down the street. The driver, a tall skinny man, reentered the Audi as Maggie entered the rear of the car. This was the first time I had ever seen the Audi peel out as it left Maggie's apartment. Although my instinct was to go after Dillon and make sure he was all right, I did not want to blow my cover, and I did want to see what was going to happen next.

Normally, after about fifteen minutes, the Audi would have returned to drop off Maggie, but not this night. A half hour later, the car did pull up. The rear door opened, and Maggie was unceremoniously shoved out onto the sidewalk. The car drove off. Maggie got to her feet slowly and began limping up the stairs. This scene did not bode well for Maggie, her baby, or in the near future, for Dillon. It seemed to me that Maggie's dealer had taken some extra time with her to, I assume, explain the "deal" to her and made sure she understood what was expected, and not expected, in the future however long or short that might be. Visitors began to appear as usual soon after, none ever staying longer than a minute or two.

It didn't look good for Dillon as well as I was fairly certain the men in the Audi knew who he was now. Would they go after him, or had they sufficiently scared him off? I couldn't chance it. I had to come up with a plan to keep Dillon, and for that matter, Liz safe. First though, I had to try to speak with both Dillon and Liz and, without giving away my awareness of what had just happened, encourage them both to disappear for a short time, so they could not be found.

Chapter 19

I drove to Liz's apartment and noticed Dillon's car in the parking lot.

That could be a good sign, I thought as I approached the door.

After knocking, I waited—I heard nothing. I knocked again and called out to Liz. The door opened slightly until Liz saw it was me. I knew that she knew what had just transpired, and that was a good thing. It would work in my favor for what had to be done.

Upon entering, Liz quickly closed and locked the door and threw her arms around me. Acting appreciative of the long hug while remaining apparently uninformed about what had happened with Dillon, I asked Liz if all was good with her day.

Liz burst out with her version of what had happened to Dillon just a bit earlier in the evening, which happened to be a fairly accurate account of what had actually happened with the exception of not knowing the condition of Maggie upon her return. Dillon appeared during Liz's explanation and confirmed his story. He was obviously still shaken and in disbelief on what had transpired. This all made my next move much easier than I had expected.

"Liz, now that we know the type of people Maggie is dealing with and working for and knowing that in all probability they now know who Dillon is and might in fact know where and who he lives with, I think it would be a good idea for you both to take a short vacation somewhere where you will not be found. Let me look into the situation in the meantime and see what I can sort out. I'm sure no one knows about me and let's see what happens in a few days."

It didn't take much convincing on my part to have both of them start packing as both were terrified of what could happen. I advised them to go to a local hotel for the night then to their bank in the morning and get cash and then to go out of state for at least a few days and try to relax a bit and to only use cash. I would stay in touch by Liz's cell phone.

They departed, driving off in Liz's car. I too left, conjuring up a plan in my head.

After work the following day, I went home and planned some more. Depending on what I saw happening in the next couple of days would dictate how my plan would unfold. I had no idea my plan would have to go into hyperdrive.

That evening, I once again got some pizza for my stakeout and parked advantageously to observe Maggie's apartment. However, something had changed. Her apartment remained dark, and no one showed up at her door for a quick visit. It was almost nine o'clock, dark with no one around. I decided to take a chance and approach Maggie's apartment. At the top of the stairs, I peered into her apartment but could not see much, but what I could see gave me little to go on. It was when I began descending her stairs that when near the bottom, one of her neighbors came out of their apartment.

She stated, "Maggie isn't home. She was rushed to the hospital this morning in premature labor. You'll have to get your drugs elsewhere." The neighbor disappeared.

Well, I thought, *I wonder if her "beating" at the hands of her dealer had anything to do with her premature entry into motherhood.*

I drove home. A phone call or two should be all that was required to find out to which hospital Maggie had been taken. My first stab in the dark was to Yale New Haven Hospital—it turned out to be the correct one. I established that Maggie had been admitted there and was currently in intensive care after giving birth. Her child was also in intensive care. That was all the information I could get from them. It was enough for now.

My next move was to call Liz and Dillon, not to tell them what had happened to Maggie as yet but to just check in with them to make sure they were all right.

"Hello?" answered Liz.

"It's me. Just checking to see how you and your son are doing. Don't tell me where you are—I only want to know you are both good and having a nice vacation."

— No Reason —

"Well, I'm not sure about a vacation, but we are as well as can be expected right now and seem to be holding our own," replied Liz as she seemed to realize that saying too much over the phone might not be a good thing not knowing how technologically proficient someone might be to hack into our conversation.

"Good, just wanted to be sure all was well. I will be in touch tomorrow and hope to have some information for you by then."

Relieved that they both were safe and doing well, I sat back to think through the process of finding out the best way to secure information about Maggie and her baby. Nothing was easy!

I poured myself a bourbon and Coke.

Chapter 20

After work the following day, I phoned Yale New Haven Hospital to see what I could find out by phone without revealing who I was. I got through to a nurse at the desk in the ICU and asked about Maggie and the baby. After a minute or so, the nurse came back on the line to tell me that both Maggie and the baby had been moved out of intensive care and into a private room on another floor. I was both relieved and astonished that apparently they were both doing well now. This was something I could now inform Liz and Dillon about as I thought they needed to know at this point.

My only concern was that if Maggie and the baby were still in the hospital, and if Dillon insisted on seeing his new offspring, things could get a little tense either between Maggie and Dillon or worse, between Dillon and Maggie's "employers" if in fact they were so inclined. It was easy to tell that they were not nice people but hard to tell how bad they really were.

I made the next phone call.

"Liz, I have some news," I reported. "Dillon is a father, and you are a grandmother!"

"Oh my!" was the surprised response. "What happened? How did you find out? Is it a boy or girl? Tell me…tell us."

I didn't want to get into the whole mess with them at this point as I didn't want panic on their part, but I knew I needed to tell them something about what had happened, so I started, "Apparently, Maggie went into premature labor and was taken to Yale New Haven. The baby and her were both in intensive care for a day but are out now and in a regular room. They are all right. And you know, dumb as I am, I never did ask if it was a boy or girl."

Liz had had me on speaker phone, so Dillon had heard all this, and I heard in the background that Dillon wanted to immediately visit his new child in the hospital. I tried to caution them both about showing up at the hospital at this point not knowing what to expect from drug dealers, but Dillon had other things on his mind, and Liz, too, thought all would be good now. I was apprehensive but knew I wasn't going to talk them out of it. We ended our conversation, and I continued to think and plan.

Liz and Dillon arrived at the hospital the following day. To my relief, their visiting Maggie and Dillon's new son seemed to go off without a hitch. In fact, Liz informed me that it was mostly all cordial. Paperwork was finalized noting both parents' names, so Dillon was officially on the hook for being his son's father, both for good and for bad. As for the good, he would have some rights as the father, but if Maggie also followed through with her threats, she might "hang Dillon out to dry" for child support if she was still so inclined. Time would tell.

After Maggie and the baby were out of the hospital and in her apartment, Dillon was allowed to visit his son, at least sparingly, but Liz had informed me that Dillon was ending up paying for everything Maggie and the baby needed. So Dillon worked as much as he could and was able to see his son only when it was convenient for Maggie to get out of her apartment for a while. It was an arrangement that Dillon was able to accept and follow through on for the sake of his son.

Chapter 21

With tensions being somewhat diffused for the time being, I went back to living my life, trying to come up with answers for my future, but with one eye still open toward the potential for Dillon's situation to blow up in his face.

Liz and I kept in touch but less so than before as she was now consumed with being a part-time grandparent and helping Dillon whenever he was allowed to take his son for a few hours. I was sure this happened only because Maggie needed a break from the trials and tribulations of raising a baby, and I was not at all convinced that she wasn't still somehow dealing.

Nevertheless, I was resolved to go on with my life, figure out what and where I wanted to be, and go for it. Vermont was my decision, mid-state somewhere near the Woodstock, Killington area near the New Hampshire border. I hoped it would be the best of all worlds. Time would tell.

The next step in the process would be to break the news to Liz that I was planning on moving. That being said, it seemed to me that it was a foregone conclusion that Liz and I would no longer be an "item," still friends but no longer dating on a steady basis. I wondered how this was going to go over, especially so soon after her troubles with Dillon's problems and opportunities. I could only be hopeful.

It was a sunny Sunday afternoon when Liz and I got together again. After normal pleasantries followed by mostly listening to what had been happening in Dillon's world which resulted in spinning Liz's world as well, I figured there would be no better or worse time to inform Liz of my impending move.

No Reason

I began… "Liz, I have been thinking of how my life has been going lately, what I want in the future, and where I want to be both physically and mentally, and I have decided that I need a change of scenery."

"What, another vacation?" Liz interjected quickly.

"No, I was thinking of a change that was a bit more permanent," I replied.

I could see Liz change her facial expression and instantly become nervous.

"I have decided to move to Vermont."

As the proverbial saying goes, "the silence was deafening." Liz just stared at me, not uttering a word. And then tears welled up in her eyes, and the floodgates opened. I could take anger, or fear, or surprise, or almost anything but this. Liz turned to Jell-O, and I could only sit there and watch.

After an eternity, a minute or two later, Liz began to calm down.

"Listen," I began again, "it is only going to be a few hours away, and we can still see each other. And it's not like I am going to just abandon you and Dillon. I promise I will be here for you both when and if needed. I know this has been really rough on both of you and that it is not something that looks like it will end soon, at least not so that everyone is happy and smiling again. But all you need do is call, and I will be here for you. I want to set up my life to be a bit more relaxed and have the time to do more of what I want to do rather than what I have to do. Okay?"

With a small sob, Liz began her response, "I know we haven't been quite as close lately since the baby came, but I have relied on you so much to help both Dillon and me through this. I just don't know what I will do."

"Liz, just keep doing what you have been doing, be patient and let's see what happens after I find a place in Vermont, change jobs, lifestyle, and become more of who I want to be. Again, I will not abandon you or Dillon. Yes, I won't be minutes away, but it's not like I am moving across the country. It is only Vermont. It will be a great place for you to visit as well, and hopefully if Dillon gets things straightened out with Maggie a bit, he and the baby can visit as well."

Liz, at least for the time being, seemed to accept what was happening.

We ended up pouring two glasses of wine and sitting out in the back of her apartment, catching some rays and mostly being silent. The day had calmed down. We sipped our pinot gris.

Chapter 22

After two relatively uneventful trips to Vermont in search of a small house and property, I was beginning to wonder if I would find what I was looking for. On my third trip to mid-state Vermont, however, I came across a cute house situated on a secluded dirt road. It was wooded all around, and the nearest house was about a quarter mile away. It needed some fixing up, but that was nothing new. The price was right, and the location just north of Woodstock seemed like a good one. I made an offer, ten thousand below asking price. It turned out to be a good offer. I should have gone fifteen!

After a few weeks of paperwork, what I would call "red tape," inspections, and such, we set a date six weeks down the road for the closing on the house. It would give me time to clear up loose ends, give notice at work, pack, say goodbyes to friends—there weren't many—and to make sure Liz and Dillon and his baby were doing all right. To that end, one Friday night, I bought a steak and cheese sandwich, some fries, and a cranberry juice and drove to my old observation site outside of Maggie's apartment. I hadn't observed what was happening, or not, at her apartment since she had the baby as reports that I heard from Liz per Dillon was that Maggie was no longer dealing and had nothing to do with drugs.

I soon found that not to be the case. People on foot and in cars were once again visiting Maggie for minutes at a time. If anything, she had increased business over what I had previously observed. I wondered if Dillon knew this or if he was covering this up for some reason. I decided to get a bit more involved.

Saturday, I called Liz to see if we could get together. She was more than pleased to have me over for dinner, so early Saturday evening, I showed up with my friend, Merlot.

The food was exceptional as usual, and the wine went wonderfully with the meal. Conversation ranged from the weather to work to how my impending move was going to Dillon and his baby. The latter was what I was trying to find out more about.

"Dillon is working so much that he really doesn't get to see the baby but once a week right now," Liz stated. "He is trying to make ends meet, and it seems Maggie keeps demanding more and more money from him ostensibly for the baby. But I fear Dillon is killing himself trying to keep up."

"Well, when does Dillon usually see the baby?" I casually asked.

"His only night off is Sunday night, so he goes to Maggie's for a couple hours each Sunday evening. He is religious in doing so and loves his son so much! And last week, he brought the baby here for a few hours. What a joy for me."

My immediate decision was to go on stakeout the next day, Sunday evening, to see what transpired.

That Sunday evening gave more clarity on the situation. Dillon showed up for his visit and stayed about two and a half hours. After he left, I continued snacking on my cold pizza and watching. Not one person visited Maggie before Dillon's arrival while Dillon was in Maggie's apartment or after. Apparently, the word was out that the "drugstore" was closed on Sundays. There was the reason Dillon thought Maggie had cleaned up her act. Nothing could have been farther from the truth.

Monday evening, armed with a homemade Caesar salad I threw together just prior to leaving for my night of surveillance, I arrived outside of Maggie's apartment and parked in my almost usual space. To neighbors of Maggie, I'm sure they thought my car belonged there by now, although I still hoped nobody noticed.

A local police car drove by about forty minutes after I arrived, just doing their normal routine drive around. Ten minutes later, the "drugstore" opened. And it wasn't like it had been when I first took up surveillance when one or two people would show up every so often at night. There were now people showing up every half hour, two and three at a time! I wondered, How did these people know when it was safe to come for their buy and when Maggie was open for business? I began to really look at what I could see from my vantage point that might be an indicator. I saw nothing.

Since it seemed that most of her clients came from the north, the direction I always looked toward, I decided to take a stroll past Maggie's apartment to see if I could see anything I wasn't seeing from my car. I didn't really feel comfortable exposing myself to the neighborhood, but I felt I had little choice if I wanted to get this all figured out.

So trying to look like I belonged in the neighborhood, I left the safety of my car and took a walk. I hoped Maggie wouldn't and couldn't identify me as I walked by if by chance she looked out one of her windows. I safely passed her apartment and kept walking. I walked for another block, and when I saw no one on the streets, I turned around and began walking back to my car. Now walking from the north, I looked up at Maggie's apartment. There in her side window was a blue flickering light. I wondered if that might be the "all clear" signal I had been looking for and the one that all her clients knew about. It was something to be considered, but I would only be able to tell if I saw it go on before her clients showed up.

But later that night, as I pulled away from my parking space after I had not seen anyone visit Maggie for an hour, I craned my neck back to see that there was no flickering blue light in her window. Coincidence? Maybe. Time would tell once again.

Chapter 23

This surveillance gig was beginning to consume my life! It was a real pain, but knowing that I was leaving for Vermont soon and knowing I cared about Liz and Dillon as I did, I forced myself into being vigilant the next night.

As I drove up to Maggie's apartment, I chose a parking spot where I was now looking south, a vantage point where I could observe her side window, which at this point was not lit. I waited. Soon, a patrol car once again drove by and disappeared. I had, as usual, ducked down as they passed so that my car looked as though it had merely been parked there. I began eating my burrito. Five minutes later, the blue flickering light appeared in her window. Ten minutes later, clients began to arrive. If this was indeed the "all clear" signal, it seemed to work well. That night, the blue light stayed lit until ten o'clock. No visitors arrived after that. I drove home.

The remainder of the evening I began to pack for my move to Vermont. I began separating items I wanted to sell before moving, those I wanted to donate somewhere, and those I was trashing. I kept telling myself that I was starting over, starting fresh—a new life—so just take the things I needed or really wanted and get rid of the rest. It's more difficult than it sounds. At three in the morning, I decided I needed some sleep. After my nap, I was up and out for work.

After work, I began looking through my collection of firearms, hunting gear, bows, ammunition, knives, and accessories. I needed to see if I wanted or needed to take everything with me to Vermont or to sell some of my lesser-used guns and bows. Ammunition was always good to keep, but I did have a couple really old guns that weren't worth much as well as an old target bow with arrows that I never used anymore I felt I could easily sell. My knife collection, I

No Reason

decided I would keep never knowing when I might need one for a special trip or future event. I had many. They didn't take up much room, and some were very sentimental. My three throwing knives were among them. Years earlier, I had brought them on a trip to Maine with my brother and one of his friends. We had camped at the base of Mt. Katahdin near a stream, made a campfire, set up our tent, and relaxed. My brother had retired for the night, but his friend and I stayed up and threw my knives at a stump of wood by firelight for about an hour. Great fun. Of course, the next morning when we were packing up, we noticed that a moose had passed between the river and our tent during the night. Then a park ranger showed up to let us know that we should not have built a campfire there and let us know if it happened again, we would be fined. As we were moving on anyway, we thanked him for letting us know about the campfire and departed. What memories!

Then there was the Buck knife I used when I shot my first deer as a teenager. This was a great knife, although I seldom used it anymore but one I would not part with. I had carried it while hunting for years but had since moved on to a really nice folding knife for gutting and skinning made by Remington and carried in a leather sheath.

Realizing it was starting to get late for me to go on surveillance, I threw an apple and some cashews in a bag and left for Maggie's. My arrival was none too soon as five minutes after setting up my observation post, the black Audi arrived. A minute later, Maggie was out the door and down the steps and into the car. There were no lights on in her apartment. And she hadn't left with the baby. Had she left it alone in her apartment, or was it somewhere else or with someone?

I couldn't help myself. I left my Jeep and walked to her steps then literally ran up the stairs to her door. I looked around noting that nobody had observed me, and I peered in. Then I heard the faint cry of a baby! She had left it alone! My god, what type of mother would do that to her child? I knew the answer, however, one that loved drugs and money over her child. My heart wretched.

But based on past experience, I knew I didn't have much time to waste standing on her landing. Although I hated doing so, I retreated to my Jeep. Fortunately, I beat the Audi's return by about five minutes. Maggie returned to her apartment and to her child. The blue light went on, and the procession began once again. I had seen all that I needed to see, a display of utter neglect!

Chapter 24

Following work the next day, I called Liz to see how she and Dillon were doing. They were both getting by, according to Liz, but were tired of all the angst caused by Maggie not allowing Dillon to see his child but once a week and knowing how she was caring and providing for him. Little did they know!

As we talked, our conversation went to my imminent move to Vermont.

Liz asked, "When exactly will you be moving?"

"It should be within a couple weeks if all still goes well with the paperwork, etc.," I replied. "I am also still trying to sell my house or at least rent it out if possible, so that could also prolong my stay in Connecticut a bit."

"I still really wish you weren't going. You know you have helped both Dillon and me so much. Not to have you around will be terrible." Liz began to sob just a bit.

I tried to comfort her with "You know I will be but a phone call away and just a few hours by car. If there is an emergency or a big party you are throwing, you know I can be here in the blink of an eye."

I could hear Liz almost laugh at my statement.

So we kept talking, keeping it light and almost nonsensical. We talked of many of the good times we had shared and even touched on a couple of the tense times we managed to get through together as well. That was how life was. But we did manage to stay upbeat and ended on a positive note that we would get together over the weekend sometime.

Satisfied that Liz's world wasn't going to explode in the next week or so, I went back to packing. It was both tedious and mind-bending in many ways. Moving to a new state, to a new way of life, was equally strenuous and refreshing at the same time. It made me think about what I was leaving behind, about what I would like to forget, about possibilities I might have in the future, and about what and how I wanted to change my life in Vermont. Would I be able to succeed?

I was jarred out of my thoughts as my phone rang, which it seldom did unless it was Liz.

This call, as it turned out, was about future employment in Vermont. One of the companies' ads I had found online and which I had inquired about filled out my résumé and all other pertinent information was interested in seeing me. The glitch was they wanted to decide by the end of the weekend, meaning I would be in Vermont for the weekend and not be able to be with Liz.

This was about me beginning a new life, however, so we did set up a time in the early afternoon on Saturday to meet, so they could interview me—and so I could also return the favor and interview them!

Possibly things were looking good for my future. At least where employment was concerned. If I got the job, it would also take pressure off me selling in Connecticut, so I wouldn't have to settle on a low bid for the house. A true step in the right direction.

Chapter 25

I felt my interview went well. I was pleased with what they were offering, and I was happy with their answers to my questions as well. It was a job managing a restaurant in a well-known resort, mainly dealing with the late breakfast and lunch crowd. Very few nights—only to fill in for a vacation or emergency. What a gift!

I drove home to Connecticut to wait. They had informed me that they had one more interview to do but that they would let me know their decision in a day or so one way or the other. I didn't have to wait long. Sunday morning, my phone rang. I had a job offer! I jumped at the opportunity. It all seemed like it was coming together nicely. The only problem was that they wanted me to start on the first of the month—just two and a half weeks away.

Then I had what I considered to be a brilliant idea. I made a phone call to Liz.

"Liz, I wanted to share the news that I have accepted a great offer at a resort in Vermont," I began.

"Wow, wonderful," she replied. "When do you begin?"

"That's the thing. They need me there on the first of the month. So I was thinking and have a question for you."

Liz hesitantly replied with an elongated "Yesss?"

"What would you think about renting my house and getting out of your apartment? Your lease is about to expire anyway, if memory serves me. And the house is bigger, in a nicer area, and I would charge the same rent as you are paying now. You would have to put up with an absentee landlord, but I think it would be a good fit for you, Dillon, and even his son when he had him."

After a brief moment where I knew Liz was considering my offer, her reply was positive, asking, "Are you sure? That would be a great deal for me and Dillon. We would have a yard for the baby, and it would be quiet and a much nicer place to live. But would the money be all right for you?"

I assured Liz the money would be fine; it would release me from trying to sell the house from a distance and would assure me a good place to stay for future visits to Connecticut. It would also keep me in better touch with Liz. She agreed. I love it when a plan comes together!

Now I had to focus on packing and getting rid of nonessentials. I managed to do a pretty fair job at that, got it all packed in a rented truck, and moved up to my new house upon closing two weeks later. It would be quite a mess inside for some time, but I made sure my bed was usable and kitchen equipment was all on hand for immediate use. Then I returned to Connecticut with the truck to use it to move Liz and Dillon into my house with the help of both of them. Dillon was a huge help in moving the few large pieces of furniture Liz had, and we accomplished their move with relative ease. After returning the rental, I drove my Jeep back up to Vermont, so I could begin my new work experience the following day. I was tired!

Chapter 26

The new job started off well. Everyone I met and would be working with seemed nice as would be expected. Being that it was a resort destination, the restaurant stayed busy throughout the day as not only local businesspeople frequented the facility, but there were built-in customers who were staying on the property.

My first week flew by in the proverbial flash. Between learning how everything worked there, learning the menus, and trying to remember everyone's names, I kept more than busy. Just like when I was deer hunting, my preferred method of finding out about all our employees' tendencies, quirks, and strengths was to sit back and observe out of everyone's way. There would be plenty of time to help those who needed some training in service, and the stronger employees appreciated the fact that I didn't and wouldn't come in as an "expert" in everything and be the destructive bull in a china shop.

During the week, I also kept in touch with Liz, wanting to make sure all was well with her and Dillon being in my house as well as checking on the Maggie and baby situation.

"Liz, how is the house treating you?" I began.

"Quite well so far," Liz replied. "Dillon and I are loving the extra room and not sharing our space with others like in the old apartment. And the woods and area around the house are magical. We love it."

"Good to hear. And how, dare I ask, is Dillon and the baby doing?

"Nothing new to really report this week so far. Maggie and Dillon aren't going to see eye to eye on much, and he is just going to have to weather the storms as they arise. I hope we can at least maintain a status quo and not have everything fall apart and become more contentious than it already is," added Liz.

With that being said, I told Liz that I missed them and bid her a good night. I went back to unpacking, trying to make sure my firearms, bows, knives, and hunting gear was all safely put away.

A couple weeks flew by in a heartbeat. Work was beginning to be as routine as it could be, and I was learning and investigating the area as much as possible. Then one morning, shortly after beginning my shift, I learned that the long-time food and beverage manager was leaving the resort for a new opportunity. Management was looking to hire. I applied immediately for the job and waited. I soon learned that there were four or five other applicants from around the country as well, and two of them were being brought in for an interview. I was picked as the third interviewee.

Two weeks later, resort management announced their decision to hire one of the outside applicants. I was informed that I was actually their second choice, but they felt their new hire would fit the ticket for what they were looking for more immediately. I accepted the decision and continued on with my job—which I enjoyed.

Upon his arrival three weeks later, I was introduced to Jesse, the new food and beverage manager—my immediate boss. He was young, energetic, had a wife and two young children, and seemed to be a no-nonsense type of guy. He expected perfection, which was fine, but there didn't seem to be much personality to go along with it. I could tell that the waitstaff and kitchen personnel were a little taken back with his attitude.

It didn't take long for Jesse to begin making changes. He let go two of the male waiters who I thought were doing a good job and hired in their place two young women who were both rather inexperienced but very good-looking.

I thought, *Well, it works for Hooters, but will it work here?*

Next he let go one of the pantry chefs, another male, and replaced him with another young, rather curvaceous young lady. Upon observing her work over the first few days, I soon learned that she was indeed slow at her job, didn't know how to step it up when the restaurant was slammed, and didn't seem to want to clean up and make everything ready for the next onslaught at the end of her shift. But I did see that the two new waitresses and the new pantry chef did

— No Reason —

like to party! And most often they were partying at one of the resort's bars with Jesse in the evening. Not that I was around all the time in the evenings as I was still mainly working breakfast and lunch shifts, but when I did work a night shift or went to the resort to grab a bite or have a drink, they were pretty much a group.

I thought, *Wow, I wonder how Jesse's wife and kids like his being out late all of the time. Wouldn't a young father want to spend time with his family?*

I decided that it really didn't matter what Jesse did as long as it didn't impact my work a whole lot. But then an interesting thing began happening. Jesse began talking with me a great deal, asking my opinion on various events taking place at the resort and becoming very friendly. Maybe overly so! I was suspicious. I couldn't help but wonder what his motives were. I was on guard. Something was changing.

Over the next few weeks, Jesse acted like he was my best friend. He constantly asked for my help with events, menus, wine selection, and more. Yet he never once invited me to party with him and the girls! Of course, I wasn't the only one to notice what was going on. There was much talk of how Jesse was conducting himself, especially after hours. Rumors were rampant about Jesse "making out" with one or more of his girls in the bar and in the parking lot and who knows where else.

I wanted no part of it. I was surprised that upper management hadn't addressed the situation by now, but then again, they had brought Jesse in to revamp and remake the food and beverage department and bring it toward five-star status. It would be a blemish on resort management if they were to discipline Jesse, or worse.

So life went on at the resort. It seemed to me that some of the "old-timers" were having to do more and more while the newly hired personnel were allowed to work as much or as little as they wanted. But the partying never stopped, and the choice shifts were routinely awarded to the young females. It all seemed a bit discriminatory to me.

During this time, I made sure to keep in touch with Liz. She reported that Dillon and she loved the house and were doing well there. And they felt safer there than in her old apartment. As far as Dillon's son was concerned, he was growing and doing well overall, although Dillon still mostly only saw him on Sundays with few exceptions. Nothing, as far as Dillon knew, had changed with Maggie selling drugs, and she still apparently claimed to not be using, but Dillon had admitted to his mother that he was very unsure about that.

I had a long weekend coming to me, and I planned to drive down to see Liz and Dillon. I wanted to be sure Liz had no other plans, so after speaking with her one evening, we solidified my trip to Connecticut. I drove down in the early afternoon on a Friday and arrived at my old house a little before Liz arrived back from work. I took the time to walk around the yard and look at my old haunt.

Shortly, Liz drove up the driveway. When she saw me, she ran to give me a big hug and kiss. It was good to be in her arms again. I took my duffel bag into the house, and I told her that the place looked a lot better than when I lived there. She had done an amazing job decorating. We sat. We talked. We shared a bottle of Merlot, and Liz later made an amazing scallop and rice dinner and paired it with a bottle of pinot gris.

Our talk covered numerous subjects, from her work and mine to Dillon and the baby, which was getting to be not so much a baby anymore, to comparing the weather and what she wanted to do on the weekend with me. We decided to take it easy, drive around a bit on Saturday, eat out at a nice restaurant, and Sunday hopefully spend some time with Dillon and his son. It was a good plan. Little did we know that Maggie was going to throw a monkey wrench into it!

Dillon arrived home late Friday night only to check his mail and find Maggie was taking him to court in an effort to further limit his seeing his son as well as collect more money from Dillon.

Dillon was beside himself. "How could she do this when I basically only have him on Sundays now, and how in the world am I going to give her any more money than I already do?" he asked rhetorically.

Liz tried to reassure Dillon that it was just another attempt at control and that Maggie would have a long way to go to prove he should not have custody on Sundays and then that Maggie needed

— No Reason —

more money for the baby. While I agreed with Liz, I knew that the Connecticut courts very heavily agreed and supported the mother virtually all the time. Dillon would have to present himself well and document all that he was presently doing to support his child. I advised him to not bring up the fact that she was dealing drugs and most likely using as well as that could only backfire on him at this point. He didn't need the drug dealers finding him and Liz for any retribution of any kind.

Liz and I did manage to have a nice Saturday together and a wonderful dinner as well. We talked, laughed, and shared memories. I know it took Liz's mind off Dillon's problems. Only I may have thought about it a little more.

Sunday, however, was a different story. Dillon, as usual, drove to Maggie's apartment to pick up his son, but as Dillon tells it, he knocked on the door and received no answer. After knocking repeatedly, he finally heard someone stirring inside. Then he heard his son crying. He was about to try breaking into the apartment when Maggie finally wobbled to the door and opened it. She was barely able to walk and looked like she had been in a coma, according to Dillon. She made no attempt to address their son, who continued to cry loudly. Dillon pushed past Maggie and went into the baby's room. He was standing in his crib and the sheets, and his clothes were stained with hours and hours of excrement. The poor child had not had his diapers and clothes changed for many hours, maybe for at least a day! And did that mean that the child had not eaten in that time as well? Maggie wasn't concerned and told Dillon to take the child and leave not letting him clean the baby at all.

When Dillon arrived back at the house, he explained everything that had happened and began to care for his son.

I felt like I had to step in and briefly stop him. "Dillon, stop for just a minute and take some pictures of how you found your child. Document what you found in the crib as well and then you can clean him up and feed him. This could all be very useful in court," I stated.

Dillon and Liz agreed, and they both took pictures and then bathed and fed the poor child.

Nice mother, I thought to myself.

Chapter 27

Tuesday was my first day back on the job. All was normal until Jesse arrived at the restaurant and wanted to talk. He wanted to inform me that he "might" have a meeting later that night and wanted me to cover for him as there was a small engagement party happening at the resort that would need to be supervised. Of course, this would make it a very long day but one that I would be earning extra money for, so I agreed.

At five o'clock, Jesse informed me that he was going to his meeting. I took over on the floor supervising the party that had just begun. The staff, as usual, all did what I considered a superb job in taking care of the twenty-eight people in the party and needed little direction. However, as the party kept getting livelier and louder, one of the waitstaff approached me and needed four special and very expensive bottles of champagne for a toast.

"Okay," I told the waiter, "I will have to go to the liquor room to get them out of the cooler. It will take me a few minutes. Set up the glasses and a wine bucket in the meantime, and I will be right back."

The liquor room was down a back-of-the-house hallway that led to a food and beverage office as well as to a room reserved for an employee or two who, for whatever reason, had to stay over on any given night. It might be because of a nasty winter storm where someone didn't want to drive home, where someone didn't feel well, or was too tired to drive home or any number of reasons. It wasn't used much, but it was handy to have available.

Upon entering the liquor room, I heard noise. I stopped to listen. I waited. It was unmistakable. Someone was in the room next to the liquor room having sex! I walked out of the liquor room and down the hall a few yards and stood outside the door. Some couple were obviously having a good time in the room. Then I heard voices.

"Jesse, Jesse... Oh, God, Jesse" came the panting voice of one of the female waitstaff Jesse had indeed hired.

Then I could hear Jesse grunting and groaning! So this was his "meeting."

I thought, *What a scumbag! Cheating on his wife with one of the women he hired to replace a waiter that actually had been doing a very good job.*

I decided as I walked back to the liquor room that Jesse would need to be watched more closely. He was a devious son of a bitch!

I grabbed the four bottles of champagne and returned to the party.

By midnight, we had everything cleaned up and ready for the next event. All had had a good time, and the service, we were told by everyone, was excellent. Jesse never reappeared at the party.

The following day, after greeting Jesse when he got in, I asked, "How did your meeting go last night?"

"Quite well" was his response. "It was quite in depth and revealing." He chuckled.

Dirtbag, I thought to myself and moved on.

Chapter 28

Throughout the week, I made sure I had as little contact with Jesse as possible. I just couldn't stomach his lying and cheating on his wife and kids and didn't want to inadvertently say something to him that could come back to haunt me and my job.

On Friday, when the lunch crowd was dying down, the general manager walked into the restaurant and approached me, envelope in hand. "Would you see that Jesse gets this paperwork just as soon as possible? It is very important that he receives this today, and we can't seem to raise him on his cell. Drop it off at his home if you can," he pleaded. "You do know where he lives, right?"

"Yes," I replied. "I can leave now since we have calmed down after lunch and drop it off to him."

Jesse lived but about five minutes from the resort, so it was no big deal to go to his home. I left the resort and arrived at his door, ringing the doorbell.

After a minute, I heard a female's voice. "I'm coming." Jesse's wife cracked the door open and saw that it was me. "Oh," she stated, "Jesse isn't here. I don't know where he is."

"That's okay," I replied. "The general manager gave me this paperwork that Jesse has to look at today as soon as possible, and he wanted me to drop it off here for him because they weren't getting an answer on his cell."

As she opened the door a bit more to accept the envelope, I noticed a bruise on her face and a somewhat black eye.

After my brief shock, I couldn't help but ask, "Are you okay? Did you have an accident, or do you need any help?"

Jesse's wife looked away and replied somewhat sternly, "No, I'm fine. It's nothing." She proceeded to close the door.

— No Reason —

I knew better. Not only was Jesse cheating on his wife, but he was also beating her! Now I wondered about the kids as well. My blood was boiling. I was going to have to sit back just a little and figure out what I could do about this situation. I didn't want it to go on.

So I became even more wary of Jesse. I watched and listened and tried to maintain minimal contact with him. It seemed more and more that Jesse was not in his office or even on the property, which of course simplified my keeping my distance from him, but it also put added pressure on me as well as the other managers and the staff as a whole. I decided to begin watching Jesse more closely and began setting up surveillance once again, this time in Vermont.

The next weekend, there was a rather large wedding party at the resort. Jesse was scheduled to be supervising the event, so I decided that I would begin watching his coming and going beginning then. It was not difficult to observe him as he was prominent during the party. I figured he would have to be there at the beginning of the reception, but as time went on, I knew as long as everything was under control, he would have time to skip out for some time or leave early for the night. Sure enough, shortly after dinner had been served and all the toasts and cake eating had been completed, I saw Jesse talking to the head waiter and then Jesse was gone. Walking out a side door to the parking lot, I observed Jesse getting into his car and pulling out of his space. I hurriedly jumped into my Jeep and followed at an appropriate distance. He didn't go far. He didn't go home. He instead pulled into a small apartment just outside the village. Upon his getting out of the car, he began walking toward the door to the apartment. Before he got there, however, the door opened, and the female pantry chef Jesse had hired ran out to greet him. They embraced, kissed, and strolled inside.

Yet another woman Jesse was cheating with, I thought to myself. *What a piece of trash!*

So I decided to wait and watch for a while just to make sure Jesse wasn't merely visiting for a minute or two because of some business at the resort. I knew that there was little chance for that, but I wanted to be sure. After an hour, I was very sure. I started my Jeep and left for home.

The next day while working, I heard a rumor that Jesse's wife had been admitted to the hospital. One of the other managers had received a call from Jesse saying he wouldn't be in for a while as his wife had had an accident, and he had to take care of his children. Later that day, the rumor expanded, and staff were talking among themselves that Jesse's wife had somehow fallen and broken her arm! How this news was known to certain members of the staff, I will never know, but it was something I wanted to verify one way or the other sooner rather than later. I made myself remain patient, however, not wanting to jump to any conclusions.

Chapter 29

Over the next few days, rumors continued to circulate throughout the resort as to what had happened to Jesse's wife and how. The rumors ranged everywhere from the fact that she merely tripped and fell to her falling down the stairs to her being pushed or even beaten by Jesse. You see, others were thinking along the same lines as me, and others had certainly figured out at least some of what Jesse was doing to his wife and children. I, on the other hand, just listened and kept my mouth shut. As I had been taught throughout my life of hunting, it is far better to listen and observe than to be noisy and seen.

Jesse returned to his almost-normal routine at the resort. Although he was there every scheduled day he was supposed to be, often he was only present part of the time. Where he was the other three or four hours he took off, no one really knew. This, however, did put more pressure on all the managers, including me, as we had to pick up the slack left by Jesse. In one way, I didn't mind as there was less time for me having to interact with Jesse. On the other hand, it did mean that we were all essentially doing Jesse's work—and making him look good in the eyes of management.

Once again, due to Jesse's absence one day, paperwork had to be signed off on over a contract for a future large wedding party. I volunteered to deliver it to Jesse's house once more not because it was convenient but more because I wanted to see how Jesse's wife was doing if I could and make sure all was as good as it could be there.

I rang the doorbell. After a minute or so, Jesse's wife answered the door, cracking it open just a bit until she saw who it was. Upon recognizing me, she opened the door fully and asked if I wanted to come in.

"Well, there is no need to bother you," I replied. "I only wanted to drop off this paperwork for Jesse to sign and get back to the resort. Is he in?"

"No, I don't know where he is. I hardly ever do" was the somewhat exasperated reply.

"When you see him, please give this to him. By the way, how is your arm doing?"

"It's feeling better every day. But the cast feels heavy, and I am limited to what I can do with one arm. And it isn't easy taking care of our children by myself. But I am getting by," she sighed.

Just then the older of the two children came running up to the door. "Mommy, mommy, come play with us," he implored.

Jesse's wife's somewhat urgent reply was "I will in a moment. Go back into your room, and I will be there in a minute. Go."

And she turned her child around and sent him back down the hallway into his room but not before I noticed that one side of his face was black and blue!

I couldn't stop myself from asking, "Is your son all right? I noticed his face is bruised." Realizing that I had pushed maybe a bit too much, I immediately tried to retract at least a part of my query with "I'm sorry, it's none of my business. I will be going now."

Looking at Jesse's wife almost now in tears but doing an admirable job at holding them back, she confessed that her son had merely fallen while running. I looked at her, she looked at me, and she knew that I knew it was a lie.

"It was good to see you again," I stammered as I turned, opened the door, and left. *Incredible*, I thought as I walked to my Jeep. *This asshole is not only beating his wife. He is abusing his children as well.* I felt sick!

Upon returning home, I poured myself a Pyrat and Coke to hopefully help calm me down. Rum was my favorite liquor and having one or two drinks would most normally take the edge off and let me relax. I ended up having three drinks!

Something has to be done about this guy, I demanded of myself, *but I have to be absolutely sure before I step in.*

Then the phone rang and broke my train of thought. It was Liz.

"Hey, how are you?" I began.

"Hi" was the staccato reply. "Not so good. Dillon had another run-in with Maggie, and she is not taking care of their son like she should be. And he has spoken with the child welfare people who either don't care or are too busy to investigate, and Dillon is worried something really bad will happen to him," Liz blurted. "He is such a happy child when Dillon brings him to the house, but Dillon tells me that normally he is left to cry and fend for himself as Maggie is either high, doesn't care, or is too busy selling her drugs to take care of him. I could scream!"

"Okay, take it easy," I started, but Liz interrupted with a firm "I can't!"

"Sorry" was my attempt at defusing the situation. "I have had a lot going on at work lately too, but I promise I will make the time to come down for a visit. And we can all hash this out a bit and see if we can find some light at the end of the tunnel."

"Well, thanks, but the only light I see is a train coming through the tunnel to wreck our lives!" was the angry response.

Little by little as we talked for the next hour, I began to settle Liz down a bit, and we eventually spoke of happier things. I only mentioned that work was busy, and I was putting in a lot of hours, making sure I did not mention anything about what Jesse was doing to his family. Liz didn't need to hear any of that, and if I was to do something drastic in the near future, no one, including Liz, needed to know about it. As it was, I might have to intervene at some point with Maggie and Dillon's situation as well.

Lucky me, I thought, *I might have not just one huge problem but two to contend with! Why does this happen to me?*

After getting off the phone with Liz, I made myself a large bowl of popcorn and a fourth rum and Coke and settled in front of the TV. I only half watched. My thoughts instead drifted to what I might have to do very soon in order to help the people I love and those who I knew needed help but were way too scared to ask for it. I fell asleep on the couch.

Chapter 30

The resort was an amazing place. People worked there from a wide array of cultures, yet almost all were very service oriented, conscientious, and diligent in their work from the groundkeepers to the cooks and kitchen help to front of the house staff to management.

Then there was Jesse. Although he did offer a facade of giving service and hospitality to guests, in many people's minds, he fell short. But somehow, in the eyes of upper management, Jesse was doing a good job. His staff really needed to stop making him look so good!

Jesse had called a meeting of his managers two weeks before a huge and important wedding was taking place at the resort. He wanted to assign responsibility to everyone during the reception as no one or two managers could take care of all that was needed to be done. As for me, Jesse assigned the tasks of coordinating all the beverages, bar and liquor stations, and the staff that would man them. It would need some extra time on my part to make sure we had enough liquor at each station and had enough of the bride and groom's choices for wine and champagne on hand. It would also mean a late night on that day and a long one.

A day prior to the wedding, I went through the liquor room to make sure we had enough liquor, wine, and champagne for the big event. Liquor of all kinds were in abundance, and the wine and champagne for the reception was still in cases piled one on top of another. I opened a couple cases of each to be sure the proper wines and champagne were in each then counted the cases I could see and reasoned that all the appropriate bottles were in stock. My part looked like it was all going to be good for the next day's festivities. I left to walk the floor of the restaurant for the lunch crowd.

— No Reason —

It was a brilliant sunny day for the wedding accented by meandering wispy-thin clouds. Beautiful in all respects. Resort staff were all busy setting up and getting everything ready for the three hundred-some guests who were expected. I began my day by making sure all the champagne was in coolers chilling for the eventual toasts. Then I began taking out the red and white wines by the case, so I could distribute them to the proper bar setups throughout the party. White wines were all delivered to the stations, and I made sure each bartender put them on ice or in a cooler. Then I went to distribute the red wine. The first couple cases I loaded on the cart were fine; however, when I picked up the third case, it was very light. I opened the case, and there were but three bottles in it! The next cases I opened, which had all been buried in the liquor room, were bottles of red wine that was not what was needed. I quickly concluded that in no way would we have enough red wine for the reception!

I immediately went to find Jesse to let him know about our shortage and to see exactly what he had had the purchasing agent order.

"Jesse," I started, "I was just taking out all of the wines and champagne for the party, and I can't find near enough red wine that we need. Do we have some stored elsewhere, or are we short?"

"What the hell!" Jesse shouted. "How could this happen? You were supposed to make sure we had everything. You're goddamned incompetent!"

"Jesse, yesterday I checked everything I could get to, and while I didn't open every case, it looked like we had enough of everything. But one case that was buried only had three bottles in it and others were mismarked and have a different wine in them," I shot back. "Let's see how much of everything was supposed to have been ordered," I added.

"That's not the problem," Jesse insisted. "I'm sure Jake ordered the correct amount I had instructed him to. You should have caught this yesterday! Go home! I mean it, go home!" he yelled. "I can't use you! You are suspended! Get out of here."

Dumbfounded and angry, I left the resort. It looked like I was going to take the fall for either Jesse not filling out the purchase order correctly or Jake, our purchasing agent, not ordering the correct amount of cases.

A week later, after being suspended for that week, with pay, I was called to a meeting with our human resources person. She informed me that after Jesse had investigated what happened, he determined that it had been my fault that the proper wine had not been received, and that fact coupled with two other disciplinary notes that were in my file, which I knew nothing about and were in fact fictitious, led me to being let go.

"This is incredible," I responded. "I wasn't there to receive the shipment of wine and the liquor room is so cramped I couldn't even get to all of the cases of wine without taking out the champagne and white wine! Jake didn't order enough red wine—not my fault!"

It didn't matter, Jesse had found a way to get rid of me. I wondered if it had to do with seeing what his wife and child actually looked like when I saw them at their home.

Here we go again, I thought. *Just when I thought all was going well here, I am let go for a lousy farcical reason, not just no reason. This is like déjà vu all over again!*

Later that evening, I called Liz to let her know what had happened. She was stunned. But we arranged that I would drive down to Connecticut for a couple days, so we could hash out the Maggie problem.

I began drinking. The rum and Cokes took the edge off.

Chapter 31

Driving to Connecticut was always somewhat of a chore made worse by idiot drivers on I-91 just above Springfield, Massachusetts, where merging traffic was next to insane and where the road curved way too sharply for traffic to maneuver it safely. NASCAR drivers wouldn't have had a problem with that stretch of road, but too many other people did! And from there down through Hartford, drivers were generally out of control. While the speed limits varied up to sixty-five miles per hour, most times, if you were obeying the speed limit, you had at least one car or truck trying to crawl into your back seat! Eighty-five and ninety miles per hour and more were not unheard of, and passing on the right-hand shoulder was apparently acceptable as well. These people never realized how quickly accidents occur, especially when weaving in and out of traffic and cutting people off just to gain a few seconds for their efforts. Maniacs were clueless that they were in fact driving four thousand-pound bullets that were capable of committing mass destruction in seconds.

Nevertheless, I was in no great rush to get to Liz's house and knew I would make it there within five or ten minutes of my expectations, depending on whether or not there was any construction delays or traffic accidents on the way. Just past Hartford, traffic opened up a bit, and everyone was doing about seventy miles per hour. I was in the middle lane when in my mirror, I saw an approaching motorcycle coming up fast. In no time, he was just feet off of my bumper, hemmed in by a car in the left-hand lane passing me slowly and one on the right that was keeping pace with me. I kept watching in my mirror when all of a sudden, the frustrated motorcyclist who obviously had a death wish leaned to the right and gunned his Yamaha and flew in between my Jeep and the car on my right. As he passed me, a semi-tractor trailer began moving from the right lane to the middle lane in front of me, and "Evel Knievel" leaned hard to the left and missed my front bumper by inches and cut in front of the car on the left and managed to miss that driver while accelerating to what had to be at least one hundred to one hundred and ten miles per hour! He was gone! He had almost killed a number of people, including himself, but had managed to merely scare the hell out of everyone.

A little while later, I pulled into Liz's driveway and reveled in the quiet and serenity for a minute before I rang the doorbell.

Liz opened the door and almost knocked me over with a big hug and kiss. "Oh, I am so happy to see you," she said. "I hope your trip was good. Come in, come in, please."

"Well, my trip was uneventful, mostly," I replied, "but outside of the normal Springfield to Hartford mess, just past Hartford, I had a guy, or a girl, I couldn't tell, almost kill me and a bunch of other people when they performed some death-defying feats in and out of traffic while doing a good hundred miles an hour or more on a motorcycle! It was insane."

"Wow, glad you made it. Sounds like you might want a drink. Are you hungry? Did you eat?" Liz asked.

"Not too hungry right now, but a drink sure would be nice. But only if you are having one too," I replied.

"Of course. Beer, wine, or a drink?

"I think a beer would be in order."

Liz handed me a stout from the refrigerator while she chose a glass of white wine. We sat and relaxed for a time, just catching up on everyday things and what was happening in our world while enjoying our beverages. We would get into more in-depth discussions later on in the evening.

Dillon arrived home a few hours later. We began our serious discussions.

Liz opened the talk. "So, Dillon, can you tell both of us what has been happening with you and Maggie lately and, more importantly, what has been happening with your son. We would like to help you get on some type of path that would be most beneficial for you and my grandson. I know when you do get to have him for a few hours and bring him here, that he is a delight, and I somehow want to be sure he is being properly taken care of when he is not. I know you had a really bad experience that one time when you went to Maggie's and found the baby crying, laying in his own excrement, hungry, and Maggie totally out of it! I would do anything for that not to happen again." Liz had obviously thought about how she wanted to have this conversation go and what she wanted to ask and say. She was calm and collected.

Dillon thought for a moment and responded, "First I just want to say that I really appreciate both of you caring so much about what has been happening and offering to help me. I feel that I have been caught between a rock and a hard place as I have to keep paying Maggie for supporting our child while knowing he is not being cared for like he should be. Ever since I found him in that miserable condition and took him out of Maggie's apartment and documented it with pictures, I have felt that I really, really need to do something to protect him from her, but it almost seems that no matter what I have come up with, that I don't think it will work because in this state, the mother is always right. And I don't want to jeopardize my having my son for at least the little time I do get to spend with him."

There was a long pause between us and then Liz looked to me. Although I would have wanted mother and son to hash this out a bit more between them, I felt I was being asked to weigh in on the subject.

"In my mind," I started, "while you obviously don't want to be even more limited in seeing your son, I don't think you can afford to be on the defensive all the time. I think you need to be on the offensive and use what you know and have documented to now use against Maggie and cause her some trouble for a change. It is not a healthy environment for your son to be with her 95 percent of the time. And I think that if child services in this state can't see what is happening that maybe a judge will. You may be able to have more visitation and be able to take him out of that hellhole for more time every week. You're right, the courts will most likely never see clear to take him totally away from Maggie, even if that would be the best thing for him, but at the same time, I don't think you have much to lose as you are basically only getting him once a week for what amounts to a few hours. At worst, it may cause more friction between you and Maggie, but who the hell cares? You have little to lose by at least trying to improve the situation."

"Then you think I should ask for a court date and try to get more time with my son?" Dillon asked.

"Yes, I think you can only benefit from it and even if nothing changes, but I think something will. You will at least know where you stand with the court."

Liz chimed in, "I think that might be a good plan, Dillon. We should be able to show that you can provide a safe, stable home here and that you have help in taking care of him with me here. Maggie really doesn't have any help, it seems. We can present the photos of the baby being in filth when you picked him up and present that Maggie had not taken care of the baby properly and was out of it."

"Well, we could certainly try," Dillon hesitantly stated, "but I'm not even sure how to go about this."

"That is what moms are for," Liz said. "I will help you get everything started and lined up and let's see where this can go." She sounded relieved that there was a plan.

I hoped it would prove to be at least somewhat helpful to all involved.

After successfully negotiating the gauntlet of I-91 through Hartford and Springfield and upon returning to Vermont, I began my search for new employment. Liz and Dillon both searched for answers and help on asking for a court date and prepared their case. A couple of weeks later, they had their court date. They had another month to wait, but at least it was on the docket. I, on the other hand, still had no job offers. Granted I was being picky on what I wanted to do and who I wanted to work for, but the pay in Vermont was certainly lagging behind what companies in Connecticut paid. It didn't help.

A month later, still with no job, I put my life in other hands and drove to Connecticut once again, so I could be in the courtroom when Dillon presented his case. I wanted to see how the whole thing would play out since, in large part, it had been my idea. I also wanted to lend moral support to Dillon and Liz.

Dillon's case was the third on the docket for that day. We all sat through the second one just to see how the whole ordeal worked. It proved to be of little help as the two "adversaries" actually still got along well and were only trying to minimally change their terms of custody with their child.

Dillon's case was called to order. Dressed in a suit and tie, Dillon looked professional. On the other hand, Maggie, arriving just as the case was called, rushed into the courtroom, apologizing for being late because of having to drop her son off at a babysitter's and being caught in traffic. She was dressed in jeans and a sweatshirt and looked haggard. I couldn't decide whether this was intentional, trying to look the part of a worn-out caring mother, or if she was just being defiant or just plain ignorant.

The judge began by addressing both of them as to overall how he wanted the case to go. He wanted everyone to be civil to each other and speak only when spoken to or when it was their turn.

"Do you both understand what I have told you?" the judge asked.

"Yes, Your Honor," Dillon replied.

"Sure" was the reply from Maggie.

Dillon was allowed to present his case. He was very well-spoken, if not eloquent. He was calm and methodical in letting the judge know about the overall condition he had found in Maggie's apartment from time to time, presented the pictures he had taken, and asked that the court grant him more time with his son. He did not bring up the fact that Maggie was a drug dealer; he had only alluded to the fact that she used drugs.

"Thank you," said the judge. "You did a nice job presenting your view of the situation, and you should be commended for your effort."

Maggie was asked to speak.

"Well, judge, I have been doing the best I can bringing up my son alone. Dillon does give some money, but I really feel that I need more to be able to take care of my son as he should be. As for the pictures he presented and his telling you that I had neglected my son, I would say that he was the one neglectful as those pictures were taken in his home, not mine. He was the one along with his mother who is not taking care of my son properly."

I thought Liz was going to jump out of her seat and strangle Maggie.

I held her arm and said, "Relax." After a few seconds, I could feel the tension subside.

"Well, that's an interesting view, young lady. Let me ask you a question. Do you use drugs or alcohol to the extent that you are incapable of taking care of your child?"

"No, I have never nor would I ever use drugs" was the emphatic reply by Maggie. "And I hardly ever have a drink either."

"Okay, I just had to ask," said the judge. He then turned to Dillon, asking, "Is there anything else you would like to say?"

Dillon thought for a moment and began, "Your Honor, I have personally witnessed Maggie using drugs and using alcohol to excess, but I cannot prove it to you. That is all."

"Thank you both," the judge continued. "After hearing both sides and seeing what evidence there is, I have to say that a mother and child's bond is sacred and that unless it can be proven without a doubt that a mother is neglecting her child, she should be the one with primary custody in cases like this. However, I see no reason why the child's father should not have increased visitation at the same time. I would recommend that the child be in the father's care on weekends and as such since he will be taking care of his son more than in the past. I see no reason to increase the child support he now pays to the child's mother. This, I believe, is an equitable solution at this time."

With that being said, the gavel came down, and the judge asked for a short recess. Everyone in the courtroom stood and began leaving.

Maggie turned and smiled as she walked by Dillon, Liz, and me and muttered, "Fuck you."

We let her pass.

— No Reason —

The next minute surprised us as the judge walked to the front of the room and asked if we would speak with him for a moment. "Son, you should be very proud of yourself the way you handled everything today. You were polite, sincere, and presented yourself well. I don't always see that here, and it counted for you. Off the record, I wish you had more factual proof to present, but what you did show the court was that you are indeed a caring father and deserve more say in your child's upbringing."

We thanked the judge and departed.

In my mind, what the judge was actually saying was that he realized what Maggie was, saw how Dillon presented himself yet needed absolute proof of what was happening. Without that, the Connecticut court system was not going to ever rule against a mother.

I asked Dillon if a pizza sounded good for lunch, and the three of us left to celebrate a limited victory but a victory, nonetheless. It was certainly a step in the right direction.

Chapter 32

Back in Vermont, I began to peruse the help-wanted ads, search online, and do some plain old-fashioned drive-by inquiries of companies, shops, and restaurants in the area. Either no one was hiring, or the pay was so low I was better off on unemployment—at least for a while.

A month later gave me little more hope of landing a job. I didn't want to settle, nor was I inclined to not work for an extended period of time. I just wasn't built that way. I kept poking around town, kept my ears open, and talked with people I knew and some that I didn't.

While the job situation didn't look good, I did manage to hear some gossip that proved extremely interesting. Jesse was leaving the resort! He had apparently been offered a job at another resort in Stowe.

Wow, I thought. *I wonder when he started working on that position. And I wonder what sense that makes for him and his family.* I decided I couldn't lose anything by visiting Jesse's wife to see if she would tell me anything about the rather sudden job change and to see how she was doing health wise.

The next day, when I knew Jesse should be at work, I drove to Jesse's house. His car was gone, so I knocked on the door. Shortly the door cracked open. Jesse's wife stood in the shadow of the door, but I could see enough to see her face. It was swollen and bruised—badly.

"Hi," I began. Taken by surprise by what I saw, I continued, "Are you okay? What happened?"

Looking down and twisting to her "good" side, Jesse's wife answered sheepishly, "I'm okay. Just had a bad reaction to some medication. How are you?"

"I'm doing fine. I'm sure you know I no longer work at the resort and have been looking for work elsewhere, but I just wanted to

No Reason

see how you and the kids were doing as I heard you might be moving to the Stowe area soon."

"That's the plan. Jesse thinks Stowe will be an even better place for us and accepted a job there. I was kind of getting used to living here, but Jesse is the boss. So we're going."

"Well, I hope it will be a good move for all of you," I replied. "Good luck with everything."

As I was about to leave, seeing all that I really needed to see and learning that indeed Jesse was moving on in his employment, his older son came running up to his mother.

"Who is it, Mommy, who is it?" he demanded.

"Just a nice man your father used to work with," she explained.

Then I saw his arm! It was in a cast. I couldn't help myself. My blood pressure was rising!

"What in the world happened to you, young man?"

"Oh, Daddy was mad at me and—"

His mother interrupted, "Oh, Jesse and the kids were playing, and he happened to fall wrong and broke his arm. Just an accident."

I looked into her eyes.

She looked down and away. I could tell she knew that I knew what really happened.

"It was good seeing you. Take care. Good luck with your move." It was the only thing I could come up with to say.

I was disgusted. No, not just disgusted, it was more bordering on rage! I knew I had to calm down.

I went home, poured a stiff rum and Coke, and thought—and began planning.

It was time that Jesse was stopped—for good. While time was on my side once again, it wasn't on the side of Jesse's wife or kids. Just how much more abuse could they handle? I didn't want to know, and I didn't want them to find out! I decided that I should make my move before Jesse moved to Stowe. It wouldn't be easy, but nothing worth doing usually is. I was going to have to set up surveillance once again but speed up the timeline on the program. He wouldn't be here too long.

The man just couldn't help himself. Even though he was leaving for Stowe in a matter of a couple weeks, he insisted on seeing his girlfriends on the side almost every night. After three consecutive nights of watching Jesse, two had been spent at that same apartment I had previously seen him at, with the pantry chef, and the other I was sure he had used the spare room in the resort to cheat on his wife with one of the waitresses, again. Quite a guy!

At least he couldn't beat up on his wife and kids when he wasn't home, I thought to myself.

But even that thinking turned out to be shortsighted. For the next day while I was in town searching for an opportunity for employment, I heard that Jesse's older son had had yet another "accident" and had somehow tripped, pulling his mother down the stairs with him! Both were in the hospital. Apparently, the police had gone to the house when the ambulance showed up and questioned Jesse about the incident. According to his statement, it had merely been an unfortunate accident that Jesse himself had called in for the ambulance. Rumor had it that it was in fact lucky that Jesse had been home when it happened. I knew better. This had to stop!

My plan accelerated into warp speed. I began thinking of the best way to stop Jesse from his continual abuse to his family. I had the outline for my plan. It would depend on what happened in the next day or two. First I wanted to see if Jesse's wife would tell the police what really happened that night. She had obviously been too scared to tell anyone the truth up till now, but after both she and her son had been in the emergency room together, maybe she would finally want to protect her children as well as herself.

It didn't happen. Both Jesse's wife and son were released from the hospital late the next day. Jesse drove them home and stayed home from work as he had had to take care of his youngest child while his wife was in the hospital. He made it all seem like he was a caring, loving husband and father.

The following day, I made it my business to know where Jesse was. He left his house midmorning and drove to work, leaving his battered wife to take care of the children. He made sure to tell everyone he saw at work his version of what had happened to his wife

No Reason

and child. After speaking with two of the waiters who were on duty for the lunch crowd that day, it sure sounded like Jesse had been an archangel through the whole ordeal. He apparently had most people convinced it had been an unfortunate accident and that he had been the "white knight" riding in to save the day.

So later that afternoon, I staked out Jesse's car once again. I still knew about when he would, or should, be leaving work, and it only took about a half hour of watching when he walked out to his vehicle. I had to quickly wash down the last two bites of my chicken salad sandwich I had brought and pulled out of the parking lot well after Jesse had driven away. I felt I knew where he was going. Indeed, I was right.

He pulled into the short driveway in front of the pantry chef's apartment. I saw him enter the house. Knowing he would be there for at least the next hour, if not longer, I decided to drive home to get what I needed. I was back watching for Jesse thirty-five minutes later, parked down the road almost out of sight of the apartment. I took a walk to Jesse's car. I knelt down beside the driver's side front tire, unscrewed the valve cap, and with the little tool I picked up at home, unscrewed the valve partway from the valve stem. Air gushed out while I replaced the cap loosely. Then I walked back to my car and waited. I was silent. I was still. I was patient. I was hunting.

Two hours later, it was dark when I saw the porch light go on outside the apartment. I exited my Jeep and walked down the sidewalk toward Jesse. It took a few minutes for Jesse and his girlfriend to finally let each other go, but as it was getting cold out, his pantry chef mistress went back inside. Jesse began walking to his car. After rounding the front fender of his car, even in the half-inebriated state he was in, Jesse noticed the flat tire.

"Son of a bitch!" he exclaimed. "You got to be kidding me! Fuck, fuck, fuck!" He then began opening his trunk.

I was by then just about five yards away in the shadows.

"Are you having a bad night, Jesse?" I asked. "Need some help?"

"Who is there?" he asked as he realized who it was. "You son of a bitch, you did this, didn't you? I'll smash your damn head in!"

And with that, Jesse took one step toward me with tire iron in hand, raising it as he approached.

While I hadn't known just exactly how this was all going to play out, I knew it was now or never. I reached for some other gear I had retrieved from home and pulled out one of my three throwing knives—the one with the red handle. With quick arm motion and a flick of the wrist, I threw the blade at Jesse. It was invisible in the night; the apartment's porch light not reaching nearly that far. I could hear it hit home. Jesse stopped. He staggered and took a slow step, dropping the tire iron, and fell to the ground gasping for air. I took the two steps toward him. I needed to reach where he lay and saw that I had actually missed his chest but luckily threw high, and the blade entered his throat, putting a huge hole in his esophagus. Blood was pouring out everywhere.

"Hope you had a good last fuck," I said as I bent over him to retrieve my knife. "You won't be beating up your wife or kids anymore."

I watched for just a moment more. He understood. His eyes closed.

I walked away but only after I took his wallet from his pants to make it look like a robbery gone bad. I took the money from the wallet and threw the wallet on the ground. Thirty seconds later, I had my nitrile gloves in a plastic bag and was driving away from the scene.

It had been quiet. It had been efficient. It had been necessary. Jesse's widow and children could now begin to lead safe normal lives. They no longer had to be so scared that they couldn't tell the truth. They might be fearful for a few days, but in the long run, they had no reason to live in fear any longer.

Jesse wasn't found until the next morning. The police investigated; the coroner confirmed he had been stabbed by knife in the throat. It looked like a robbery gone wrong, and there were no leads. This type of crime never happens in a nice little tourist town nestled in the hills and mountains of Vermont.

But it did. It needed to.

Chapter 33

Although Jesse's wife and children were horrified with what had just occurred, they were also relieved to know that none of them would be beaten and abused anymore. They wouldn't be moving to Stowe; they could remain where they were if they so choose, or they could move on with their lives in a location of their choice. Sad to know that two children now had no father to look up to, but had Jesse continued on his ways, who could tell if his two children would have even made it into adulthood.

I allowed a couple of weeks to go by—just to be sure that Jesse's family, the town, the police, and the newspapers had settled back into their normal routines once again. Bad things happen all the time, but generally people either have very short memories, or they have more pressing problems to deal with and tend to forget what happened in the past. Or they go through a combination of the above.

I stopped one evening to see how Jesse's wife and children were doing. As I pulled into their driveway, the two children were outside playing in the yard. Jesse's wife saw me through the kitchen window while she was watching out for the safety of her two boys and came out onto the front porch as I approached.

"Good evening," I started. "Looks like the boys are having fun."

"Hi. Well, yes, they are. They are feeling better and better about things and are generally doing better each day."

"And how are you doing?" I asked.

"Me? Oh, I am doing pretty well too. I am adjusting to the fact that it's just me raising the boys, but it had already been mostly me raising them anyway. At the same time, it has made certain things easier on us all." She stared into my eyes, almost like she knew, or at least wanted to ask more so that she would know, but she didn't.

I didn't let her stare faze me.

I looked back for a few moments and then turned to watch her boys play tag. When I returned to finish my conversation, Jesse's wife was smiling. I smiled back. I could tell all was going to be good with them. They were having fun. They were smiling. They were laughing. They were getting over their loss and moving on, together.

"Well, I just wanted to see how you were all doing. Please feel free to let me know if you need help with anything. Anything at all. Here is my card from when I worked at the resort, and my cell number is on the back. Good to see you and the boys. Stay well."

"Thanks so much for caring and for stopping by. Feel free to visit when you can. And if I do need help in the future, I will be sure to contact you."

As I turned and began walking toward my car, she gave me a heartfelt thanks. I kept walking and opened the door to the car, waved, and backed out onto the street.

Jesse's wife and two boys were better than I had ever seen them before. I smiled.

My good feelings were short-lived. Halfway home, my cell phone rang. It was Liz. Once again, she was frantic. I tried to calm her down so that I could understand her better, but it just wasn't happening.

"Liz!" I shouted into the phone, "I am driving and will probably lose you in a minute, but I will call you right back. I am almost home." And then I hung up.

Liz would think I merely lost service, but I needed to concentrate on what was happening with her as well as keep my eyes on the road and watch for Vermont sheriffs whose only job, as I saw it, was to issue traffic tickets of one sort or another to otherwise law-abiding citizens. This would include using a handheld device while driving.

Three minutes later, I was pulling into my driveway.

The first thing I did after visiting the bathroom was to make myself a nice tall rum and Coke. I felt I would need it for what I projected was about to happen. Then I called Liz.

Without my uttering a word, Liz declared, "My god. I need to talk to you! I don't know what to do. Dillon is falling apart, and his son is in danger. And I don't know if there is anything we can do about it!"

"Okay, Liz. Calm. Calm," I encouraged. "Take a deep breath and then another one and begin slowly and succinctly and tell me what has happened."

I could hear Liz taking a deep breath and then a second, and I could tell she was beginning to calm her nerves.

She began, "Where do I start? God!" After another long breath, she began, "Dillon came home today after trying to see his son, and it basically happened all over again! Oh, why does this keep happening?" And I could hear the tears rolling down Liz's face.

"Calm. Breath. Calm, Liz." I waited.

The tears stopped, and I could instead hear anger in her voice. "That bitch can't take care of Dillon's son, and something needs to be done! But I doubt the Connecticut Child Welfare people will do a damn thing about it until it is too late! And that is just not acceptable!"

"Liz, just tell me slowly what happened. So I can understand. Then we can figure out what to do or who to go see. Can you do that?"

"Yes" was the somewhat meek response. "Dillon went to see Maggie to…of all things, give her money for child support as well as pick his son up. After knocking on her door, as he told me, for over two minutes, he managed to push the door open only to find Maggie passed out. This is in the middle of the day today, Saturday! So he went to find his son, and once again, he is in his playpen, filthy. He hadn't been changed again in who knows how long, and Dillon couldn't believe he wasn't crying and screaming his head off. So he immediately starts to undress the baby and begins to clean him up when some guy Dillon has never seen before comes into the apartment, walks right past Maggie who is still out like a light, and asks Dillon, 'What the fuck are you doing here?' Dillon tries to tell this guy who he is, but instead the guy pulls out a knife and threatens Dillon and tells him to get out. So Dillon backs away and, not wanting to escalate the situation, begins to leave. At that point, Maggie begins to wake up and, in a half-lucid state, wonders why Dillon is there. The boyfriend, friend, derelict, whoever he is, continues to come toward Dillon with his knife, and Dillon hits the stairs running. He was scared for his life. But it is his word against Maggie's and the asshole! We don't know what to do!"

"Okay, Liz. If I understand all of this, the bottom line is that the baby is not being taken care of properly, and with Maggie being drugged, drunk, whatever, and a hostile guy showing up and threatening Dillon, it would appear that Dillon's son may be in danger, let alone not being taken care of properly. I would suggest contacting either the state child services or the police—or both—just to at least be on record about this even if they do little or nothing about it. I think you have to begin establishing a record of all this for possible future use in court or whenever."

"Yes, that sounds great, but what about now?" Liz blurted back. "How is that going to help the situation now? You know damn well that the state or whoever will never do anything immediately, and I just don't want whatever they do to be too late."

"Liz," I responded, "you can only start the ball rolling now. It may be slow, but at least you will have notified the proper authorities and be on record. Who knows what may happen after you report this? Maybe the police or child welfare will find out what Maggie is up to, and the whole situation may turn around in a second." I didn't believe what I had just said to Liz for an instant, but I needed to get Liz on track and start her and Dillon down a possible road to recovering some sanity about this whole mess.

After making a bit of small talk with Liz and making sure she stayed calm, I began to formulate my own plan to help alleviate the situation…one that might just be a little more immediate than going through the state.

I sipped my rum and Coke, nibbled on a few roasted cashews, and planned and plotted. Liz was right. Anything that she and Dillon might get started would take literally forever to get through the court system or any other pathway that Connecticut had set up. And there would be no assurance whatsoever that Dillon would even meet with any success given that Connecticut tended to lean heavily in favor of the birth mother, even if they were totally unfit to raise a child.

— No Reason —

Dillon would have a huge uphill battle that could literally last until his son turned eighteen if in fact he made it that far!

Sitting, drinking, popping a few cashews, and thinking the problem through seemed to give me the perspective I needed. It was to my advantage that I knew as much as I did about Maggie's drug dealing, the coming and going of her clientele as well as her supplier, all while never having let on to Liz or Dillon that I had ever staked out Maggie's apartment or even knew where she lived. And I also felt it to my advantage that I now lived in Vermont rather than Connecticut. Sure, it meant more travel and time, but I also felt I could come and go with relative ease and not have anyone know where I was at any given time.

The following day, I phoned Liz just to check up on her state of mind and to see how Dillon was doing as well.

"Liz, good afternoon, how are you doing today?"

"Well, quite frankly, Dillon and I are frustrated to the point of no return! We called Child Services and explained the situation and voiced our concern. They listened and apparently registered our complaint, but they also couldn't give me a good estimate of when someone would go to Maggie's apartment to see what was happening and observe how Maggie is living with and taking care of Dillon's son. And the police were no better. They took our statement, told us that it was really a Child Services matter, and said that unless a crime was committed, they would have no real jurisdiction. Even the fact that Maggie's boyfriend or whoever threatened Dillon with a knife was not enough to get the police involved. It would be a case of two people telling opposite stories and then there was the possibility that they could charge Dillon with trespassing as he had let himself in when Maggie was passed out. What a system!"

"Liz," I calmly responded, "at least you have registered a complaint with the authorities so that if anything else does happen, they can build on it. Please convey my concern to Dillon and let him know that he must remain calm and patient through all of this and that he should document everything that happens between him and Maggie and her so-called friends."

I tried to get Liz's mind off of the subject, so we chatted for a few minutes and finished with Liz asking when I thought I might be in Connecticut again. I didn't want to let her know it was going to be in a few days.

Chapter 34

I began my trip to Connecticut the following Tuesday afternoon. I was in no particular rush, only needing to be in Maggie's neighborhood in the early evening, as it was getting dark. Down I-91 in Vermont was, as usual, uneventful as there was normal traffic which by anyone's standards would be seen as minimal. I saw no Vermont State Troopers.

Upon entering Massachusetts, I concerned myself with driving the speed limit, making sure I did not go over five miles per hour more than the law allowed. I made this a routine whenever I drove in Massachusetts as I did not want to get pulled over and give the police an excuse to either search my car or myself and find that I was either carrying my 9 mm or other guns. There was just little future in it as far as I could see, and I knew that it only really meant a minute or two difference in the time I would arrive at my destination.

Approaching Springfield, I began hitting their normal traffic, which by my standards was anything but normal. Cars were doing seventy-five in the right-hand lane, eighty and ninety in the middle and left-hand lanes. But worse, cars were weaving in and out in order to gain seconds as they put not only themselves in danger but everyone else. Drivers were right on my bumper and then passing me on the right and weaving to almost take my front bumper off my Jeep! What insanity these people lived in. Why they didn't realize they were driving four thousand-pound bullets and could cause a mass murder in the blink of an eye was beyond me. Nevertheless, I continued on at my pace until I came upon some light construction, restricting the lanes down to two for about a half mile.

Upon merging to the right, an older silver pickup truck rolled up behind me and decided to almost live in my back seat. I watched in the mirror closely and gently applied the brakes so as to warn the idiot driving the truck that I had to slow down. A moment or two later, he shot out to my left and pulled alongside of me and began squeezing me over to the shoulder. He was beeping furiously at me, and I could see him gesturing with his right arm and giving me the finger. I had done nothing to him. I couldn't imagine what his problem was. Yet he continued to try to push me off to the side of the road. I managed to get ahead of him in my lane by about two car lengths and kept looking in my driver's side mirror. He was nuts! It was obvious he was again trying to catch up with me.

As luck would have it, my lane began to open up while he remained boxed in in his, not moving at all, nor could he move as he had crawled right up onto the bumper of the car in front of him. I accelerated as fast as I could once free of the work zone in order to put distance between myself and the pickup. A few miles later, I once again approached a work zone and came to a crawl. To my disbelief, the silver truck came up behind me once again and soon managed to get alongside of me as before. Again, he began to cut me off. I managed to avoid him by darting in front of a car to my right and rear. Traffic began to move freely once more, and I hit the pedal. I wanted nothing to do with this guy.

Shortly, I passed the Connecticut welcome sign and traffic was moving as usual above Hartford. I continued onto the Wilbur Cross Highway below Hartford when all of a sudden, there he was again! Right on my tail then passing me and trying to cut me off. I decided that the upcoming exit would be a good one to get off on since I knew the area and could hopefully ditch this idiot. I made a last second right-hand turn onto the exit ramp, but to my amazement, the pickup made an even sharper turn crossing the right-hand lane and making it onto the ramp as well. He then raced to catch me, pulled alongside of the Jeep, and began trying to push me into the railings to my right. I managed to not sideswipe the railings, and as we approached the traffic light, I hit my brakes as he flew past me. He ended up at the light with two cars in front of me. I still had no idea why this guy was after me.

As we waited at the light, this maniac threw his door open and began running back to my Jeep! Still not comprehending all that was happening, I went into survival mode. Reaching into my inside-the-belt holster, I began extracting my Smith & Wesson 9 mm. I don't know if he saw me doing this, if he finally realized that I was not who he thought I was, or what, but as he came up to my car door, he abruptly turned around, still ranting and raving like a looney tune, and climbed back into his truck. I replaced the gun I was prepared to use in its holster and watched this guy pull a U-turn back onto the entrance ramp to the parkway and race up the ramp. He continued to yell and give me the finger as he drove the other way. I will never know what provoked this guy.

What I did know, however, was that there were far too many people who had the chance to observe what had just happened and who could possibly identify my Jeep as being in Connecticut. I aborted my mission. Instead, I drove to Liz's and surprised her. She was more than happy to see me.

"What are you doing here?" she demanded. "Why didn't you tell me you were coming?"

Though I would never tell her the real reason, I said, "Just wanted to surprise you and see how you and Dillon are doing. What's for dinner?"

Liz laughed. "Well, I hadn't planned anything really, but now that you are here, maybe we should go out somewhere."

We visited one of my favorite area restaurants, had a few drinks, had great steaks, and I told her of my wild encounter with the silver pickup on the way down. She was aghast.

"Well, did you call the cops?" she asked.

"No," I responded. "It would be my word against his, and there isn't much the police would do at this point anyway. I do have the guy's license plate number though in case something should come up in the future or if I should be so fortunate, or unfortunate, as to see his truck somewhere."

"I would just steer clear of him no matter what," Liz cautioned.

It was actually good to see Liz talk about something other than Dillon's problems and be concerned about something else for a change. Liz continued to lighten up, and we laughed and chatted until leaving the restaurant.

I stayed two days. I had a nice visit, although it wasn't what I had planned for or hoped to accomplish.

Chapter 35

Back in Vermont, I went over my plan to "visit" Connecticut again—soon. In the meantime, I kept looking for a job. The "right one" this time. And it was getting more difficult for me. The more I didn't work, the more I got used to not having a schedule to conform to. My flexibility in where I wanted to be and when seemed to be overcoming my need for money. But I knew that couldn't really happen. So I looked. I interviewed. But rather than a company interviewing me, it was more like me interviewing the company. I wanted my next move to be a good fit.

A week later, I finally had an interview that I thought went well both ways—for the company and for me. It was a small almost start-up company with only four people currently working there. Two were full time and one was part-time. One was the owner. He was looking for another full-time person, and my background seemed to fit their needs, or so I envisioned. They seemed to be professional yet a bit laid-back. Not wanting to bring up the fact that sometimes I needed to visit Connecticut or take a trip elsewhere with little notice, toward the end of my interview, I did ask about taking time off as needed and what their policy might be. To my relief, they didn't seem to mind when and if that would happen, as long as it didn't happen too regularly. Assuring them that it wouldn't, we briefly spoke about learning their systems and operations. When we parted, I was sure I would be hearing from them soon for a second interview.

The phone rang two days later. It was just after nine in the morning. I was somewhat disappointed when I looked to see it was Liz. Apparently, nothing was changing between Dillon and Maggie. The previous evening was yet another bad one for both Dillon and his son. Maggie was strung out again, and their son was not being taken care of properly. I listened to Liz, tried to calm her down once more, and reiterated that Dillon needed at least to try going through proper channels with the court, etc. She understood; she knew the reasoning, yet she was frustrated and scared beyond belief. And that I understood.

Life, as I knew it, continued in its plodding mundane fashion. The weekend came and it really was like any other day of the week for me. I did chores around the house, went shopping for food, and topped off my tank. Unfortunately, that didn't take all day. I did a lot of reading.

After what I considered was a very quiet weekend, Monday started off on just the opposite foot. Again, shortly after nine while I was having my morning coffee, the phone rang. It was Liz.

"Hello. What's up?" I answered in hopes of having an upbeat conversation.

The reply was anything but uplifting. "Oh, I just had to call you again as I just need to talk to someone about Dillon and the baby. You are the only one I can trust to listen and maybe come up with some good advice."

"Well, let's see what the ongoing saga brings today," I replied.

With that, Liz led into a tirade about Maggie, her lifestyle, her lack of taking care of her son, and her utter disrespect for Dillon. What could I say? She was right as far as I was concerned. I was running out of ways in which to console Liz. And while I paused to think of something new to say to Liz, my phone let me know I had another call coming in. I told Liz I was putting her on hold for a minute to take the other call.

But her reply surprised me with a gruff, "That's okay, we can talk some other time. I'm sure the call is more important than what we are talking about. Bye."

And Liz hung up the phone.

I was more than startled by her action. Obviously, Liz was more bent out of shape than I imagined as she was now striking out at me. It was disheartening to say the least. But I had another call to answer. It was the owner of the small business that had interviewed me some days ago.

— No Reason —

He began with the normal niceties. "Hello, this is Chris calling. How are you?"

"I'm fine, thanks. I was hoping to hear from you. As I had told you before we ended our meeting that I thought you and your operation would be a good fit for me and hoped to discuss the possibilities further."

"Well, that's what I am calling about. Frankly, I don't see a need for a second interview."

My heart began to sink. *Did I not impress him at all during the initial interview?* I wondered, questioning my own perception of how the talk had gone. I didn't know how to respond to that, so I didn't.

There was a pregnant pause.

"No, I mean, I would like to offer you the job. I don't see a need for another interview unless you have some misgivings or questions about the job, our business, or anything of the sort. I do believe that you would be a good fit and become an important asset to the company."

Stunned just a bit once again, I thought for a moment and responded with "Well, yes, I do have a few questions for you, but they are nothing that can't wait until I start. I would be happy to accept your offer."

"Fantastic," Chris replied. "Now, if it's okay with you, I would like you to start here in two weeks, on the Monday. We should have your space and everything set up by then, so you can move in. How does that sound?"

"That works for me! I'm looking forward to it. If you need anything from me before that, just let me know. I appreciate the opportunity."

With that said, Chris assured me that he didn't need anything from me until the day I started. He was a man who would rather deal via handshake and in person rather than go strictly by formalities. I liked that!

I was elated. I had what looked to be a great job, decent pay and benefits, and looked forward to working closely with a few good people. I sat back and smiled.

But only for a moment.

For then I remembered my shortened conversation with Liz and how she was obviously angry with me for taking another call and all but hanging up. I didn't deserve that—but I realized her frustration.

Now, I thought, *I need to plan my strategy for helping Liz, Dillon, and his son.*

With the new job in the wings, I had limited time to do what needed to be done. I knew the schedule Maggie and her drug-dealing friends were on in Connecticut. There was no reason not to still use the same plan I had had when my efforts were thwarted by some idiot in a pickup truck trying to run me off the road and kill me. No one needed to know where I was going to be or not be next Tuesday, six days before the start of my new job. It would be "Connecticut drug bust—take two!"

Chapter 36

The following few days flew by but with one exception. Friday brought me into town for a few essentials that I needed as well as to do some banking. Walking into the bank, I was greeted with the usual hello, and after saluting back, I proceeded to sign a check I needed to deposit. Upon turning around, the teller that was free was a gorgeous young lady, that is to say about my age, who smiled at me, and we made small talk while she processed my transaction. She had no ring on her finger. I was intrigued.

"So I haven't seen you here before. Are you just filling in or permanent at the bank?" I somewhat clumsily asked.

"No, this is my third day. I transferred from another branch, and I will be here permanently now unless of course I give all the money away," she joked.

"Well, even if that were the case, they might keep you on anyway. I'll be sure to put a good word in for you."

"Oh, do you have pull here?" she quipped back.

"You can probably see from my account that my pull here is quite limited. No, I'm just a nobody."

"Why, hello, Mr. Nobody! I'm Hope. Very nice to meet you and hope you will come back soon."

"I will certainly try." I smiled.

"Have a good day," said Hope.

"You have a better one," I responded. *Wow*, I thought as I walked out of the bank, *if that was what I think it was, I haven't flirted or been flirted with in I don't know how long!* If nothing else, my ego received a real shot in the arm. *It was certainly better than what Liz was dishing out to me recently*, I mused.

My weekend was quiet—the way I liked it. I kept going over my plan for my trip to Connecticut on Tuesday, one that I hoped would go off without a hitch and allow Dillon to become a real dad and Liz to be a lot less stressed and a bit more congenial. But my other thoughts were about my encounter with Hope.

Monday I again had to, or more wanted to, visit the bank. I needed cash for my upcoming little trip to Connecticut and back. I could not use credit cards and even just having my cell phone on me was bad enough for tracking purposes; I felt the pros outweighed the cons in carrying it. I made a mental note of not keeping it on all the time.

I walked into the bank and was greeted by a chorus of three hellos by various staff—two tellers and the branch manager. I did not see Hope. After finishing filling out my withdrawal paperwork, I turned and saw her. She had apparently been in a back room, the bathroom, or taking a break somewhere, but now she was back, and as I approached the window, she looked up and seemingly recognized me.

With a smile, Hope asked, "How can I help you today…sir?"

"Well, I have an easy one for you today. Wouldn't want to make you work too hard, you know," I responded.

"That's good because I wouldn't want to disappoint you," Hope quipped back.

I liked her attitude and style. She was not only beautiful but bright, quick, and personable. I hadn't seen much of that lately. I felt invigorated.

As Hope counted out the money I was withdrawing, I quickly turned my head to see another customer enter the bank. It was a young man enveloped in a hoody, making it difficult to see his face. Bank personnel didn't care for people coming in with hoodies on. The hair on my neck began to bristle, and I went into hunting mode. I watched and listened and positioned myself just in case something nasty began to happen. And it did.

In a split second, the young man produced a small revolver and waved it in front of the teller two windows to my right.

"Everyone, stay exactly where you are!" he demanded. "I need all the money you have, and I will shoot anyone who gets in my way.

— No Reason —

Don't even think about hitting an alarm because if one goes off, I will just start shooting," he rambled.

The tellers and branch manager who were all behind the counter at this time froze, including Hope. The poor young women directly in front of this lunatic was gasping for oxygen and shaking visibly. I was the only customer in the bank at the moment, unless you count this idiot who the more I observed of him, the more I was sure he was strung out on something which made him more of an uncertainty and threat to everyone. He began waving the gun at the bank personnel more and more and glanced my way, trying to make sure I complied as well. He didn't see me as a huge threat. His second mistake!

I allowed him to continue ranting about getting all the money from the tellers. The more he demanded, the more frantic he became. He was whipping himself into a frenzy, and I felt becoming more unpredictable every moment. I could see this situation escalating into a really, really bad event at the drop of a hat.

"Hurry up!" he shouted at the tellers. "Put all of the money into one bag and hand it over! Now!"

The poor scared tellers were trying, but they were so fearful they could hardly move as fast as this assailant wanted them to. I felt I was watching a time bomb which could explode at any moment.

"Listen," I said calmly, "these nice people are doing all they can to help you with what you want."

With that, he turned toward me, pointing his gun, and shouted, "Shut up! I will kill you if I hear from you again!"

After a moment staring at his gun, I began to laugh! He looked at me incredulously and took a step closer, still pointing his six-shot revolver at my face. He thumbed back the hammer of the weapon and ordered me to get on my knees.

"You don't want to do this," I said with a smirk. "You are already in trouble. Don't make it worse. Just put the gun down and leave—now!"

He apparently couldn't believe what was happening. He hadn't prepared for anyone challenging him like this, and he was becoming confused and more agitated than ever.

"I will kill you!" he exclaimed. "Get on your knees now!"

With his attention focused now totally on me, it allowed the two tellers and bank manager to quietly and quickly flee into a back room. This man was a mess. He had lost any control he had had and now couldn't comprehend the situation he had put himself into. Only I stood directly in front of him with Hope standing behind the counter to my left and to the right of this master thief.

I continued to focus on his revolver. He was now close enough that I could make a final verification that the six chambers in the handgun were all empty. As he trained his .38 on me, I could see into the chambers and see some daylight, indicating that the gun was not loaded. Standing and showing him no fear, I instead slowly and purposefully drew my concealed 9 mm from my inside-the-belt holster. He was in disbelief and began looking for an exit strategy.

"Now put your gun on the floor and lay down facing the floor. You see, my gun is actually loaded and yours isn't! Do it now," I insisted. "Hope, hit your alarm just in case your friends haven't already done so," I instructed.

She reached out her arm, hit the button, and our assailant hit the floor—face down.

I kicked his revolver away and stated, "We will wait."

The wait wasn't long. Local police arrived within about a minute and a half. Upon their ascertaining who was who and finding out that I was actually a good guy, I had done as instructed and laid my Smith & Wesson on the floor and backed away as the police handcuffed the failed robber and read him his rights. Of course, the police were a bit skeptical of me until Hope and the other staff in the bank told them what I had done. They were very apologetic after that and, in fact, thanked me for what I had been able to accomplish.

This, I thought, *was going to ruin the rest of my day—and sure as hell cancel any ideas I had about traveling to Connecticut.* I felt almost cursed at this point.

So the police interviewed me and got my side of the story, which happened to coincide with all of the bank staff's version of what happened. Nevertheless, I was now in the spotlight, so to speak, and knew I wouldn't be able to get to Connecticut in the near future given the fact that I was now somewhat of a town celebrity. So much for staying under the radar!

On the other hand, the staff at the bank loved me—including Hope! In fact, after the interviews were all done and over with and the police advised us that we could all go, Hope came over to me and threw her arms around me. She hugged me harder than I can remember and then broke out in tears. I held her in my arms and allowed her to cry. After my shoulder was thoroughly wet, she finally relaxed her grip on me and looked into my eyes.

"Thank you. That's all I can say right now. Thank you," she said softly.

In my typical smart-ass way, I answered, "No problem. Always happy to come to the aid of a damsel in distress!" And then I pushed my luck almost without thinking, "Can I buy you dinner tonight?"

Hope looked at me, smiled, and burst out laughing. "I should be the one taking you out to dinner or cooking for you or something!" she blurted.

"That may all come to pass down the road," I responded, "but for today, I think you had enough on your plate that you really don't need to cook tonight. What do you say?"

There was somewhat of an awkward silence.

"Listen, if you would just like to be alone and not deal with anything else today, I understand. Don't worry about it," I stammered.

"No! No! I would love to have dinner with you tonight. Oh my. I don't know why I hesitated. That would be great. So where do you want to meet? Or when or I don't even know what I am saying at this point."

I put my index finger against her lips softly. "Okay, okay. Breath and get calm. How about if you tell me where you live, I pick you up around seven, and hopefully by then I will figure out a good place to eat? Anything you don't like?"

"Only one thing," Hope responded, "I don't care for chain fast food."

It was my turn to laugh. "I'm with you there. That is the farthest thing from my mind. No, we will go to a nice restaurant so we can relax, talk, have a drink or two, eat some really good food, and maybe get to know each other a little better."

"That sounds great! Are you sure though?" she asked.

"Positive." I smiled.

Hope smiled back.

After finding out Hope's address, I reiterated that I would be by at 7:00 p.m. She confirmed the date and started to thank me again.

I stopped her by holding up my hand, smiling, and saying, "I know. It's in the past. Let's get to the future."

She nodded her agreement.

We parted company for the moment, and as I was walking away, my thoughts turned to what had just transpired. *Wow, this has really messed up everything to do with helping Dillon and Liz, but on the flip side, what an introduction to Hope. This will be interesting to see where this goes.* I felt really good.

Then I snapped back into reality.

My phone was ringing. It was Liz. I actually hesitated for a moment wondering if I should answer it. But I did.

"Hello."

"Hello" was Liz's reply. "I need to talk to you about this whole mess down here once again. I can't bear to see what is happening to Dillon all the time. Maggie called him last night and told him she was going to bring him to court if he didn't start to give her more money and pony up more things for her to have for the baby. She is totally out of control and ruining Dillon's life. And mine!"

I couldn't get a word in edgewise.

"She won't allow Dillon into her apartment to pick up the baby now either. She has to bring him down to the road. That just makes everything take longer, and Dillon has to wait for her to come to the car. It's awful. I don't know what to do. Can you help us?"

Finally, I had a chance to talk.

"Well, thanks for the call," I started sarcastically. "I understand you are frustrated beyond belief and feel helpless, but my first instinct tells me to ask you once again if Dillon has started any type of process where he goes on the offensive and takes Maggie to court over what has been happening."

"He is going to do that. He promised me he would do that this week," Liz fired back.

"Well, it has to start somewhere, Liz. And I have no say in the matter—I'm not related to anyone involved in this whole mess. Dillon has to step in and begin swimming on his own. He can't just tread water and hope someone comes along to save him. It may not happen."

"I know, you are right. But Dillon is young, and he is unsure about all of this. And I don't know much about it either. You said you would help, even if you were in Vermont, and we thought we could count on you."

"I can only help as much as I can," I responded. "I can't do it all for you and Dillon."

"I know that!" was a somewhat emphatic response.

I could tell Liz's anger was growing and not just with the situation but with me! I couldn't let on to her that I had been thwarted twice now to solve the situation and that sometime in the near future, I would try for a third time to make the problem go away.

Liz began again, "Maybe you shouldn't have moved to Vermont! You might still have a good job here and been able to help Dillon more if you were around. Maybe everything would be different."

I heard tears begin to roll down her face. They were angry tears.

Following a bit of silence on my part and sobbing on hers, I started to calmly reply, "Liz, you know I had to do what was best for me first and that I would help..."

I was cut short as the conversation was cut off.

Wow, what a change in Liz, one that I am very happy to find out about now.

I might normally have been devastated, but with me stopping the bank robber earlier, which I didn't even get to tell Liz about, and with actually getting a date with Hope, which I wasn't going to tell Liz about, I still felt pretty damn good about how my life was going. Not to mention a new job coming right up.

I drove home thinking, *No matter what happens with Dillon and Liz, I will still try to help them out of the situation they are in if for no other reason than the good of Dillon's child. But whether or not anything comes out of my date tonight with Hope, I think it is in my best interest to cut social ties with Liz after her problem is solved. She could continue to rent from me, but I think it would be best if my relationship with her didn't cross over the landlord-tenant line.* I would cross that line when necessary.

Upon arriving home, I was trying to think of the best place to take Hope for dinner. There were a great many good restaurants in the area but only a few really great restaurants. I poured myself a good stiff rum and Coke—I was pretty sure I deserved one—sat down and thought.

The bank incident felt like it was eons ago. Instead I was looking forward to going out with Hope. And then it hit me. I knew where to take her. Just because I didn't work there anymore didn't mean I shouldn't go there. It was a great place. Great food, atmosphere, and service, and since I knew most of the personnel, I felt confident we would get the proper attention I was looking for. I booked a table for two for seven thirty. I finished my drink.

Chapter 37

Seven o'clock took forever. I was showered and dressed and ready way too far in advance and thought about pouring myself another glass of courage but thought better of it. I didn't need to make a bad impression after making a good one. I waited. A few minutes before seven, I took off in my Jeep. I figured it to be about a ten-minute drive to Hope's address and from there another ten minutes to the resort and the restaurant. It gave us an extra ten-minute buffer in case Hope wasn't ready.

For some strange reason, I was nervous as I approached her door. I was already her hero. What could possibly go wrong? I knocked. After a minute, I knocked again. Then I heard someone walking toward the door. I was relieved when Hope cracked the door open and peered out. She smiled as she opened the door fully and ushered me in.

"Sorry I took so long to answer the door, but since I didn't know where we are going and how casual or fancy it might be, I kept trying on different outfits and finally settled on this, if this is all right?" Hope had on a simple gray dress with a silver necklace and matching earrings.

I was awestruck. "You could have showed up in jeans, and you would have been okay. You look wonderful," I beamed.

"Thank you. And please," Hope continued, "let me thank you again for what you did today. I—"

"Stop," I cut her off. "It was something that just happened, and it happened to work out well. It's probably something we might talk about and even laugh about in the future, but right now let's just look toward the future and to our dinner tonight. Okay?"

"Sounds good. Let me get my purse. Are you going to tell me where we are going?"

"I'll let you know when we are there. You will have to let me know if you have been there before. Since we know so little about each other at the moment, it's going to be fun getting to know you," I offered.

"Yes, it will" was the somewhat meek reply.

I opened the door to my Jeep and allowed Hope to settle in before shutting it. After climbing in on my side and putting on my seat belt, Hope asked me her first question of many we would undoubtably have for one another this evening.

"So do you always happen to have a gun on you, or was that just a lucky coincidence?"

"Well…I will tell you this. When I am out and about, my gun doesn't do me any good sitting locked up in my house. If you are uncomfortable with that, I understand, but—"

"Oh, no! I am very comfortable with that," Hope interrupted. She smiled at me, and I mirrored her smile back. She touched my wrist and said, "Thank you."

We were off to a great start!

Dinner was fantastic. The company was even better. Hope had never been to the resort. She had only heard about it. We began with a cocktail and some mindless conversation. We followed that up with appetizers—stuffed mushrooms for Hope and fried calamari for me. I ordered a glass of Merlot for each of us to enjoy with dinner as she ordered a filet mignon, and I opted for an end cut of prime rib. By the time we got to thinking about dessert, we both concluded that we were just too full to order.

"My lord," exclaimed Hope, "that meal was awesome! I can't thank you enough again for all you did today. And you managed to keep my mind off of what happened at the bank today throughout the meal. You are a wonder."

"Overall, I wish we didn't have to go through what we did today, but by the same token, look where it has gotten us. I really enjoyed dining with you tonight and learning a bit more about you. I hope we can do this again."

"You bet!" was the more than enthusiastic reply. As we got up from the table, Hope stepped toward me and gave me a soft kiss on my cheek. It was accompanied by a beautiful smile.

In turn, I took her hand and we walked to the car. This was one of the best days of my life. It looked like there was Hope at the end of my tunnel.

The drive back to her apartment was full of laughter. We had found out enough about each other during dinner to enjoy each other's brand of wit. Hope could be very sarcastic at times, something that paralleled my dry, sarcastic humor that some found extremely objectionable. But Hope did not.

Pulling into her driveway, I was about to get out of my Jeep, so I could open the door for Hope when she pulled me toward her and gave me a real kiss. I responded in kind.

After a few more loving pecks, she stated, "We might be more comfortable in the house and top the night off with a nightcap."

I followed her inside.

We collapsed on the couch after Hope poured us each a glass of wine, and we continued to talk. We were great for each other. As it was getting really late, or really early depending on your viewpoint, I knew Hope would have to once again be at work in the morning.

"I should go. You have to work tomorrow, and I have things to do as well. I might stop into the bank just to see how everyone is doing, but other than that, I hope you have a wonderful day. I had a great time tonight."

Again, Hope took the lead. She pulled me to her and gave me a huge hug and followed it up with a heartfelt kiss. I think we had both died and gone to heaven.

"I can't thank you enough. But you already know that. I hope I will see you tomorrow, but if not, please call me at night."

"I will be in touch. And thank you for a great evening." I turned and walked to the Jeep.

My life, I felt, was going in the right direction.

The following day, I wandered into the bank in the early afternoon. All seemed like it had gone back to normal. Hope was busy with a customer, but the bank manager saw me come in and greeted me and thanked me once again for what I did the day before.

Hope continued to be busy, so when she looked up, I mouthed to her, "I will call you later."

She smiled.

Later, while snacking on some popcorn at home, I went to pick up the phone when in fact it rang. Thinking it might be Hope, I answered with an enthusiastic "Hello!" It was Liz.

"Listen, I want to apologize for how I acted when we last talked. I was upset, well, I am still upset. But I think I am more in control of my emotions now. I know I sometimes expect a lot, but I just don't know what to do."

My response was measured but firm, "I realize you are under a lot of pressure about the whole mess with Dillon and Maggie, but you have to realize that some of what is happening has to be taken care of by Dillon. Although I would love to be able to wave a magic wand, I can't do that, so I actually need a little bit of slack from you as well. And believe it or not, I have been trying to make a life for myself up here too, and I want to stay on the right track. Do you understand?"

"Yes, I guess I do" was Liz's sheepish reply.

We made small talk for a few more minutes, but I thought it not important to fill her in on the bank robbery and all that followed. There would be time for that if necessary.

After we said our goodbyes, I sat and thought, *How am I going to pull all of this off now that I am going to be working, have a new "friend" here in Vermont, and need to get away to Connecticut soon but that so no one knows I was there?*

It was a quandary I was going to have to work out.

I picked up my phone and called Hope. "You were a busy girl today," I opened with.

"Well, yes, I was. We were! Not only were regular customers coming in, but it seemed like the entire town stopped in to visit after what happened yesterday. So of course, we all took extra time talking to everyone about it. It's kind of getting old already—talking over and over about what happened and what could have happened. And of course, lots of people asked who saved the day. I know you had wanted to stay under the radar, and I didn't tell anyone your name or anything like that. But I bet the newspaper on Thursday will have the whole incident spelled out, and you will become a real celebrity."

"I'm sure that will happen too," I responded. "I just hope the whole thing can blow over in a short time, so I can go back to just being me instead of some savior figure. I don't need the publicity."

"I know. And that is just another reason why I like you so much. You are very humble about it all and what you did. You are amazing!"

"Okay, yep, that's me. Now can we talk about other things?"

Hope realized that enough was enough on that subject. "You bet! How about let's talk about us getting together again soon not only to relax a bit but also to have you instruct me in learning how to shoot. We talked briefly about it over dinner, but I have thought about it more today and really do want to learn more about shooting and all that goes along with it, both for fun and for self-defense. Would you still be willing to teach me?"

"Only on one condition," I quickly responded. "You will have to make your lasagna for me that you were bragging about at dinner. I want to make sure you really can cook."

I could tell Hope was smiling. "But of course, it's a deal. How does this Saturday night sound for a lasagna dinner?"

"Awesome! I'll bring some wine. And if you want, I can begin your introduction into handling firearms. But we will have to do that before we pop the cork."

"Sounds good. I'm looking forward to it."

We continued to chat over the phone, finding bits and pieces about each other that only enhanced our newfound friendship.

Almost a bit of déjà vu, I thought. *I remember going on a somewhat similar journey with Liz not too long ago.*

This, however, felt even more real to me than before.

When we began wrapping up our conversation and started saying our goodbyes, I interrupted and inquired, "So I just had a thought. How about if we get together for a drink or two this Friday evening? I want to be sure you think I'm worth a lasagna dinner on Saturday," I quipped.

"Oh, I already think you are worth one lasagna dinner. But it's a good idea, so I can be sure of it," Hope countered my serve.

We laughed.

Friday evening was upon us like a flash. We met at a local tavern, had a few drinks, relaxed, talked, played a little pool, and shot some darts. Hope was fun!

Saturday afternoon, I began getting a couple guns and teaching tools together for my lasagna firearms class. I wanted to be sure to make Hope's instructional experience fun yet give her enough substance to allow her to want to learn more and more. I packed up my Smith 9 mm, my Ruger .10-22 rifle, and my Weatherby Orion over-under shotgun. The shotgun was more to impress her with than really teach her about at this point, but I did want to give her a good overview on what these three firearms could do and how to handle them. I brought appropriate ammunition to show Hope for all three firearms as well.

At four o'clock, with guns in hand, I knocked on Hope's door. She soon greeted me, and after finding out where I could put the guns for the moment, I set them down and excused myself to the car. I reentered her house with two bottles of one of my favorite white wines, Tiefenbrunner Pinot Grigio.

"I think these should go well with your lasagna," I said.

"I'm sure they will. After all, you know, I'm not much of a wine snob, don't care if there is red with red meat or white with fish or whatever, as long as I like it," Hope declared.

I felt the same way. And there had been times in my past when I had had a $100 bottle of wine and also had a $30 bottle of wine and couldn't really tell the difference.

"As long as you enjoy them, that is what matters most," I agreed.

I liked someone who thought along the same lines as me! No pretentious thoughts, just simple honesty.

I put the wine in her refrigerator to chill.

Hope was still busy putting together her great-looking lasagna before putting it in the oven, so I started taking the guns out of their cases and placed them on her coffee table, together with a selection of appropriate ammunition as well as a cleaning kit. Both semiautomat-

— No Reason —

ics had the magazines removed and receivers open, and the shotgun I left in three pieces—stock and receiver, barrel, and the forearm. I wanted to show Hope how easily the gun went together. By the time I finished tinkering with the three firearms, Hope was ready to put the lasagna into the oven.

"I am ready to begin the class if you are," stated Hope. "The sooner we do the class, the sooner we can taste this wine you brought! I'm looking forward to it."

"I'm ready too. But we are going to take the class nice and easy. There is no rush. And anytime you have a question, feel free to stop me and ask. Okay?"

"No problem."

I began with the 9 mm handgun, first going over basic nomenclature and parts of both the gun and the ammo then went over overall safety when handling a firearm. Hope listened attentively and seemed to take it all in in her stride. I moved on to the .22 rifle and did pretty much the same thing, posing simple questions to Hope on where she thought a safe direction might be while holding a rifle rather than a handgun and how best to carry a rifle versus other guns. She was an eager student.

Finally I showed Hope the twelve-gauge shotgun. I put the pieces together in a few seconds. She was not only amazed at how quickly it could be done but thought the gun was just beautiful. It was! We talked about the use of a shotgun, both for fun and for self-defense, and I made sure she knew there were also pump actions, semiautos, bolt actions, and side-by-sides as well. We would get into more depth on these as well as other guns should she want to keep learning at a later time. Hope was enthralled!

"When can we do this again? I want to learn more, and I want to be able to shoot them all too."

"We will, we will." I laughed. "It is going to be a process, so patience. Right now I want to show you how to hold each of these three guns correctly, load them, and get used to handling them a bit. It will take some time for you to get comfortable with these and other guns, but again, we are in no big rush. And I can't emphasize enough that safety is the first concern."

"Yes, I know. I want to learn it all and go shooting with you and be just as good as you." Hope smiled. "But now I should check on the lasagna. It should be about done. And now I have to keep up my end of the bargain."

Dinner was just starting to bubble, so Hope was going to leave it in the oven for another ten or fifteen minutes so it could brown. It gave me time to put away the guns and open a bottle of wine. I poured two glasses, and we toasted.

"Here's to your becoming another Annie Oakley," I proposed.

We clinked glasses and sipped.

"Wow, this is great! It's going to go well with the lasagna," she said.

"Time will tell," I responded with my dry humor and a smile.

Hope extracted the lasagna from the oven and uncovered a garlic bread that she had made from scratch earlier in the day. She placed it in the oven to warm.

"The lasagna is too hot to eat anyway, and the bread will warm up nicely in the meantime. Maybe you could pour a little more wine while we talk?"

My eyes and nose were both in hyperdrive. The garlic bread not only looked great, but now as it heated, it began to smell even better.

"You are a wonder," I said. "This is obviously beyond the call of duty. I love garlic bread! How did you know?"

"Just a hopeful wild guess. I wanted to make this dinner as memorable as possible. I hope we can have many more as time goes on."

"Judging by the smell alone, between the lasagna and garlic bread, I think that it's pretty safe to say we could keep doing this on a regular basis. But I will let you know for sure after I taste everything," I quipped.

We both laughed.

Minutes later, we sat down to eat.

"This lasagna is awesome! As good as my mother used to make," I ranted. "And I can't believe this garlic bread. Wow! I haven't had anything like this in ages! I can't thank you enough for all of this."

"No!" Hope responded. "I can't thank you enough for all you have done already. I mean it! You go around not wanting to be thanked and all humble and all, but you must realize what you did in the bank the other day and now starting to teach me about guns and safety is way beyond what anybody normally does." She reached out across the table and took my hand. She began to cry.

I got up and went to her and held her.

"I'm sorry," she started.

But I interrupted. "No, you let it all out. It was a very traumatic experience the other day, and you have to let yourself acknowledge that. It's okay. Besides, now you have to put up with me being around more and more and learning more about shooting than you ever wanted to."

Her tears began turning to laughter. She started pushing me away, but I held her. When she gave in, she looked up at me and we kissed.

After having seconds, we sat and talked and enjoyed our wine. I helped clear the dishes and clean up the kitchen, and I thought dinner was over. I wanted to relax with Hope and keep conversing. I was wrong.

"We still have one more course to enjoy," Hope said. "I hope you like tiramisu."

I was astounded. I had found a woman who was not only smart, intelligent, fantastic looking, fun, and nice but who could also cook better than me!

"What!" I exclaimed. "I suppose you are going to expect me to save you every week all of the time after all this. You are something!"

We had a great night. It could not have gone better.

Chapter 38

Monday, I began my new job. It began by sitting down with Chris and filling out all of the required paperwork needed for working. What a bore! But while doing so, Chris also filled me in more on some of their procedures, holiday schedule, sick time, and most importantly, he told me how since everyone working there goes deer hunting every year, they shut down the first week in the season so everyone can commit to getting venison in their freezer.

"Yep," said Chris, "it's one of our benefits that I initiated so that anyone who cares to relax in the woods, go on a hunting trip, or just merely sit home can do so for that week each year. You have to be here ninety days to get paid for the week, and since you won't be here that long by the time the season begins, you will not be paid for that week. But after that, it is a paid week."

"That's fantastic," I responded. "I'm not worried about losing one week of pay but being able to hunt the first week of the season is a great benefit! And next year getting paid to hunt will be even better. Thanks for that."

Not only did I already like the attitude in the company, but this would afford me my time to do what I loved to do as well as give me time off so that I could sneak down to Connecticut for a day and take care of a certain problem, hopefully with no one noticing my being gone. I would merely be hunting as far as anyone knew.

My first day went by in a blink of an eye. Everyone seemed really nice and helpful, but then everyone always seemed nice and helpful on your first day anywhere. But it was more than that—they all seemed genuine. I got to talk about hunting with almost everybody and felt this job was going to be a great fit as everyone seemed to love the outdoors—hunting, fishing, kayaking, hiking, and walking or jogging to stay fit. What a deal. What a nice change.

In the evening, while preparing some meat loaf for myself, the phone rang.

"Hello," I greeted the caller.

It was Liz.

"Hello," she responded. "How are you? We haven't talked in a while, and I wanted to make sure everything is okay—between you and me, I mean."

"Well, I have some good news and some bad news. I started a new job today, and I feel really good about it. It's a small company trying to grow, but everybody seems to be really friendly and team oriented. Quite a change from what I'm used to."

"That's great. Congratulations. I hope it all works out well for you."

"Thanks. But I have also been thinking a lot about our relationship and our lack of communicating well lately, especially when it concerns Dillon, his son, and Maggie. I know the whole ordeal has been tough on you and Dillon, but I feel I have been made the sounding board for you, and it hasn't always been pretty. I don't deserve anger, and I don't deserve to be hung up on. It's not what I call a good relationship any longer. And don't get me wrong, I still want to help where and when I can as far as this whole debacle, but I'm not going to be the bad guy here anymore. I have a life to live too, and it is just starting to turn around and get to where I want it to be."

There was silence on the other end. I was sure Liz didn't expect that out of me, but I had to air my thoughts and feelings and be honest.

A somewhat meek response followed, "Thanks for that. I know I have not always acted like I should, and I expected way too much. But what happened between us over this thing has happened. I can't change that. But I have also had a deep conversation with Dillon, and he has talked to the child welfare people and the court system. And he is trying to go forward to get more parental rights through them than he now has. It is a start. As for me, I will continue to support him in any way I can even if it means me being frustrated, angry, and terrified all at the same time. I also wanted to let you know that I really don't want us not to be friends but that Dillon and I will not rely on you to fix all of our problems. It's just not fair or right. I would like to stay in touch, be friends. You can continue to be my landlord if you still choose to allow me to rent, but I will expect nothing more."

Now there was silence on my end. It was a lot to absorb—especially when I didn't expect it.

"Of course, you can continue to rent the house from me. And I do hope we can continue to be friends. You know I care about you and Dillon and his son—a great deal. I would like to be kept abreast of what happens in the future."

"Thanks for understanding where I am at," responded Liz.

And almost without thinking, I took a shot in the dark and asked, "So have you found someone new?"

I knew the question could go wrong in a hurry, but I had to know. If Liz had in fact found another man she was interested in, it would at this point be something favorable to me as well.

"Well, I think so," she said. "We have seen each other a couple of times, and we seem to have some of the same interests. And he is a lawyer and is willing to help out Dillon as he can. He has cautioned us as to what to expect the courts to do to help Dillon, but there is a chance we could see some positive decisions made. I could only hope for Dillon and his son's sake. But who knows how long it will take?"

My "shot in the dark" turned out to be a bull's-eye!

"I'm happy for you, Liz. I really am. And for Dillon too. I hope something good can come out of this relationship for both of you." I was smiling.

Now I wouldn't have to feel bad about dating Hope or worrying about hurting anybody's feelings down the road. Life was getting better and better.

After saying our goodbyes, I hung up the phone and fashioned myself a bourbon and Coke. I contemplated my good fortune of late. The meat loaf was in the oven. I began preparing some brussels sprouts to steam and cut up a couple of potatoes to boil for mashed potatoes. I punched in Hope's number.

— No Reason —

"I've had a great day! How about you?" I asked after Hope picked up on her end.

"Mine just got better now that you have called" was the response. "I take it you had a good day at work."

"Yes, I did. Work didn't seem like work, and that is always a good sign. Everyone was helpful and nice showing me around and letting me know where things are kept, etc. but then that is almost mandatory on anyone's first day at work."

"Well, that's great," Hope responded. "Sounds like this will be a good fit for you."

"I hope so. And one of the nicest perks of the job is that they give the first week of deer season off so everyone can go hunting and hopefully get some venison while communing with nature. Better yet, they pay for the week off too. Although since I just started, this year I won't get paid for the week, but as of next year I will. What a deal!"

"That is remarkable! It sounds like the owner really cares about his people and how they live and play. You know it really doesn't take much to gain enthusiastic and dedicated people who actually want to work. It just takes some thought and effort. But I'm sure giving the staff that week off with pay comes back in spades for the company over the course of the year."

"I'm sure you are right," I responded.

We then talked about more mundane things like the weather, what was happening in town and at the bank, and about getting together during the week in the evening for a drink or whatever. After saying good night, I sipped my bourbon and Coke and took the meat loaf out of the oven, mashed the potatoes, and sat down to a meal of comfort food.

Chapter 39

The following two weeks flew by. Work continued to be great. I was getting to know people, what I needed to do each day, procedures, and by all accounts, Chris informed me that so far I had been exceeding expectations. I liked the way he communicated, was forthright in his criticism and accolades, and I knew where he was coming from and what was expected of me.

On the home front, all was going great with my relationship with Hope. She was a very calm and collected person, especially when bank robbers weren't pointing a gun at her, but she was also extremely caring and thoughtful, most often thinking of me more than of herself. She was just what I had been looking for and needed. We met for drinks at night once or twice a week and usually managed to eat over each other's house at least once a week.

At our last dinner together, I informed Hope that since deer season opened on Saturday, I would be in the woods most of the day and for the week for that matter. She understood that it was my haven, my "church," and my time away from all the rat race of daily life. But I did mention that I might just pop over some evening after hunting to fill her in on my escapades in the forest.

"I'm cool with that. You can drop over anytime," Hope encouraged.

So the Saturday of opening day, I entered the woods midmorning. I actually hoped not to get a deer too soon in the week, as I had planned my trip to Connecticut on Tuesday. I really didn't want anyone to think I wasn't hunting that day, nor did I want a deer hanging in my front yard where someone might come by, see it, and wonder where I was that day. I was satisfied to scope out new territory, relish in the great outdoors, and observe nature at its best.

I managed to see some good deer sign but only saw a few does all day. Sunday and Monday where similar, although I scouted different areas, seeing some good tracks and a few scrapes where bucks were leaving their scent. Outside of a handful of small does, I finally got to watch a four-point buck wander through a mountain field. It was great fun to watch him, and I hoped he would grow into a big ten-pointer in the years to come and sire more bucks.

Monday evening, I decided to drop in on Hope. She was happy to see me and hear about my experiences in the woods for the past three days. It was obvious that Hope wanted to learn more about hunting with all of the questions she posed to me, so after some wine and cheese, I popped the question.

"Would you like to go out with me sometime and get a feel for how I hunt and what it does for me?" I asked.

"Really? You would take me out into the woods with you? Wouldn't I ruin your hunting?"

Laughing, I replied, "Not in the least. I would love to spend the day with you in the woods. Who knows, if I get a deer that day, you could drag it out for me!"

"Or I suppose you could have me gut your deer for you" was her quick response.

"That would be another option," I joked. *What a gal!* I thought to myself. *She is actually interested in what I love to do and is willing to learn about it firsthand. How did I get so lucky?*

I didn't stay late knowing that I had to prepare for my trip south the next day. I was hoping the third try at this would be the charm. I also wondered if I really needed to do this thing anymore as Liz seemed like she was moving on with her life, and Dillon had finally started the ball rolling with the court system. But on the other hand, his son deserved better, and Maggie was a slimeball in my estimation, not a good mother, a despicable person, and low-life drug dealer who actually helped or caused at least two deaths that I knew of. And then there were Maggie's suppliers, even more lowlife as all they cared about was money. They didn't value anyone's life, as could be attested by Maggie if she cared to admit it, and they could certainly have gone after Dillon with a vengeance if Dillon had not beat feet out of there as quickly as he did.

No. I decided the court system was far too uncertain in Connecticut, giving every opportunity to mothers no matter how bad their care of a child and to lord over fathers who were treated like second-class citizens. I felt I needed to make a difference in this child's life, and I knew Dillon and Liz could give him a good life if certain obstacles were removed. I hoped to take care of that.

I packed all the gear I could possibly imagine I would need to make my trip a success. Something I hadn't thought of before, but something that might be advantageous to me was to bring along my old Connecticut license plates, complete with magnets on the backs so that when parked on the road, I could simply snap them over my green Vermont license plates and blend in with all the Connecticut cars on the road.

Tuesday morning, I was in no rush. I wanted to be in Connecticut for as little time as possible to lessen my visibility in the state. I needed to time everything right so that I could do all I needed to do in the least amount of time and get back to Vermont in a timely fashion. I ate lunch at home, waited, and checked to see what the weather was going to be like in Connecticut. To my initial dismay, the forecast was for light rain and sleet. While making the trip a little more dangerous, the poor weather might actually be of benefit to my undercover operation.

I started the car in the early afternoon. All packed and ready to do something I no longer really wanted to do, I still felt obliged by my conscience in some indescribable way. I suppose that, in the back of my mind, I still knew that law enforcement was either too busy, not knowledgeable enough about what was happening in Maggie's neighborhood, or just plain looked the other way when it came to drugs coming out of Maggie's apartment. But again, at least two people had died as a direct result of those drugs that I knew about, and how many might in the future? I reassured myself that I was actually doing the right thing.

The day was rather dark, damp, and dismal as I started south. There was no precipitation coming down, but I was sure that would

No Reason

begin somewhere in Massachusetts or Connecticut. The drive through Vermont was uneventful as usual. No traffic to speak of, and where there was, it was only in small pockets of eight or ten cars that could easily be passed and observed in my rearview mirror. I constantly reminded myself that I had to stay within five miles per hour of the speed limit on this trip so as not to get pulled over going either way during my excursion.

Seeing the "Welcome" sign coming into Massachusetts was always a double-edged sword for me. On one hand, it should only take about one hour to get through the state, but on the other, traffic was almost always a nightmare, especially when approaching Springfield. People began being nuts in their effort to traverse these roads in the minimum time possible. It was somehow a right, I suppose.

The rain began around Holyoke. It was just above freezing, and I took it down another notch just to be sure I didn't hit some black ice or to be defensive about it, to ensure that should someone else hit some ice that I could manage to be safe. All was good until nearing Springfield, where traffic was beginning to slow because of all the merging and overly cautious drivers who probably shouldn't be allowed to drive in bad weather but did. Some idiot in a red Honda Civic blew by the group of cars I was mired in going just forty-five miles an hour while this guy had to be doing ninety in the shoulder! Obviously, he was more important than anyone else on the road.

Not a minute later, traffic slowed to a stop and then we crawled. Not surprisingly, less than a mile ahead when I finally got there, there was a three-car accident. One of the cars was a mangled red Civic. From the way the cars were piled up, it appeared that the Civic sideswiped a car merging onto the freeway and careened into another car in the right-hand lane. No police or emergency vehicles were on scene yet. A couple cars had pulled over to try to help those involved, but outside of talking with these people, there wasn't going to be much to do until medical help arrived. The Civic looked like it was part of the middle of a sandwich. I was betting they would have to cut the car apart to get the driver out.

Finally getting past the accident scene, my speed which was more or less dictated by all the cars around me eventually sped up to about forty-five once again. It's truly amazing however how short people's memories are as about two miles below the accident, there were more and more cars tailgating, weaving in and out of their lanes and trying to make up for lost time by accelerating and then braking unnecessarily. I stayed in the right-hand lane waiting for the first Connecticut exit, where I could pull off and apply my blue and white plates to cover my green plates.

After quickly accomplishing the plate switch, I got back on the road and continued to blend in with traffic. Shortly thereafter, I saw blue lights flashing in my mirrors. A Connecticut State Trooper was coming up fast, and traffic began parting like the Red Sea. The trooper was much too busy to notice me, and he was soon out of sight as I observed him exiting the interstate two exits up. It was raining a bit harder now. I plodded along through Hartford, where traffic began to ease just a bit. I was ahead of rush hour as I had expected to be. Shortly thereafter, I was approaching the exit I would take to get onto the Merritt Parkway and then to the exit for Maggie's apartment.

It was beginning to get dark a bit earlier than normal as it continued to rain with dark clouds overhead. The wind had also picked up and leaves were blowing off trees, covering the road with a new slickness. As I approached Maggie's "place of business," I drove around the area for a few minutes making sure there were no police in the immediate area, performing some duty that might make them too close for comfort. All seemed to be quiet as the weather continued to worsen.

I found an advantageous parking spot where I was camouflaged by other cars and could observe Maggie's apartment. I sat in the Jeep for about ten minutes. Only one person had walked by on the other side of the street during that time, in part due to the nasty weather, I was sure. I was feeling more and more confident about making this happen. My confidence grew even more as it started to sleet, and the wind picked up. I loaded six rounds into my little Charter Arms Revolver and put it into my jacket pocket. I also made sure my Smith & Wesson 9 mm was safely tucked into my inside-the-belt holster just in case all hell broke loose. I exited the Jeep, closing the door but leaving it unlocked—something I never did but wanted to make sure I could get away quickly.

I crossed the road, walking toward Maggie's. There was no one on the street. No pedestrians, no cars—the weather couldn't have been better for my purposes. If I had everything figured correctly, the Audi carrying the drug dealers would be pulling up waiting for Maggie within five or ten minutes. It was now or never. I began ascending the stairs to Maggie's. As I quietly took each step, I heard shouting coming from inside. I stopped for a second. There were two voices. I listened. I was in hunting mode. Then I heard crying. It sounded like a small war. I approached Maggie's door and peered into the small window beside it. It appeared that both Maggie and her boyfriend were not only shouting at Dillon's son but also beating on him mercilessly. This couldn't go on!

I hesitated for a few seconds wondering whether I should politely knock on the door or kick the door in. I decided to be as unobtrusive as possible and knocked. Still hearing utter turmoil inside and receiving no answer, I rapped on the door with authority.

"Go away! We are not open, you fucking moron!" was the response by Maggie.

I took that as a welcome and tried the door. To my amazement, the door was open, and I turned the doorknob. Stepping into the room, I was unnoticed for a few seconds as both Maggie and her friend were way too busy shouting and wailing on Dillon's son. Then Maggie saw me. I could tell she was trying to figure out who I was but couldn't quite come up with it. Her boyfriend turned, and I could see rage in his eyes. He looked like he was possessed. Maybe he was. As both their attentions were now turned toward me, the boy realized that he had an out and ran into his bedroom, closing the door with force as he did.

This was indeed a good thing. A young child should not have to witness what was about to happen. And it began.

"Who the fuck are you!" shouted the enraged boyfriend. "Get the hell out or I'll kill you!" He began moving toward me, and as he passed the kitchen table a short distance from the door, he picked up a French knife from the table and started waving it at me. "I will cut you from ear to ear, you son of a bitch! Get the hell out!" he continued.

Meanwhile, I could see Maggie putting together just who I was. It all just took seconds, but it all felt like slow motion at the same time. Then time stood still. With one more step, this child beater came as close as I dared let him. With one smooth motion, I raised the little gun from my pocket, aimed, and gently pulled the trigger. He was stunned and his approach stopped abruptly. He looked at me incredulously not believing what had happened. As blood ran down his forehead, the knife hit the floor followed by his collapse. His eyes were wide, and as he stared into nothingness, the life went out of him. Whether he had been high or just mean or maybe both, I didn't care. He wasn't going to beat on little kids anymore! Yes, he was collateral damage of sorts, but as far as I was concerned, he had no right to be alive after what I had just witnessed.

I turned my attention to Maggie. I could see the fear in her eyes, yet I also saw her trying to figure out how best to kill me. She knew the knife had not worked for her boyfriend, so she moved toward a small closet and began opening the door. As she did, I could see on a shelf about four feet from the floor was a semiauto handgun.

"Don't even think about it!" I yelled. "You're a piece of trash that deserves to be disposed of!" As she paused for a second, I added, "How could you beat your own son?"

Maggie began to turn toward me and tried to distract me, saying, "He keeps shitting in his pants. I'm tired of it." Her hands had by now picked up her gun, and she was swinging it my way.

My little revolver barked, and Maggie stopped. Just as her boyfriend before her, blood began trickling down the side of her head. She crumpled into the closet with her gun falling on top of her as she went down. She would no longer care whether her son soiled his pants or not!

The hunter in me made me kick the two bodies lying in front of me to be sure they were dead. No movement. My attention turned to Dillon's son in his bedroom. I slowly opened the door and heard whimpering. It was coming from under his bed. Not wanting to imprint my image in his brain, even though being as young as he was, he would most likely not remember me, I felt that basically he was all right, just scared and hurting a little from his beating. I gently closed the door to his room.

I now had to focus on what was happening outside on the street while the storm continued. Peering out the window, all appeared quiet except for the sleet raining down, making everything icy and slippery. I watched, hoping the black Audi would be on time. After ten minutes of waiting, I began to worry that Mr. Drug Dealer had either altered his schedule that I had come to know of or that indeed the weather was causing him to be late. Thankfully, after five more minutes, I could see the Audi pulling up on the street to its usual spot.

Perfect, I thought. I turned on the flickering blue light in Maggie's window.

As the wind and sleet continued, I opened the door of Maggie's apartment and almost slid down the stairs. I caught myself. Visibility was terrible, something unexpected in my favor as I made my way to the car. My approach was from the rear of the passenger side of the car as they would always wait for Maggie to open the rear passenger door and slide in before transacting their business while driving for the next fifteen minutes. I was confident all they would see was a customary form of someone coming to the car and opening the door.

As I approached, my right hand grasped the little Charter .22 knowing that I had reloaded the gun while waiting for the dealer's arrival. I had six shots if I needed them to make this happen. All was quiet but for the sound of the sleet hitting their mark and the sound of the windshield wipers of the Audi. I opened the rear door with my gloved left hand and produced the revolver as I slid into the rear seat. Crossing over my body with my right hand, I only heard the drug lord exclaim, "What the—" when I pulled the trigger. He had no other time to respond. The bullet entered the side of his head, instantly killing him.

The driver tried to pull out his gun and turn toward me, but he too had no chance as he was taken totally off guard. Another little .22 bullet entered his brain, and he slumped forward. I exited the car leaving the car door open. The engine was still running, and the windshield wipers still tried to fend off the sleet. I began walking toward my Jeep. No one else was on the street, either walking or driving. I hoped it wouldn't be too long before someone found what had just transpired only because I hated leaving Dillon's son alone in the apartment but knew I really could do nothing about it.

I opened the Jeep's door and slid in, started the car, and buckled up. I put the little revolver in the console and pulled out of the parking space. I drove slowly passed the idling Audi and continued on toward the parkway. No one had seen me or my Jeep, at least that I knew of, and I was certain that it all looked like a drug deal or drug war gone bad. All four had been shot in the head with a .22, execution style. They were all people who hurt and killed other people. They had lived far too long in my mind.

I kept driving along the back streets of the small city, obeying all speed limit signs and stoplights. I didn't want to be in a hurry, but I did want to get out of town as quickly as possible. My conscience wouldn't allow it, however. I was thinking too much about the safety of Dillon's son. So the best I could do was to pull over a few blocks away from the "hit" and wait to hear sirens speeding toward the scene. About two minutes later, I heard the faint sound of multiple sirens coming closer. The louder they got, the better I felt. Then I could hear them getting a little farther away as they approached Maggie's apartment. These were all good signs.

As I pulled out of my parking space, I once again heard a siren coming ever closer. With blue lights flashing, I pulled to my right in order to give the cruiser a wide berth as the officer screamed by me, I was sure, to the scene of the crime. Relief overwhelmed me. I knew Dillon's son would be all right, and I knew that he now had a real chance at life. I smiled as I continued toward the interstate. The weather was terrible. I managed what I considered a safe speed on the highway of about thirty-five and progressed toward my goal of getting back to Vermont—and safety.

An hour later, I pulled off just before the Massachusetts border and filled up the gas tank, paying with cash. After doing so, I pulled ahead and onto a little side road, where I was safely off the travel lane and ripped the front and rear Connecticut plates from my Jeep. I

— No Reason —

placed them under a blanket in the back seat and looked around. The weather had been my best ally as no one was anywhere in sight to see me stop and "become registered in Vermont" once again. I drove on continuing north.

It took an extra hour to get to the Vermont border as the sleet was panicking everyone and slowing traffic to a crawl in some areas and rightfully so as there were quite a few cars that had spun out or managed to hit a guardrail. Once into Vermont, however, the weather improved as the precipitation was mostly snow, and generally, the Vermont DOT did a great job on the roads.

I continued to keep my cell phone turned off as I wanted to limit any chance of traceability as to where I was. I knew I would be getting a call from Liz at some point. I was sure she would be horrified by what had happened but, at the same time, relieved that her grandson would now be safe. Should she have called prior to my arriving home, I had it set to tell her that I had hunted all day, a somewhat true statement of sorts, and I had had my phone off during the hunt and failed to turn it back on. Stretching the truth, maybe; lying, I didn't think so.

Upon arriving home, I immediately retrieved a shovel from my garage. It was dark, snow was beginning to accumulate, but I managed to wend my way through the evergreens on my property and dig a hole about three feet deep under a forty-foot pine. Not without sadness as it had done a great job, I dropped the little revolver into the hole, hopefully never to be seen again. I covered in the hole and scrapped pine needles over the top as snow continued to fly and helped cover the burial site.

I then continued on to a small stream again on my property and in a tiny pool, but one which was about six feet deep. I threw the remaining .22-caliber bullets from the box I had used into the pool, so they could all settle at the bottom and most likely be covered up by springtime. Call me paranoid, but I wanted no evidence whatsoever of what I had done.

About two inches of snow later, I opened the door to my house. I was hungry and thirsty, but it was getting late. I turned on my phone to check to see if I had missed any calls. I hadn't. I decided to make a quick call to Hope. It would aid in verifying my whereabouts if it ever became necessary.

"Hello, my brave hunter" was the greeting I received from Hope. "How was your day?"

"Not bad," I responded. "I had a good day hunting, although I didn't get to bring anything home. How about you? A good day?"

"I, too, had a pretty good day. Nothing out of the ordinary except for the snow we are getting."

"I know, I'm looking forward to be able to do some tracking tomorrow. And the woods will be a lot quieter for walking," I added. "And I wanted to ask, what you have planned for the weekend? I was wondering if you wanted to come hunting with me Saturday?"

"Really, you mean it? I would love to. Let me know what I need to bring or do."

We talked for another ten minutes, some of which time I advised her about clothing and footwear and sustenance. She was excited, to say the least.

After saying "good night," I cracked a bottle of Pyrat and mixed it with a little bit of cola. It tasted superb after my long day. Then I began boiling a pot of water, which was meant for pasta, and chopped some onion and garlic and began sautéing that together with some ground beef. I drained the pasta, poured the sauté mixture over it, added some grated cheese, and sat down to let my stomach know that my mouth was still working. It tasted good. I relaxed. The day had gone well, and I was satisfied.

But I was also waiting to hear from Liz.

Chapter 40

At nine thirty the following morning, my phone rang.

Caller ID told me it was Liz, but I answered with an unknowing, "Hello?"

"Have you heard what happened?" Liz blurted. "You won't believe what we just went through. It was horrible, but it's going to be great."

"Okay, okay. Slow down. I have no idea what you're talking about," I responded, not wanting to commit myself.

"Well, it's all over the news. If you would bother to listen to a radio or watch the news, I'm sure you would have known about it by now, even up in Vermont!"

Convinced that saying less was the proper way to go, I merely waited for Liz to continue.

"Last night, there was a mass shooting at Maggie's. She is dead, along with her boyfriend and apparently two drug dealers outside. The police think it was a 'hit' by the way it was done. My god! Thank God Dillon's son is all right. He is with us now. Isn't that wonderful?"

Wanting to know more about the scene the police found, I led Liz down a path to tell me more. "Liz, tell me what happened, or what do the police think happened? Go slowly," I encouraged.

"Well, they think someone went into Maggie's apartment and shot her and her boyfriend in the head with a .22. The police told us that is a common caliber for hit men to use. Then they also shot two guys outside the apartment while they were sitting in their car. The police found a whole bunch of drugs in the car—so they think the whole thing was drug related. The saving grace was that they found Dillon's son under his bed in the apartment. It looked like he had been bruised up quite a bit and was scared out of his mind, but otherwise, he is good. And so last night, it was on the news as a breaking story, and when I saw it, I told Dillon. And we called the police. We went down to the station and spent the better part of the night there answering questions about where we were and our relationship with Maggie. After we convinced the police we had nothing to do with the shooting and Dillon proved that he was the father, we were able to take Dillon's son home here. Now it will be for good! We are both so exhausted but so relieved at the same time. There should be no more courts to deal with and a lot less problems as Dillon will now have sole custody of his son. Isn't it wonderful?"

"Wow! It sounds almost unbelievable! Terrifying and great at the same time. As long as Dillon's boy is good."

"Oh, I think he is or will be. They don't think he actually witnessed anything but was just really scared. That's why they think he was hiding under his bed. In fact, they don't think that whoever did this even knew he was there! Oh, we are both so happy."

"I'm very happy for you both. I'm sure all three of you will mold into a very loving family."

"Thanks," Liz replied. "This is all still sinking in, but I wanted to call you to tell you the news. And of course, I should ask how you are doing."

"I'm good. I have the week off and have been hunting every day, so I have had a lot of calm in my life. I haven't shot a deer yet, but with new snow on the ground now, I have a better chance. Hopefully, I will have meat hanging by the end of the week. Tell Dillon I hope all continues to go well for him now that he is going to be a full-time dad. Let me know if I can help in any way and let me know what you hear about what happened with Maggie. Take care."

"I will and you do the same," said Liz in a more relieved way than I had heard from her in a long time.

While eating my morning oatmeal and enjoying my coffee, I turned on the TV and the morning news. The incident was a major news item, even in Vermont. Liz had pretty much summed up what the police knew or what they were telling the media, and it all went along pretty well with what I knew. They were missing a few details, the biggest of which was the fact that Maggie and her boyfriend were beating on a child! But other than that, not only did the police find a large amount of drugs in the car in the street, but they found a good amount in Maggie's apartment as well. The police, however, said they had known nothing about any drug dealing that may have been happening out of Maggie's apartment prior to the killings. I wondered how true that was. In any event, some other low-life drug dealer would now be taking on increased territory, I was sure. It wasn't like the drug trade was going to stop. The only thing that would really stop was the beating and abuse by someone not fit to be a parent and her boyfriend. This was good.

I turned off the TV and got ready to go hunting. It was a cold, crisp day, most brilliant with about four inches of new snow, fairly ideal for deer hunting. While I wasn't convinced I would shoot a deer before the weekend, I knew I would have fun tracking and exploring new territory. I kind of wanted to have Hope experience the full extent of deer hunting with shooting a deer when she was with me and let her decide if this was something she was still interested in or not. Nevertheless, I decided that if, and it was a big if, I happened to see a really huge deer, I might shoot it in spite of the experience I wanted Hope to have. After all, I could use a nice head mount hanging in my house.

It was soft and quiet in the woods. The snow had not had a chance to freeze and get crunchy and noisy. Stalking rather than sitting on stand was in order. I walked. I tracked and slowly made my way up a small mountain to a high meadow in the midst of a forest. Obviously, this was a field that some years ago was farmed but had long since been abandoned. I decided to wait at the edge of the woods and the field, watching for the slightest movement that would allow me to identify a deer. Success found my efforts a half hour later when I saw the flick of a tail. A good-sized doe walked out into the field followed by a smaller doe. Both were in no hurry, and the larger doe kept looking back into the woods. I waited. They were about one hundred yards away, a fairly easy shot with my scoped .30-06. They both grazed for about ten minutes and then I saw a third deer join them. It was an impressive eight-point buck. I watched to see what was going to happen. The buck walked right over to the larger doe and began to mount her. All of a sudden, I heard something crashing through the underbrush from the other side of the meadow about fifty yards from where the three deer were trying to mate. I was amazed by what I saw through my scope. This buck was huge! I quickly counted twelve points, but the rack was by far bigger than any I had ever seen in Vermont. He stopped for a moment and then made a charge toward the eight-pointer. Knowing he was no match for the larger deer, despite his urge to mate, the lesser deer backed off and ran to the edge of the woods. The big buck chased after him, and they both disappeared into the woods.

There was no time for a shot at the big buck, but now I knew where he hung out. The two does ambled off into the woods shortly thereafter. It was a great day to be out enjoying the grandeur of nature. As I stayed put and watched and waited to see if anything more would happen, I was startled enough to bring my gun up to my shoulder and swing to my right. I was almost run over by a rogue chipmunk traversing the stone wall near me! This guy made as much noise as a freight train and stopped not ten feet from me, looked right at me, chattered, and took off the other way. What could be better?

My decision was an easy one. I would not hunt this area again until Saturday when Hope was with me. I didn't want to spook these deer, and even if the twelve-pointer never showed up again, that eight-pointer was a fine deer. Either would be a good choice for putting meat in the freezer. I slowly departed the area to explore other parts of the mountain. On the way, I ate an apple I had brought with me and offered the core to the deer, leaving it on one of their trails. It was a glorious day.

As evening approached and darkness fell over the woods, I climbed into my Jeep for the return home. I felt really good about everything that had happened in the day and felt even more confident about harvesting a deer in the near future now that I had found what looked like a great spot. My lights lit up my driveway, and as I pulled up to the door, I noticed car tracks and footprints in the snow leading up to my door. I cautiously got out of the Jeep, retrieved my cased rifle, and looked around the yard more closely.

No Reason

Footprints went all around my house. It certainly wasn't UPS or FedEx trying to deliver a package! I drew my sidearm from its holster and entered my house. After checking each room and finding no broken windows or doors that had been jimmied and nothing out of place, I holstered my gun and sat down to think. Five minutes later, I saw lights coming up the driveway.

Two local sheriffs' cars approached the house. I had a hunch what this was about. Upon hearing the two men knock on my door, I opened it smiling.

"Hi, officers," I greeted. "What can I do for you?"

I knew these two men from the time I helped thwart the bank robber in town. And they in turn were familiar with me.

"Good evening," replied the smaller of the two, him being only about five feet nine and 250 pounds.

The other officer was massive—probably six feet two and 350 pounds. I would be able to easily outrun either, even on a bad day.

"Don't know if you have heard what happened down in Connecticut, with the drug killings, I mean. But we have been asked by the Connecticut State Police to come by and ask you a few questions about what happened yesterday and where you were."

"Well, yes, I did hear about it from the lady that rents my house in Connecticut. I used to date her for a while and so I know her son as well. Liz called me this morning to let me know what happened. Startling to say the least."

"We are sure it is nothing since we know you from stopping that bank robber in town. But apparently, your former girlfriend mentioned your name to the state police down there, and so here we are. We actually stopped in earlier, but you weren't home."

"No, I was out hunting like I was all day yesterday as well. Finally saw a couple good bucks but couldn't get a shot off. I'll hopefully catch up with one of them by the weekend and put some venison in the freezer."

"So you were hunting all day yesterday and today? Is there anyone that can attest to that?"

"Not totally," I replied. "I did talk with Hope, one of the tellers at the bank and who I am seeing now, in the early evening yesterday.

We talked about my hunt for the day, and she wants to come out with me this weekend and learn more about deer hunting with me. But as far as I know, no one actually saw me hunting yesterday—or today. I tend to be pretty good at staying hidden."

The big officer chuckled. "Yeah, we understand. We just had to ask. Hope, I'm sure, can corroborate your story. It would be a good trick to be down in Connecticut and then back up here in that amount of time. Not that it couldn't be done, just improbable."

"We'll follow up with her tomorrow at the bank," the smaller officer chimed in, "just to tie up loose ends. Thanks for your time, and good luck hunting."

With that, the two men departed.

I was a little perturbed that Liz had failed to mention she had said anything about me to the police when she had been interviewed, yet I kind of understood she would forget to let me know. Nevertheless, I thought about all of my planning and the details of how I had carried everything out. I couldn't find a mistake anywhere. My only possible flaw was having no concrete alibi for yesterday's supposed "hunt," but it seemed like the two sheriffs had no problem with my story and would report it as such.

I turned to my bar, poured a Pyrat and Coke, and began boiling water for my pasta. I began chopping onions while the water heated and began to make a meat sauce. I was hungry!

After eating too much, I rang Hope to let her know about my day—seeing two good deer and about my being questioned by local sheriffs. Her reply was just what I was looking for.

"Well, if they are coming to see me tomorrow to ask me if we talked last night and about your whereabouts during the day, I can assure them you had been hunting and neglecting to see me as a result!" Hope laughed and I joined in.

We talked more of our upcoming hunt together and about how we missed each other when we didn't see each other every day. Our relationship was wonderful.

Hope indeed had a visit from the two local sheriffs the next morning. After entering the bank, they had to patiently wait for customers to clear before they could speak to Hope.

— No Reason —

"Hope, we would like to speak with you in private for a minute or two if we can," began the smaller sheriff. "We need to verify a few things that you can hopefully clarify. It would be best to speak behind closed doors."

"Sure," responded Hope. "Let me just tell the bank manager that I will be in the room over there for a few minutes, and I should be able to meet you both there in a minute."

"Great," the larger sheriff said. "We'll meet you over there."

As the two men walked slowly into the small meeting room, Hope advised the bank manager that she would not be at her window for a few minutes. The bank manager had no problem with Hope leaving her post.

"What can I help you with?" asked Hope upon her entering the room and closing the door behind her.

Both sheriffs simultaneously began answering by saying, "Well…," and after looking at each other, the smaller sheriff continued with "Don't know if you heard about the drug shootings down in Connecticut two days ago, but it seems that your boyfriend who helped us catch that bank robber here is kind of involved in the investigation down there. Apparently, he used to go out with the lady there, who is the mother of a young man, who was the father of a child found at the scene. The mother of the boy was apparently dealing drugs and got herself shot and killed as well as another guy in her apartment. In addition, two more drug dealers were killed in their car outside of her apartment. The Connecticut State Police asked us to speak with your friend, which we did last night. He indicated that he was hunting all day as he had been pretty much every day this week and that on the day of the shooting, you spoke with him in the early evening. Is that right?"

"Yes, absolutely. My friend, as you put it, has been hunting every day this week. We have been seeing each other since shortly after the attempted bank robbery and have become good friends. We do talk most nights and did in fact talk that evening. He was home after hunting all day. It is his passion. And after this week, he has to go back to work, so he has been trying to make every day count in the woods."

"That's pretty much what we thought," responded the smaller sheriff. "He told us you would verify his story, and it all seems to come together for us. We appreciate your time. Have a good day."

"No problem, officers. Take care."

As the two sheriffs exited the bank, Hope returned to her teller station.

The bank manager walked up to Hope and whispered, "Everything okay?"

"All good," responded Hope. "I will tell you more about it if you like later today."

"No, no worries. Just needed to know that you are okay and nothing is the matter."

The bank manager returned to her office, and the bank returned to its normal routine.

Chapter 41

Saturday morning rolled around, and Hope was knocking on my door at about eight o'clock. She was ready to go on this new adventure. Obviously excited, she had her newly purchased hunter-orange overalls and jacket on and wore a big smile.

"I'm ready," she chimed. "Are you?"

"Almost." I smiled back as we gave each other a kiss. "I thought we should have a good breakfast first before we head into the woods for the day. You never know what might happen, and who knows when we might be able to eat again."

"Well, that sounds a bit ominous, but okay, I'm up for eating. What are we having?"

"I was just starting to make some bacon and eggs and toast. Coffee?" I asked.

"Sure. Sounds good. I guess I hired the right guide for this trip." Hope laughed.

"Well, if nothing else, you get a good breakfast. We might not even see a deer, but hopefully, this guide will show you a good time out in the great outdoors!"

We both laughed, and she helped me out by getting the toast ready while I finished cooking the bacon and frying the four eggs we would share. Finishing our coffee, we rinsed off our plates and put them into the sink.

After loading up the Jeep, we headed out. I made sure that Hope understood that we would be doing very little actual talking in the woods, but we would be using more hand signals and gestures. Most importantly, we would be listening to the woods and watching for all of its creatures. She understood.

I parked the Jeep and uncased my rifle. Hope stood by and watched. As we walked into the woods heading for the high meadow where I saw the two nice bucks earlier in the week, I loaded three rounds into the gun and made sure my safety was on. I made sure we walked slowly. Hope soon figured out that there was no rush, that stealth and quiet were what we were looking for. She learned quickly.

It took a good forty-five minutes to get to where I wanted to be. Both because I wanted to be quiet and not be seen by any deer. I also did not want either of us to start sweating under our hunting gear. Nor did I want an alarmed murder of crows signaling our presence or even agitate a squirrel into chatter.

Stopping at a stone wall which bordered the field and the woods, I found a flat rock upon which Hope could sit comfortably—or almost comfortably. After all, the longer you sit on a cold rock, the more uncomfortable it gets. I motioned for her to watch the field and the other side of the woods. In turn, I found an advantageous spot about twenty yards from Hope where I could stand and also sit on a rock. Hope could see me; I could see her, and we slowly became one with nature. We waited, nearly motionless. I had advised Hope that if she needed to move, to do it all at once—moving tense muscles, scratching an itch, or changing an uncomfortable position. Then to remain still for as long as possible. She was a good student and probably moved less than I did. I wasn't sure if this was because she was fearful of me admonishing her over moving too much if she was afraid of ruining the hunt or if she was just really good at not moving, but she would certainly not be my downfall if I did not connect with a deer.

We waited. We waited some more. A few sparrows flitted between us, and crows filled the air with their raucous noise from time to time. I was about to get Hope's attention and let her know we should eat the sandwiches I had made the night before when I heard a snap in the woods to my right. I stopped, got her attention, and motioned for her to be still. She understood. We sat and listened for five minutes. Then ten. Out of nowhere, a small doe appeared from the woods about seventy-five yards away. It grazed. Hope saw it too, a few seconds after I did. We watched. The doe was young and was in no hurry to move from the field. It pawed at the snow to reveal succulent grasses underneath. Slowly, the small deer moved across the field and disappeared into the woods. I looked at Hope. She looked at me, and we both smiled.

We continued to wait, both of us becoming increasingly hungry. Finally, I motioned to Hope that we should eat. The gourmet peanut butter and jelly sandwiches I had made were exceptional! It filled a void. We went back to waiting. Ten minutes later, Hope decided she had sat long enough and stood to stretch. As she did, another doe appeared at about the same spot the first one had come from. This doe was much bigger. Shortly, another doe appeared in the field, and they both fed on the grasses under the snow. We watched and waited.

Twenty minutes later, I could see the two does begin to act differently. Their white tails flicked more and more, and they began looking around the field more often. They seemed tense. Then they both picked up their heads and stared straight down the mountain. In a flash, they were gone! Literally two or three bounding leaps and they vanished into the woods. Then I heard it too. I knew from experience it wasn't a big buck crashing through the woods to get to the does. Instead, I soon caught sight of two men dressed in camo hunter orange (I hesitate to call them hunters) traipsing through the forest with their rifles slung on their backs, talking and making all kinds of noise. Hope saw them too and remained motionless. The two men blindly passed by in the middle of the field not fifty yards from us and never saw us! Though we were both dressed in hunter orange, these men were blind. How would they ever see a deer?

Hope and I hunkered down once again and waited until almost four o'clock. Not seeing another deer, I put the safety on, on my rifle and walked to Hope.

I whispered, "Well, you got to see a bit of almost everything today. Let's start to walk out of here."

Hope smiled and nodded her head.

We made it to the Jeep just as darkness fell. I unloaded the rifle, cased it, and I put the heat on as we began to make our way to my house.

"Well, what do you think?" I asked.

"Those two hunters were idiots!" she answered.

I laughed that that was the first thing out of her mouth.

"They couldn't sneak up on a deer if their lives depended on it. Those two does heard them way before I did, and I know you heard them before me. So how could they possibly expect to find a deer? Are there any deaf deer?"

We both laughed.

Hope was right! But she continued, "The rest of it was great though! We got to watch those two deer feed and be deer. Certainly, people in the city never get to see anything like that, and other than hunters, I dare say a lot of country people never get to see that either. It was awesome! And it was so peaceful, except for when those two jerks went by us. But just listening to the birds and having that little chipmunk come up to me was terrific."

"Wait, what chipmunk?" I asked.

"Oh, there was a chipmunk on the stone wall to my left where you couldn't see that stopped and stared at me for a couple of minutes, not two feet from me! It didn't seem afraid, just curious. And all of a sudden, it jumped and turned around and sped off into a crevice in the stone wall. I had to stifle myself from laughing out loud."

"I have to say," I said, "you did one hell of a job sitting and standing still for as long as we were out there, especially for your first time. It's too bad we didn't see a buck, but at least you saw the does."

Before I could go on, Hope interrupted, asking, "Could we do this again tomorrow? I know it is Sunday and didn't know if you wanted to do anything else before you go back to work, but I would love to try to see a buck with you tomorrow."

How could I be so lucky as to have found Hope? I thought. "I was just going to ask you if you would be up to trying again tomorrow, but I guess I have my answer. Let's do it!"

After arriving back at my house, I wiped down my rifle with a silicon cloth and put it away for the night. It felt good for both of us to take off our heavy hunting jackets and overalls and relax. I offered Hope some wine, but she declined.

"Can you make me a gin and tonic instead?"

"I think I can manage that." I poured two.

— No Reason —

We toasted to a good day in the woods and to a better day tomorrow. We decided on breakfast for dinner, and together we whipped up some French toast made with sourdough bread, slathered with butter, and Vermont maple syrup. We talked and laughed, sharing more about our first day in the woods together, what we saw, heard, and felt. We fell asleep in each other's arms while sitting on the couch after we finished eating. We napped for about an hour.

Hope later gathered her things and left to go home. She needed to do a few things before going to bed, and I needed to finish cleaning the kitchen and then take a shower, making sure there were no ticks on me. We would do this again tomorrow, hopefully with greater success!

Sunday morning at eight o'clock, I heard a knock on my door once more. This time, I opened the door to a smiling Hope with pastries from the local bakery in hand.

"Wow, good morning," I greeted. "This is a treat. Don't like my cooking I guess."

"Not at all. Just thought this would be nice and fast too, so we can get into the woods as soon as possible. I have a good feeling about today," Hope replied and gave me a kiss while walking into the house.

We had coffee, pastries and were off for the woods. Hope wanted to know if we would hunt the same area again. I informed her that I thought it was a really good spot, and we should keep watching that area. She was excited.

Again, we worked our way slowly up the slope to the high meadow. Flurries were in the air, and the temperature was getting noticeably colder. I found a spot for Hope to sit about ten yards from where she had been the day before. I, too, moved down the field a bit, settling in on a vantage point that offered me good shooting lanes not only within the field but also down into the woodlands. An hour later, the flurries had changed to a true snowfall. We both sat in silence and waited. The forest, field, and even the air above was quiet. It seemed like the snow had put a silencer on all of the woodland animals as well as the birds. Crows were not talking and the red-tailed hawks usually in the area were missing as well. Songbirds were silent.

Both Hope's and my own orange outfits were now turning white. We were being camouflaged whether we wanted to or not. Another hour went by uneventfully. I wondered if Hope was getting bored or disappointed. Finally, I heard a noise. It came from my right in the woods. I could see a ways into the woods but saw nothing coming our way. I looked over to Hope—she had heard it too. She was sitting at attention, listening intently. We waited. Ten minutes later, we both heard another snapping noise. I tensed my muscles and gripped my rifle a bit more. I finally saw movement in the shadows in the woods.

A dark object was slowly making its way toward us down through the trees. With the snow now almost preventing me from seeing into the woods and the inherent darkness in the forest because of the thick clouds and heavy snow, I could only wait, hoping that whatever I had seen would continue to come closer for a shot. Following a stout gust of wind which made the snow almost impenetrable, I finally saw the animal. It was large with a great rack. But I couldn't shoot.

I quickly looked to see if Hope also saw what I saw. I could tell she did. She was now standing, looking directly at the animal. The animal continued toward us and crossed a mere thirty yards in front of us both, offering me a very simple broadside shot. But Hope and I just watched. This great bull moose was not legal to shoot; I had no license for it. But merely seeing it in the wild and knowing Hope saw it too made my day. I didn't care if we saw anything else all season.

The bull just kept ambling along. It was curious that the beast seemed like it was moving in slow motion, yet it covered a huge amount of territory with each step. Moose are truly amazing animals. Finally, this one stopped. It stood still for a minute and turned its massive head toward us. Looking as dumb as ever, it stared toward us, possibly not being able to make out what we were. With very few predators able to bother a large moose, apparently the bull figured we were not going to be a problem either, and it began walking off toward a stream and pond to our left. What a sight. Soon, it had vanished completely.

I took the opportunity to make my way slowly over to Hope to see if she was all right and to see what she thought of seeing the moose. When I got next to her, she was starry-eyed.

No Reason

"My god," she began quietly, "that thing was huge! I have never seen a moose before, and they are gigantic!"

"How did you like the size of that rack?" I asked.

"I am speechless. I can see why you love to be out here as much as you are. It's not like looking at a picture or watching TV. This is awesome. I want to get my hunting license next year and hunt with you if you will allow me." Flakes of snow melted on her lips as she looked up at me.

"Sounds like a plan! Are you hungry, shall we eat quickly? Or have you had enough for today?" I asked.

"Are you kidding? Let's eat our lunch and get back to watching for venison to cross our paths. This is great!"

I decided that I was falling more and more in love with Hope by the minute. We gobbled down our ham and cheese sandwiches, downed a fun size Snickers bar each, and I left Hope where she was and hoofed it back to my post. I have never been able to get it straight in my mind why a bite-size chocolate bar would be "fun size." I always thought a "fun size" would be a very large bar! The wait continued.

By three o'clock, the snow was beginning to subside, but we now had a good foot of snow on the ground. It would allow us to walk through the woods in silence if we wanted to, but it also allowed the deer to be silent as well. I chose to wait. My patience was rewarded a half hour later when two does poked their heads out of the woods and sauntered into the field. I could tell they were both nervous, flicking their tales incessantly. They seemed like they had a plan and kept moving through the field.

A minute later, all hell broke loose. The eight-pointer I had seen here previously exploded from the trees with his head down, following the does' scent. He was moving fast. Then as before, I heard more commotion, and the large twelve-pointer appeared. These two bucks apparently had quite a rivalry going on! With the angle the larger deer was making toward the two does, my shot was not an easy one. The smaller buck offered a sure shot as he was broadside about fifty yards out. I made a decision.

My rifle came up to my shoulder. My right cheek hit the wood on the stock, and I peered through my scope, resting the crosshairs on the buck's left front shoulder. The .30-06 broke the deafening silence, and the nice eight-pointer collapsed. The larger buck stopped. He was startled by the sound and couldn't locate where it had come from. He knew, however, which way the does were headed, and he decided to head the same way. The rutting urge was strong.

My decision to allow this impressive buck to pass on his genes to more offspring was a good one in my mind. Not that the deer I had just shot was inferior, but the twelve-pointer not only had a great rack but was also a very heavy deer. Chances are the smaller eight-pointer would be more tender eating anyway.

Hope had watched the entire drama unfold. I looked over to see her reaction. She was laughing, not knowing if she should stifle her enthusiasm.

I released her of her concern as I yelled, "How was that?"

She made her way through the snow over to me and gave me a bear hug! "That was something! It all happened so fast. Why did you decide to shoot the smaller buck?" she asked.

"Well, I had a much better shot at the smaller buck, and I wanted the big buck's genes to get passed on to more deer. The rack would have been great in my living room, but I'm very happy with this deer. Let's go gut it out!"

"Okay, you will have to show me."

We walked over to the deer lying in the new fallen snow. I poked at him with the barrel of my rifle not wanting to start working on a deer that was only wounded and stunned. He didn't move. I relaxed. Taking out my knife, I began showing Hope how the process went. She helped hold the carcass open and aided me in turning the deer over, so the entrails would fall out. She was not squeamish. Now the real work of getting him into the Jeep would start. Although most of the terrain was downhill and the dragging was made easier by the new snow, there were still areas where both brush and slight rises made the drag difficult. I had Hope carry my rifle, and that made my chore easier, but when we finally made it to the Jeep at dark, I was sweating profusely.

— No Reason —

After loading the deer into the Jeep aided by Hope, we drove to the local deer check-in station. The buck did not have the biggest rack taken in the area, a ten-pointer beat it, but by weight, I had the heaviest yet taken, 187 pounds dressed. This was a large deer for Vermont. I could only guess the twelve-pointer I passed up would have weighed in at about 220! Oh, well.

Upon arriving home, the next chore was to hang the deer in my garage. I threw a rope over one of the rafters, looped it, and tied the other end to the rack of the deer, which was still in the rear of my Jeep as I had backed the vehicle halfway into the garage. With Hope's help, she guided the deer out of the Jeep while I pulled on the rope to get it out of the vehicle and off the ground. Then I tied it off and put a piece of cardboard underneath it to absorb what little blood was still dripping. With the temperature still dropping, the carcass would begin to freeze shortly.

"That's done," I said. "Thanks for all the help! It certainly is easier with two people than just doing it by myself. Let's go inside and have a nice cup of hot cocoa or something stronger if you like."

"Cocoa would be fine. Maybe something stronger a bit later," Hope responded.

We sat for a while, sipped our hot drink, and agreed it had been one spectacular day. I assured Hope that the day had gone just as I had planned in order to try to lure her into getting a license next year and becoming my hunting partner.

Hope's response was "You know, I don't usually talk like this, but you are full of shit!"

We laughed and sipped our cocoa.

While I have always enjoyed hunting by myself, these past two days had proven to me that there was even more to enjoy when another person is as enthusiastic about hunting as Hope was. It made me want to hunt even more—with the right person.

Our reminiscing of the past two days was cut short when my phone began to ring. It was Liz. I thought about letting it go to voice mail, but I took it anyway.

"Hello."

"Hello yourself," Liz began. "Hope you are doing well. I just wanted to call to let you know that we are doing great, and Dillon and his son are wonderful together. The little guy is running around all of the time and keeps us busy, but we love it. And it is so good to see Dillon being a father."

"That's great," I responded. "All's well that ends well, I guess."

"You bet! It certainly was a strange and tragic way for Dillon to get his son here full-time, but we both can't be happier with the outcome. You know, from what the police have told us, they still have no clue as to who killed Maggie and the other three people. They figured it was all drug related, but they don't know why all the drugs at Maggie's and in the car outside were still there unless someone got scared off and ran. The police said they questioned everybody in the area and anybody that had a connection with any of the people killed."

I hesitated but wanted to get it out in the open, "Yeah, they even had local sheriffs up here ask me about my relationship with you and Dillon and had to verify my whereabouts for that day. It was quite a surprise that they did that."

"Oh, well, I guess maybe I should have said something to you about that because I did mention your name and that we used to see each other and all that. But I didn't expect that they would actually interrogate you about it. I hope you withstood the torture," Liz said sarcastically.

"Yep, it was no problem, but it still would have been nice to have had a heads-up about the sheriffs coming to talk with me about it. As it turned out, I hunted all day as I have been all week. I finally got a nice deer today, so I can go back to work tomorrow with a clear head and no regrets over my areas I chose to hunt."

"That's great. Congratulations. I'm glad your hunt was a success."

Liz had no idea just how successful my week of hunting had been for all involved. We soon ended our conversation, and I turned my attention back to Hope.

She was asleep on the couch. It had been quite a day, and she had been a real trooper, sitting in the cold for the greater part of the

— No Reason —

day then seeing the moose and then watching me shoot the deer and helping gut it and drag it out. She was beat. I realized I was too. I sat down beside her and closed my eyes.

Two hours later, I awakened from my nap to find Hope in the kitchen making some spaghetti for us. Ten minutes later, we drained the pasta. She finished sautéing the chop meat, onion, and garlic, and after adding that to the tomato sauce, we poured it over the pasta, grated some parmesan over it, and celebrated the gift of the deer with a bottle of pinot gris. The meal was exquisite!

Chapter 42

The next morning came early as workdays always seem to. It was good to get back into a routine, however, and my "church" in the woods had satiated my thirst for peace and quiet and solitude. I was again ready to be with people. So I engaged wholeheartedly in my new job and continued to enjoy my work. I also kept up my relationship with Hope and enjoyed that even more.

Winter flew past in a flash. When weather gets nasty, other than people you see at work, most normally everyone is in hibernation mode. So when the crocuses and daffodils begin poking up from the ground, more and more people exit their dwellings on a more consistent basis than in the colder months. People begin to congregate in their neighborhoods, talk, get together for drinks, go for walks, and enjoy the warmth of the sun and fresh air.

Hope and I engaged in some of the springtime frivolity, but our main focus was on getting Hope used to handling all types of firearms. After getting a good bruise or two on her shoulder, Hope loved shooting my shotguns. It only took those two times to teach her that the gun needed to be tucked in firmly against her shoulder so that no bruising occurred. And with a rifle, she proved to be deadly within one hundred yards. Handguns gave Hope the most problems as the recoil was something she was not used to when she fired my .357 Magnum and even my 9mm. The other problem which befalls many slightly built women, or men for that matter, is a certain weakness in operating the slide properly on a semiautomatic. It took some work, but Hope became proficient in their use as well.

We also studied a lot for her hunter education course she was going to take online. She began the course being nervous about the tests but soon found she knew what she was talking about and could apply her knowledge to what was being asked on a test. Hope passed the final test with flying colors. Now she would only have to travel upstate for a day to pass her practical portion of the hunter safety course. She would most likely get to shoot a wide variety of firearms, and I assured her that she would do well with the safety aspects of the course.

Hope had wanted me to accompany her on the day of her practical test, but I refused.

"No! This is something you can and need to do on your own. You know you know all of this, and now you just have to rely on your own confidence."

Hope knew I was right, nevertheless she was a bit nervous. Off she went. It would be a good adventure for her and help make her into a strong, safe hunter. After I knew Hope was on her way, I puttered around the house doing chores that needed doing. I walked out into the woods to check to see the spot where I had buried the little .22 revolver was still intact and undisturbed. It was. I felt confident no one would ever find that gun. There was now no sign whatsoever that something had been buried there.

As I walked back to my house, my cell phone rang. To my surprise, it was one of my sons calling. We hadn't talked in months, nor had I spoken with my other children in a long, long time. Somehow, it seemed I had fallen out of favor with them, and I really had no idea why.

"Hello," I answered noncommittally.

"Hi, Dad" came the response. "What are you up to?"

"Just doing some things around the house."

"Oh, good. How do you like your house in Vermont?"

None of my three children had ever visited me yet in Vermont. They seemed to get together with their mother a few times a year but, with me, not so much. I accepted it for what it was. I didn't like it, but it was reality. We made small talk for a few minutes and then we said our goodbyes. It was nice to hear from him, but it was strange at the same time as we no longer knew enough about each other's lives to really get into a good conversation. I was actually a little depressed after getting off the phone.

I attended to my chores that I wanted to get done and then took a few minutes for myself. I poured myself a robust porter beer and sat outside for about a half hour just relaxing and taking in the clean, fresh Vermont air. Although I really had no idea when Hope would return from her day at the hunter safety course, I thought I would prepare one of her favorite dinners for us that night. So I went to the kitchen to prepare. I first took out a backstrap of venison that I had thawed and seasoned it on all sides and put it back in the refrigerator. I then cut up an onion, cleaned and cut about a half pound of button mushrooms, and washed and cubed four potatoes and immersed them in water, so they wouldn't brown. Now all that was needed was to sauté the onions and mushrooms, boil the potatoes and later mash them with a little milk and butter, and put the venison on the grill. It was time for another porter.

A half hour later, Hope called me to let me know she was on her way home. She had had a marvelous day and was excited to tell me about it all over dinner. She had accomplished her goal of passing the course and did it handily. Forty-five minutes later, she pulled into my driveway. I met her with a glass of pinot noir. Hope smiled from ear to ear. We toasted to her success and walked to the porch hand in hand. I started the grill and began boiling the potatoes. After putting the venison on the fire, I returned to the kitchen to sauté the onions and mushrooms. Hope was tired, I could tell, but at the same time ecstatic over what she had accomplished.

Upon sitting down for dinner, we toasted once again to our future hunts together. The venison melted in our mouths, and the meal was just what Hope had wanted. It topped off her day of shooting shotguns, rifles, and handguns safely and showing her instructors how proficient she had become. She had been the only female in this class, unfortunately, as women, when instructed properly, can hunt and shoot just as well if not better than men. Hope had proven that. I was proud of her!

We both kicked back after dinner, and Hope continued to tell me about her day. She had been given the chance to shoot a variety of guns, from little .410s to 12-gauge shotguns, semiautos, pumps and over-unders, a .22 rifle, a .223, a seven-millimeter, and a .30-30 and

— No Reason —

.30-06. Handguns ranged from .22s to .38s, .357s, and a .45. Hope's worst nightmare was apparently shooting a Smith .44 Magnum. The recoil after two shots was all she had wanted to punish herself with, and she politely let her instructors know it.

"I had braced myself knowing what I thought I was going to feel but really had no idea how much I was going to get rocked by that .44!" Hope told me. "And then stupid me, I went and fired a second shot! I really don't need a gun that big, I don't think. Unless maybe I'm going after an elephant—and that ain't going to happen! I managed to hold on, opened the cylinder, made the gun safe, and gently put it down. I thanked my instructor and he laughed."

I smiled and let out a small chuckle. "You did the right thing. Everyone has limits. Some big hulking guy would have kept shooting and punished himself just to be macho. It is the kind of thing you have to get used to. You can't do it all at once, but if you wanted to, you could get used to it over time. But like you said, you have no real need to shoot such a large caliber gun."

We continued talking. I had switched over to helping empty the pinot noir, and we sipped our wine and nestled next to each other. Things were going well.

Chapter 43

Throughout the summer and into the early autumn, Hope and I continued to practice shooting in the woods behind my house. We both loved doing it and doing it together made both of us better. I could still outshoot her, but by the same token, she was damn good. For her birthday, I bought her a nice little Smith & Wesson .380 with which she immediately fell in love with. She handled it easily, and she was confident in using it. Even though Vermont isn't known for high crime, I thought it a good idea that Hope would carry it whenever possible. One never knew when it might just save a life. Plus, I always think it a good idea to carry a handgun when hunting as one bad slip or fall out in the woods coupled with the possibility of losing your rifle in the mishap could be the difference between life and death. Having a handgun securely holstered can make sure that you can signal to others your location in the case of injury. Even having a cell phone is not as sure as a handgun. Sometimes, there is just no signal.

A few weeks before deer season, Hope and I purchased our hunting licenses online. We also began taking walks in the woods, scoping out new territory and visiting my old haunt, where I had scored the nice buck the previous year. We loved being in the woods. We loved being with each other, and with each sojourn into the forest, we were becoming more and more one with the animals, plants, and nature. Hope was learning to become very quiet, even when the forest floor crackled with dry leaves. I showed her that hunting was not a marathon, where the finish line was in sight, but instead sometimes it was more of a snail's crawl where movement could not even be discerned by the sharp eyesight of a deer or heard with their radar-like cone-shaped ears.

No Reason

Work also continued. My place of business was about to shut down for a week once again in honor of deer season, but this year, I was going to get paid for it! What could be better? Hope had scheduled a week of vacation from the bank. I really didn't care whether I connected with a deer this year, but I wanted Hope to have the thrill of bagging her first buck.

Opening day dawned with clouds and rather warmish weather. There was no snow, nor was any expected until possibly the middle of the week. It would make hunting a bit more challenging but keep it interesting.

Hope and I headed out midmorning. We covered ground slowly, keeping about twenty-five yards between us while traversing up the mountain to the upper fields, where I had shot last year's buck. We saw nothing, but in all honesty, the deer had the upper hand as even traveling as slowly as we could, we couldn't help but announce our presence with each footstep. It was noisy!

So we decided to find two good spots to sit and wait for the remainder of the day. I dropped off Hope at what looked like a good stand overlooking the same field I had been successful with the previous year when Hope accompanied me. I went about two hundred yards further into the woods to Hope's right and found an open bit of forest that gave me a selection of up to about seventy-five yards of shooting lanes. I adjusted my scope for about that distance and sat on a large, downed tree.

Birds flitted by every now and then. I did see a small mouse or vole, I couldn't tell which, run by in the leaves but saw nothing else. A half hour before dark, I began making my way toward Hope. I soon found her sitting where I left her, but she was paying no attention to my approach. I slowed my already slow pace. I looked and listened. Nothing. I took a few more measured steps and stopped again. Hope continued to stare in the opposite direction, and I froze. Finally, I saw what had Hope's attention. A small doe had grazed within about fifty yards of her but was in a depression in the field where I could not readily see. I waited with Hope to see if a buck would follow. None appeared, but the cloak of darkness continued to fall, and I finally broke ranks and walked up to Hope.

"I hope I didn't scare anything off for you," I began. "But we had better get out of here before we begin to run into trees in the dark."

"No, no, you were fine. There was only that small doe which I assume you saw. I was just hoping for something bigger with horns! Oh, well. It's getting really dark and now past legal hunting, I'm sure, so let's get out of here."

With that, I led the way down the mountain as it progressively became almost too dark to see where we were going. Then a shot rang out! I instinctively crouched down, as did Hope.

"What the hell," I whispered. "That couldn't have been two hundred yards away and way too dark for a shot—unless someone is jacklighting deer! Let's slow down and angle off this way a bit and stay away from whoever is over there."

Hope agreed. "Let's not get shot today."

We finally made it out of the woods and back to my Jeep. With guns unloaded and safely put into their cases, we climbed in and drove toward my house.

"Not a very interesting day," I said, "but interesting nevertheless."

Hope knew what I meant. "Yep. Outside of seeing that small doe, nothing really happened all day. But then that shot was more than a little concerning. Nobody should have been shooting that late, right?"

"Exactly," I responded. "Either a gun was fired accidentally, or someone was poaching deer. In either case, not good. Now if we heard three shots spaced evenly and then another three shots spaced evenly, that would have meant that someone was in trouble, and in that case, we would have tried to help. But one shot means something totally different. And that's why I wanted you to have the handgun on you, so if you did get lost or injured, you would have a gun on you that could be used to signal for help."

As we drove, we planned for the next day's hunt. My theory had always been that deer are on a two- to three-day cycle, and if they do not show up one day, there is a better chance for them to appear either the following day or the day after. If they don't appear or show any signs of appearing during that time, chances are deer are not frequenting that territory as often as needed to be successful. It would be time to move on.

After arriving home and getting out of our hunting gear and cleaning the guns, I poured a glass of wine for each of us. Hope used the bathroom to take a shower, and I followed after she finished. I was taking her out for dinner at one of the local restaurants to both celebrate her first day of hunting as well as maybe hear some of the scuttlebutt from other hunters.

As we walked into the restaurant, I noticed a pickup truck that looked like one I had seen about a half mile from where we had parked for hunting and that we passed on the way home. Looking around the dining room, I soon figured who owned the truck. Three out-of-state hunters were sitting at a table, drinking beer and being loud. They still had their hunting clothes on, and one had what appeared to be blood on his sleeve. They continued to make noise and, after listening to them, learned that they were indeed celebrating bagging a deer late in the day. Apparently very late in the day!

About ten minutes after we sat down, I couldn't help it. I excused myself from the table and walked over to where the three men continued to cause a ruckus.

"Excuse me," I began, "I guess you gentlemen had some success today hunting. Congratulations. I would just ask that you try to contain yourselves a bit as there are others here trying to have a nice quiet meal, not to mention that there is a family over there with young children who don't really need to hear your language." I smiled and began walking away.

"Who the fuck are you to tell us what we can and can't do? Go sit down and leave us alone, or better yet, leave if you don't like it! We have every right to drink and celebrate here! Nobody else is complaining!" shouted one of the three.

I looked at Hope. She was motioning me to leave with her. She didn't want to get into it with these three. Nor did I, but I would if need be. Instead, I put a twenty on the table to pay for our round of drinks, and as we had yet to order any food, we left.

The last thing I heard as we walked out was laughter from the three as one of them said, "Good riddance, asshole."

And then another of the three added, "But the bitch he is with is a keeper!"

As I slowly turned around, Hope pulled at my arm. "Let's just keep walking," she said.

Walking back to the Jeep, Hope kept her hold on me until I opened the door for her.

"Well, where do you want to go from here?" I asked.

"Why don't we just go to my place, and I can cook something."

"No," I said emphatically. "I want to celebrate your first day of hunting and don't want those jerks to ruin our night. Let's try somewhere else."

"Well, we could go to the resort," suggested Hope sheepishly. "It is probably too expensive for those idiots to go to." She laughed.

I too laughed. While I hadn't expected to spend that much on dinner, I figured we both deserved it now.

I drove to the resort. We had a lovely, quiet meal. We commiserated about what had just happened, and I questioned whether or not these three were the ones who shot something in the dark. I knew their truck had at least been in the area.

Hope ended our talk about the three with "Oh, well. Hopefully, we will never see them again. Maybe they are here just for the weekend."

I could only hope as well, but knowing they were from out of state, I knew many hunters, or in this case "so-called hunters," traveled to Vermont for the week.

The next morning, Hope and I struck out once more for the high fields we were getting to know pretty well by now. With no real change in the weather, conditions remained similar to the day before. When we walked, we traveled about as slowly as we could manage, and it took a while before we decided to sit and wait. Again, I dropped Hope off at a likely looking spot near where we had been the day before, and I continued on finding a nice spot to sit about 250 yards from Hope. I not only wanted Hope to become independent with her hunting, but I wanted her to become comfortable being alone in the woods with no help in sight, even if I was just a couple hundred yards away. My goal was to build her confidence.

— No Reason —

We sat in silence, listening to the sounds of the woods. The wind began to pick up, and the trees in turn swayed with the gusts, creaking a bit more than I liked. I wondered how Hope felt about it. Nevertheless, we both stood our ground and continued to survey our respective areas for the movement of deer. Shortly after noon, two small does bounced into my view. They had no notion of me and continued on their path to my right, just fifty yards from my stand. I waited with expectation of seeing a following buck. It didn't happen. It just didn't seem like the deer were moving. We needed it to get cold to instigate the rut. And some snow and less wind would be very nice as well.

At about three thirty, I decided to visit Hope and let her know I was going to circle around and hopefully push a deer or two toward her while she continued to sit. She had seen nothing all day but a few songbirds. Wanting to keep her interest up and not wanting her to begin to get discouraged, I hoped I could push something out for her.

After circling a good hundred yards or more, slowly, I began to enlarge my circle and not care about the noise I was making in the dry leaves. I walked with purpose, not fast but didn't try to hide the fact that a human was rambling around in the woods. Twenty-five minutes later, I knew that I was once again approaching Hope's stand. All at once, three deer got up from their beds not one hundred yards from where Hope sat and exploded into the woods running toward Hope. I stopped and held my breath, wishing to hear a shot from her .30-30. There was only silence.

Ten minutes later, I approached Hope.

She was smiling. "Well, thanks for that," she said. "At least I got to see some deer today, even if they were only does. I can't believe they were that close to me all this time just hanging out until you pushed them. And I'm not sure I would have even been able to get a shot off if one had had antlers. They were moving pretty quick!"

I snickered a bit. "It all just goes into your memory bank of hunting. You can never let your guard down anywhere. Deer in the woods can magically appear and disappear when you least expect it. It's their woods. We are just visitors."

"You got that right," Hope agreed.

As we began to wend our way down to the Jeep, I was extra cautious after hearing the late shot the day before and made sure we were exiting the woods by the time dark really set in. As we drove off on the back road we had come in on, a good-sized six- to eight-pointer crossed into my headlights ten yards in front of the Jeep.

"Where were you today?" I muttered.

Hope laughed. "Anywhere we weren't apparently!"

"But at least it's good to know that they are around," I added. "I'm confident we will catch up to one soon."

I could only hope. I wanted to keep positive for Hope's sake and not let her become discouraged at all. I had always professed that nothing breeds success like success. And so far, we had had none.

Hope cooked that evening. She put together a nice meat loaf with baked potatoes and brussels sprouts. Very simple but great comfort food. We both decided on a good dark porter beer to accompany her efforts. During dinner, we talked about the day's hunt and how she felt about being somewhat on her own in the woods.

"I'm pretty good with being alone. I know you are near if something ever happened. It's just that what if something ever happened to you and I wouldn't necessarily know where you were? What if it was dark? What would I do then?" Hope queried.

"That is what we have our cell phones for," I replied. "While I hate using them in the woods, I certainly do not want you to feel abandoned or concerned if I do not show up when you think I should. There could be a multitude of reasons for me not showing up, but again, when in doubt, by all means, call."

"I would just hate to have your phone go off just as a deer approached you," she replied.

"So would I." I laughed and added, "But you need to feel secure about everything that is happening in the woods, and I am only too happy to make any sacrifice I have to, to make that happen" was my somewhat sarcastic answer.

Hope looked at me and chuckled.

The following two days were much the same as the previous days hunting. Nothing in the freezer to show for our efforts. We did manage to see a few deer here and there, but nothing that we could identify with antlers or that was within range. The forecast, however, was becoming more promising. A cold front was due to arrive by midday and snow was to be on its heels. Eight to twelve inches were forecast, a little more than we needed for sure, but balancing the fact that it might be a struggle to walk in that amount of snow, we would surely be able to track and remain silent.

The next day's temperature was in the teens. Snow began dumping just past noon. Hope and I were already in place in the woods. As we began to be covered in snow, the two inches that had fallen would be great to move in—quiet and allowing to show us any tracks to be new. I walked over to where Hope was sitting and motioned to her that we were going to start walking. She was more than willing to get up and move around, warm up a bit, and hopefully change our luck.

A half hour later, as we walked about twenty-five yards apart, we cut the track of what should be a good-sized deer, quite possibly a buck as it was alone and leaving large impressions in the snow. We began tracking. I motioned for Hope to stay on the path of the deer, and I moved off about thirty yards. I wanted her to become more knowledgeable about tracking and more comfortable with reading the tracks while still making sure that she knew all that was happening around her. We moved slowly but with purpose. We were within sight of each other often, and I made sure that she knew not to travel too fast as not only might that spook a deer, but between the snow, the temperature, and our warm clothes, I didn't want either of us to sweat. That would only lead to becoming colder.

An hour passed. Hope kept on the track of the deer, but we saw nothing. Snow was mounting even under evergreens in the woods. As we came up to a small stream, Hope seemed to hesitate. She looked over to me, and I slowly made my way to her.

"I'm a bit confused," she stated as I came close. "I'm not sure which way this deer went. There are a bunch of tracks before the stream and then they seem to disappear."

"Let me see if I can figure it out," I offered.

It looked as if the deer rambled around on our side of the stream for a while, possibly took a drink of water in the stream, and then from what I could tell, the deer traveled downstream for about twenty yards before it got out on the other side. Luckily, the stream was less than a foot deep anywhere. Nevertheless, I cautioned Hope to be very careful as we crossed on the more than slippery rocks. There was no future in swimming in the stream when it was so cold out. As I was almost out of the stream on the other side, I heard Hope sound alarmed as she let out a small yelp. She had slipped on a rock but managed to not take a plunge into the water. She was relieved to reach the other side as I held out my hand for her to hold onto.

We picked up the deer's track once again and moved on. The terrain began to get steeper, and the underbrush became thicker. This was not easy hunting. Ten minutes later, we stopped. I knew it would take us a while to get back to the Jeep, and I didn't want to be in the woods in the dark. It appeared the deer had won once again. The snow continued to fall as did the darkness. As we approached the Jeep, we both felt good even though we had not connected with bagging a buck. It was a good hunt. Hope had learned a great deal, and we were both tired from trudging through the ever-deepening snow.

As we drove home, we analyzed our day and planned for yet another day in the woods. By tomorrow, the snow would have stopped, and we should enjoy good tracking all day. We laughed a bit over Hope's almost dive into the water, but as I rounded a curve in the road, we both stopped our frivolity as we looked at an out-of-state truck on the side of the road. We both knew what we were looking at. It was the three musketeers masquerading as hunters. They were still not out of the woods, although it was now pitch-black. However, we knew they were still in the area.

"Damn," I uttered.

"My sentiments exactly," Hope chimed in and added, "How about us getting a burger for dinner?"

"Sounds good to me. We had a tough day out there, and we could use some downtime to relax and recuperate."

I drove to the local diner.

We collapsed into a booth and ordered burgers and fries to go along with two hot cocoas. Our only fear was that the three idiots might show up there. They didn't.

Chapter 44

The next day dawned sunny, bright, and cold. An almost ideal day for hunting. It had snowed about eight inches overall, but drifts could be found to depths up to two feet or more in some spots. Trekking through the woods would be slow and laborious but quiet and trackable.

I had arranged to pick Hope up at her place that morning, so she wouldn't have to drive in the still somewhat unplowed roads leading to my house. My Jeep managed the road with relative ease. After shoveling off Hope's porch before I entered, I knocked on her door and waited for her to open up. The latch sounded, and the door opened a few seconds later, and I walked in. Hope had turned and walked back to the kitchen as she was preparing breakfast, bacon, eggs, toast, and coffee.

"Thanks for shoveling the porch," she opened. "Thought I would make a nice breakfast to start the day and didn't get out there to do that."

"A small price to pay for getting such a gourmet meal," I responded. "Are you ready for a big day of hunting? I have a good feeling about this. Conditions should be very conducive to at least one of us getting a good shot at something. Maybe both."

"That is my wish. Wouldn't it be great to shoot something today? Voila! Here is your breakfast," Hope said as she turned to me with a plate filled with eggs and bacon. "The toast should be ready in a second…oh…there it is," Hope added as the toaster beeped at us.

I added two pieces of toast to my plate and sat down. Hope followed with a mirror image of my plate followed by two cups of coffee. Butter was already on the table.

We were on the road a half hour later. The scenery was gorgeous. Snow hung on every branch of every tree. Sun glistened on each snowflake, and most everywhere lay virgin snow, untouched by man or beast. I drove the Jeep hard into a parking spot to be sure the vehicle was not in the road. We uncased our rifles, put three rounds into each firearm, and began our slow ascent through the woods and up the mountain. I wanted to go back to the open fields near the top to do some sitting during the day and also do some tracking if needed. The new fallen snow would also enable Hope and me to separate even more than we had been able to up till now. As if she needed me, following my tracks would be easy.

Traversing the mountain, we cut the tracks on what appeared to be two small deer. Reaching the first destination, I dropped off Hope at a spot which offered her good views of the woods coupled with open shots of up to 150 yards in the field. I kept walking. Still traveling uphill, I stopped at another small field about what I figured was a quarter mile from Hope. I cleared a spot in the snow, found solid footing, flicked the safety off on my .30-06, and waited.

Chickadees flitted by, knocking snow from branches where they landed. A squirrel chattered high up in the forest canopy, and about an hour into my wait, a small red fox silently strode by me not twenty yards to my right. He too was hunting.

Another hour passed. Waiting wasn't working, and since we had great snow for tracking, I decided to walk back to where I had left Hope and try to pick up some fresh tracks from a good-sized deer in hopes that it was a buck and see if we couldn't get a glimpse of a future dinner. I slowly turned, engaging my safety once again. As I did, a shot rang out. It came from Hope's direction, but it didn't sound like a .30-30 to me.

The snow must be making the sound of her gun sound different, I thought to myself.

While cautious, I was at the same time elated to think that Hope might have just shot her first buck. I began making my way toward her, always with an eye toward movement ahead.

Before I took three steps, all hell broke loose! It sounded like a war. I knew the gunshots were not coming from Hope's rifle. I

No Reason

counted seven shots, maybe more, within the scope of about five seconds. I held my ground for a couple of minutes, waiting to see if deer would be running my way. Nothing appeared. I started walking with purpose toward Hope. Soon I stopped, listening intently. While faint, it sounded like people laughing and carrying on. I moved on slowly until I came to an opening in the woods, where I could begin to see into a small field which I knew was near to where Hope had been waiting. The talking and laughter became louder as I approached. Peering down into the field from my vantage point still in the forest, what I saw was almost unbelievable. I could count four deer lying dead in the field. But I could not see any hunters near them or in the field. I hesitated a minute. Laughter once again filtered through the trees, but now I heard the faint sound of a female voice. It was Hope, and it didn't sound like she was talking in a normal tone, rather one that was very anxious and nervous.

It was time for me to move—to find out what was happening. I cut into the field, walking past the four dead deer. As I did, I noticed that three were does with one being a small fork-horn buck. That was the only legal deer lying in the field! I picked up my pace through the snow, being still careful to watch for any movement or hunter-orange color that would denote another person in the woods.

I moved through the final patch of woods before approaching the spot where I had left Hope. The laughter and talking was now clear. It didn't sound good. I used a couple of pine trees as cover and looked out into the field. Midway through the field was another deer lying dead. But the real problem was I could not even see Hope. She was not where I had left her. I watched for a few seconds and finally saw movement. The talking and laughter was again getting louder. I homed in on the location. Just past the field, maybe ten yards into the woods, I saw what appeared to be at least three people, none of them wearing hunter orange but in normal camouflage garb. The laughter became louder and then I heard Hope screaming.

I began to run through the drifts in the field toward her. Adrenaline cursed through my body, and I didn't notice the depths of the snow. The laughter continued mixed with more frequent screams. As I ran by the buck in the middle of the field, I noticed it had good-sized antlers, but my focus was on what lay in front of me, not on the size of the buck.

Finally, coming to a small rise in the field, I could view the scene. Rage set in. Hope was pinned down in the snow with two of the three men on top of her. I could see them trying to rip off her hunting clothes. She was doing all that she could, but with one holding her arms down and the other trying to disrobe her, collectively they were trying to rape her!

Now being just fifty yards away, I yelled at the top of my lungs. I kept running. The two who were attacking Hope looked my way. The one who had held her arms down let go and lunged to the left, picking up a rifle that was leaning against a tree. I was in disbelief that hunters could be doing such a thing. Then I realized these were not hunters but the same three poachers we encountered at the restaurant earlier in the week. They were monsters!

As the one rapist raised his gun to his shoulder, I stopped, lay out prone in the snow, and leveled my gun at him. He pulled the trigger but had not expected me to hit the ground, and his bullet whizzed past me harmlessly. In turn, I steadied my crosshairs on his torso and fired. The impact of the 180-Grain Remington bullet hitting his chest sent him backward into a bush. The snow around him began to run red.

With that happening, the man still on top of Hope and who had had his back to me was now trying to get to his rifle. I had to ascertain which of the two men still standing was the biggest threat to me and to Hope. However, that decision was made for me by Hope. Little did the attackers realize that Hope carried her .380 Smith & Wesson inside her bib overalls. As the would-be rapist got off her and as he picked up his rifle, Hope managed to reach inside her overalls and extract her handgun. While still lying on her back, Hope took her gun off of safety, and I heard a shot and then another. Hope fired twice, hitting her assailant in the chest and the side. He crumpled to the snow, kneeling at first and looking at Hope in disbelief. He then fell forward, dead.

The third man now was hiding behind a tree not ten yards from Hope. I could see his rifle being raised to his shoulder and knew he was trying to take out Hope before worrying about me. Now kneeling on one knee, I leveled my .30-06 at him. Although I could barely see him due to the tree that he was hiding behind, I fired. It was enough to jolt him back and lose his aim at Hope. Bark from the tree flew everywhere. His final mistake was to stand and yet try aiming at Hope once again. Now Hope was in the process of trying to roll over and get in a position for a shot at this man. However, I made her escape attempt a moot point when again my crosshairs settled on this man's chest. I pulled the trigger. I blew out his heart in an instant. I instinctively reached into my pocket for another round and shoved it into my rifle and closed the bolt. I was unsure if there were more than three attackers and did not want to make the mistake of thinking all was well.

I yelled to Hope, "Are you okay? Are there more?"

"No. Just three. I'm okay." I could hear here panting.

As I approached Hope, I could see that I had been none too soon. Her overalls had been cut with a knife, and her shirt and thermals were cut and ripped. I could see her chest, although they had not yet ripped off her bra. Another minute or two would have been devastating. She arose from the snow and embraced me as I ran to her. We held each other forever!

Following our "forever" hold on each other, we both looked around at the carnage in the snow.

"What the hell happened?" I asked.

"Well..." There was a long pause. "I was just sitting here waiting for a deer to show up, and all of a sudden, shots rang out just a little over there. It sounded like a war. At first I thought it was you, but then there were way too many shots. So I waited and watched. Finally, that nice buck came running from the woods. As I was putting my gun up, the buck just dropped dead. I was a bit flustered by it all, so I let my guard down. And when I saw two guys coming out of the woods, I just figured they were in a hunting party that got lucky. I didn't recognize any of the guys and so when they saw me, they waved and walked over to me. It was only then that I recognized them, and they saw that in my face I'm sure. That's when one of them pushed me down, and I lost my rifle. He started talking trash, saying that I had better be quiet, or he would kill me and told me he and his friends were going to have some fun with me. They obviously thought I was alone and then the one guy held a knife to me and started cutting my clothes off. The other guy held me down. Meanwhile, the third guy showed up and kind of stood guard as the other two continued to attack me. They were laughing and calling to one another about what they were going to do with me and how they were going to take turns with me. I was so scared! And I couldn't get free until you showed up! Thank God you did."

"Okay, let's settle down now and make sure you are good to walk out of here," I said.

"Sure, I am," responded Hope. "But what are we going to do? Do we just leave them here and get out of the woods? What do we do?"

"Well," I began, "there are four other deer in the next field that I saw lying dead."

"Four?" Hope questioned. "My god!"

"Yep, four and then this one that made it to this field. Three of the deer are does and are illegal. And seeing how there were five deer killed and only three hunters, or more like poachers, they shot two too many anyway. These guys were just bad! And then they started attacking you and then trying to kill both of us! I would love to just leave them here to rot, but I would hate to get caught. No, I think we have to report what happened to the state police and to the local game warden and let them investigate. After all, we did nothing wrong and had to defend ourselves, or we would be laying in the snow instead of them. And one more thing. It would be a shame to let five deer go to waste. At least if we report this, the meat can go to feed some people in a shelter or something," I added.

"I guess you're right. It just seems like a lot to go through. I don't want to be looked at like we are criminals. But really, like you said, we were only defending our lives. And not for nothing. Between you and me, these three sons'a bitches deserved to die!"

"You all right?" I asked, thinking that Hope might just be in shock. After all, she had just killed her first human being.

"I am now, thanks to you." Hope sighed. "You shot two of the bastards, and I never would have been able to defend myself if you hadn't spent so much time with me teaching me how to shoot and what to do in an emergency, not to mention making me take my .380 with me hunting in case I needed a weapon. And boy, did I!"

"Yep. I guess you will be indebted to me forever now," I joked, trying to keep the situation as light as possible under the circumstances. "Okay, so let's walk back to the Jeep, collect ourselves a bit, and call the police and wardens," I said. "We can wait for them near the Jeep and show them the way up here, so they can do what they do. It's going to be a long day and night!"

We began walking down the mountain toward the Jeep. What was to have been an enjoyable day hunting had turned into a nightmare! I was still so angry, but moreover, I was concerned about Hope and wondered how a long-term memory of what had just happened would affect her. I wondered, too, if she would ever want to go hunting again.

A couple hundred yards from the Jeep, a large buck crossed our path. It would have been a relatively easy shot for me, but I figured that we had had enough excitement for one day, plus the fact that I really wanted Hope to shoot her first deer, and she had no opportunity for a shot with me walking in front of her breaking ground through the snow.

"I guess we'll leave that buck for another day," I said as I turned to face Hope.

She smiled back. "Next time," she responded.

I was encouraged.

Upon reaching the Jeep, we unloaded our rifles and placed them in the Jeep. I had Hope get into the passenger side as I started the engine, so Hope would stay warm. I dialed 911.

"Hello, what is your emergency?" the dispatcher asked.

I filled in the state police dispatcher on what had happened and where we were and told her that we would be waiting for them by my Jeep. I also asked that they call the Vermont Game Wardens who were needed as well. About ten minutes later, we heard a parade of sirens. Two officers showed up together followed by a third about one minute behind them. Together, Hope and I began telling the officers our story. In the meantime, more officers began showing up, followed by medical personnel. Within another ten minutes, two game wardens were on the scene.

The police and game wardens joined forces and inspected our rifles and took them into their possession as evidence. Forensics would have to clear us for not shooting the five deer but for defending our lives. They also took Hope's .380 and inspected my 9 mm, but as it hadn't been fired recently, they allowed me to keep it. We also showed them what had happened to Hope's clothing. She was not embarrassed by it at all, just justifiably enraged by what had happened. After assuring the authorities that Hope and I were both all right, we began showing them the way up the mountain.

Upon reaching the large field where Hope had been attacked, the policemen and game wardens were speechless. As they cordoned off the area and looked around and took pictures, they had us both separately explain what had transpired. Shortly after doing so, all seemed to agree as to what had indeed happened and how it had all unfolded. The tracks in the snow aided greatly in verifying our stories, which matched to a tee. I also took the game wardens into the further field where the other four deer lay in the snow. That, too, was clear to see what had happened with the aid of the new snow.

As it was getting dark, generators were pulled, pushed, and carried up the mountain by ATVs and manpower in order to give light to the scene. There was no question in either the state police's or the game warden's minds as to what had happened. Their real question was why it happened. After everyone was satisfied that the scene had been well-documented, the officers went in to find identification on the three dead poachers. Taking wallets from all three men, their names were called into headquarters, put through their system, and soon came back with hits on all three. To our amazement, two of the three were wanted fugitives! The two who were directly trying to rape Hope had escaped from prison in Montana while being transported to a hospital about a month earlier. They had both been convicted of rape and attempted murder there. The third man had also been in jail but had gotten out of prison a few months earlier. He had only been convicted of robbery and had served his time, although it had been shortened due to overcrowding.

When the state police checked the license plate on their truck parked at the base of the mountain, it was found to have been stolen out of New York.

"You two are lucky to be alive," one officer relayed to us both. "These were extremely bad men with nothing to lose. They apparently thought they were above any laws and were invincible only to be taken down by two law-abiding hunters and one of them a woman!" As soon as he said it, the officer knew he shouldn't have. "I mean, I didn't mean—"

"That's okay," interrupted Hope. "I don't suppose it's every day that you meet up with a woman that hunts and who knows how to defend herself. But really, I only managed to shoot one of them, someone else managed to get two," Hope said as she looked over to me. "And he taught me everything I know." Hope smiled and sighed at the same time.

Wanting to change the subject just a bit, I asked, "When do you think we might get our guns back? After all, neither of us has shot a deer yet."

All of the officers looked at each other and snickered a little.

"It will be a little while before our forensics team can clear them for you. Until then, you will have to use other firearms, I'm afraid," replied one of them.

"That's what I was afraid of," I said. "Oh, well, I have more." Then I turned to one of the game wardens and asked, "Can the five deer be butchered and given to a shelter or home of some sort so that all that meat isn't wasted?"

"We should be able to take care of that. All the carcasses will be kept cold until the meat can be butchered. Barring any unforeseen problems with this case, we should be able to have the meat used by soup kitchens or shelters," one of the wardens replied.

"Excellent, at least something good might come out of this," Hope chimed in.

"Although you might not want to think of it this way," an officer stated, "you both have been able to stop three very dangerous men who will never hurt anyone again. Your community should be thankful for that!"

The temperature could be felt to be dropping like a rock. Hope and I were escorted back to our vehicle and allowed to leave. The authorities still had a long cold night ahead of them. I didn't envy them their jobs.

The following day, one of the officers stopped by my house. He was happy to find Hope with me, so he could talk with us both at the same time. He explained that they had removed the three bodies of the attackers, and the game wardens had in fact been able to get all five deer carcasses down the mountain and felt that the meat would be salvaged for use at one or more of the local soup kitchens in the area. We felt good about that.

"Is there anything else either of you can remember about the incident that you didn't tell us yesterday?" the officer asked. "After all, I was amazed that both of you weren't in shock yesterday. You were both very coherent and calm, all things considered."

Little did the officer know what my background was with ridding society of bad people. Yet I, too, was amazed how well Hope was doing. She was a rock!

"No," I answered. "At least for me, I believe I told you my side of the story. It all happened pretty fast, and I don't know all of what happened to Hope firsthand. But of course, she could tell you that."

As I turned to look at Hope, she started by saying, "Well, I told you most everything yesterday. However, there is one more thing that I don't think I told you yesterday. When I was being attacked by the two men, the third man never actually participated actively. He more or less stood guard. But when he started shooting at us, we had to defend ourselves, and thank God we managed to win."

"I'm glad you two came out of this all right. You were lucky as well as prepared. If there is anything else either of you remember, please let us know. Here is my card. I hope you have a better day than you did yesterday." The officer left.

We looked at each other and smiled. We had both dodged the proverbial bullet. We had done nothing wrong.

We decided to take the day off from hunting, but we started planning our hunt for the following day. Hope would have to use one of my rifles that she was totally unfamiliar with, and I decided to break out one of my brother's old rifles that I hadn't used since he passed away and that I had inherited. It was an eight-millimeter Mauser. Not known for being terribly accurate, this particular gun had always been a nail tacker. Wicked accurate at up to 150 yards, just heavy to haul around all day. I told Hope we would go out in the backyard later and fire off a few rounds to make sure both rifles were good to go and to familiarize Hope with the new gun. She was happy to do so.

The next day broke with the sun peeking out from clouds for the first few hours. But clouds moved in again and covered any sun we had had earlier. The temperature remained in the midtwenties—what I considered good hunting weather.

After having a quick breakfast of bacon, egg, and cheese on toasted sourdough and coffee, we drove to where we normally parked. I was hesitant to trek up the mountain to where we had been two days earlier. I didn't want Hope to relive her attack. She, however, assured me that she was good and ready and willing to go back to the scene.

"I'm fine," she stated. "I would like to go back there to see what it looks like and to finalize getting it all out of my mind. I also want you to take me to where the other four deer were slaughtered, so I can put the whole thing into perspective."

"As long as you are all right," I replied. "If you feel queasy or bad about any of it, we can always go somewhere else or stay down the mountain lower and hunt. Let me know."

As we traveled up the mountain, I allowed Hope to lead the way. The tracks from all the people going up and down the mountain made it easy to walk on top of the snow, and should a nice buck present itself, Hope would have a clear shot. We walked in silence, slowly climbing the slope in search of movement ahead. I wondered how many more deer were local to this area as five had been unlawfully taken from it.

Upon reaching the field Hope had been hunting, we surveilled the area. We relived what had happened and walked to the spot where Hope had been knocked down and attacked. We saw blood in the snow where her two attackers had fallen and where the third man had fallen following my fatal shot. It was not pretty. We also walked into the field to see where the buck had fallen after being shot. I took Hope to the next field to show her where the other four deer had been shot. Hope began to cry. With my rifle in my right hand, I put my left arm around her and held her tight.

"It's okay," I said softly. "We don't have to stay here. We can go somewhere else or just go home."

"No!" Hope said emphatically. "I'm not upset about me being attacked or about killing those three assholes. I'm sad that five deer were slaughtered for no good reason! That is a travesty. Do you think more deer will show up here today with all of this blood still on the ground?" she asked.

"I'm not sure. Never had anything happen like this in my life," I responded. "It's up to you. Do you want to go somewhere else or sit here a while and see what happens?"

"Let's stay and sit for a while. But can you stay within sight today? I would feel a little better if you did."

"Certainly," I assured Hope. "Let's find a couple of good spots and sit, enjoy nature, and see what happens."

We did just that. We sat and waited.

I set up about seventy-five yards from Hope where we could see each other. I wanted her to be confident. After about an hour, two does walked by on the edge of the field. It was good to know they were still in the area after the carnage two days before. Besides a couple of chickadees and a murder of crows, all was quiet for the next two hours. I decided to gather up Hope and begin a slow decent off the mountain, still hunting our way down.

We walked about twenty-five yards apart, watching for movement ahead. As we began to explore the lower part of the mountain, I looked over to Hope. She had stopped. I looked ahead but could not see anything moving Nevertheless, I knew that when one of us stopped for whatever reason, the other stopped as well. I waited.

— No Reason —

A minute or so later, Hope raised her rifle. As she peered through her scope, I waited. I, too, readied my gun. Finally, I saw what Hope had been focused on. I raised my rifle to see the magnificent buck better. It was the same deer with the massive antlers I had encountered once before. This was going to be Hope's shot. The buck ambled in front of both of us. I estimated him to be big for a Vermont deer, maybe 225 pounds dressed. A tree cracked in the breeze, and the animal looked straight at Hope. He took a hard left-hand turn and disappeared.

I walked to Hope. She was standing there all smiles.

"Didn't you have a good shot?" I asked.

"No, I had a perfect shot," she answered. "I just think that he was so beautiful that he should be able to sire a whole bunch more deer, especially after losing five on the mountain. He deserved to live. He'll be around next year, I'm sure." She smiled.

I smiled back, proud of her and her hunting ethic. She was right. The deer in the area could use a shot in the arm, so to speak, after the poachers killed five deer in a matter of a few seconds.

We continued down the slope to my Jeep. After putting our rifles away and climbing into the front seat, we looked at each other, smiled, and kissed each other lightly.

We both started talking at the same time, but I stopped to let Hope finish.

"There has been enough killing on this mountain this year. We have both been through a lot! I can only speak for myself, but I think I can wait until next year to bag my first buck."

"That was just about what I was going to say too," I responded. "I would like to have meat in the freezer, but one year without it is no big deal. We can just relax for the rest of the season. Let's go back to the house, freshen up, and go out for dinner."

After thinking it over following the close of the regular deer season with the start of muzzleloader season, I decided to get out into the woods one time with my CVA and see if I couldn't track down a deer. It was a snowy Saturday, and I still hunted in the late morning near where all the killing had taken place. I was alone as Hope was working, and I had not introduced her to the intricacies of using a muzzleloader. The solitude was invigorating.

After reaching a good spot from which to watch and wait, I settled in. Snow continued to fall, and even though I was dressed in hunter orange from head to foot, I was soon camouflaged in white. Just before two o'clock, I saw movement about fifty yards from me. A nice fork-horn buck wandered out of the woods into the edge of the field. He sniffed the wind continually, either trying to find a doe that had not yet been serviced or trying to make sure he was safe. I was downwind. He had no idea I was there until I squeezed the trigger, the muzzleloader roared, and a cloud of smoke rose up through the snow. When the smoke cleared, the deer was nowhere to be seen. As I approached the spot where he had been standing, I saw that I had indeed killed the animal cleanly, and as he fell, he had slid back into a dip in the field. Now began the chore of dressing him out and dragging him out of the woods. But now I had venison for the winter.

Chapter 45

The following months flew by. Work for both Hope and I went well. After a while, townspeople finally began treating us as normal people, forgetting about how we "saved them from getting raped and murdered" by the three convicts. Hope had changed my thinking about things when she decided not to shoot the big buck. Had I been alone in the woods and had that buck in my sights, I would not have hesitated to shoot. But she was right—that buck would be better served to live another year and sire countless offspring. Now we were beginning to get ready for the upcoming hunting season.

On weekends, Hope and I practiced with our rifles. All our firearms had been returned by the police following their forensic analysis and all had checked out satisfactorily. And too, Hope's handgun had been returned. We both continued to challenge each other by seeing who could draw our pistols from their holsters and shoot our targets the quickest and with the most accuracy. Hope managed to best me about one out of every five tries! Sometimes, I wished I wasn't such a good teacher.

A week before opening day, Hope and I took a walk in the woods. We wanted to scope out the terrain and look for fresh sign of deer, tracks, scrapes, and/or fresh droppings. There was no snow yet. It made for easier walking, but it was a bit crunchy and noisy. We found a number of trails dotted with tracks, a few piles of droppings, and spotted three deer in the distance as well. All looked like it would be a good season ahead.

The following Friday, everyone at work wished each other luck in the next week. We would compare notes on the Monday when everyone returned to work. After thanking Chris as always for the paid time off, I was lovingly reminded about the previous year's hunt.

"Good luck this year filling your tag," Chris stated, "but please, this year, just stick to shooting at deer! No more shoot-outs at the OK corral!"

"That sounds awfully good to me," I responded.

Hope made a thick venison stew for dinner from the deer I had shot the previous year. As with everything Hope did in the kitchen, it was superb. We paired it with a bottle of Merlot and relaxed on the couch after dinner, talking about the next week of hunting. We were both in need of having Mother Nature envelope us in her wonders.

After eating a nice breakfast of eggs, bacon, and coffee, we loaded up the Jeep and drove off to our destination. I still wanted Hope to get a chance at that big buck we had seen. There was still no snow.

We took our time, as usual. Our goal was to be as silent as possible and limit the usefulness of the big ears on the deer in warning them of our presence. Still, we managed to make some noise. It was ultimately unavoidable. Sitting was the best option. I dropped Hope off at a spot near where we hunted the past year, and I took up a spot on a rock wall about one hundred yards further. She could see me, and I could see her, but we both had different areas to cover.

Soon, I heard rustling in the leaves. Then a grunt. Through the trees, a large black object lumbered forward. It was a bear! I had never been able to shoot a bear while hunting. I had seen one, one year, but it was busy running up a mountain with amazing speed and agility, and the underbrush it was busting through made it an impossible shot, not to mention I estimated the bear to be two hundred yards away and increasing the distance with every bound it was making. But now was a different story. It was bear season, and as the bruin walked closer, my heart actually began to flutter, something my heart used to do when deer hunting but no longer did. I was nervous. In fact, I never had this anticipation when I had done any of my other shootings.

At about thirty yards, the bear stopped. It scanned the terrain, but bears having poor eyesight couldn't see me, but I could tell its fine-tuned olfactory system had picked up my scent, and he didn't like it. He stood on his hind legs, making himself as large as possible and let out a loud "*wuff.*" He knew exactly where I was. In one swift motion, I raised the .30-06, aimed, and fired. The 180-grain bullet tore through his heart and collapsed the bear in an instant. The three hundred-pound bear never knew what hit him. It was a humane kill.

Hope had heard the "*wuff*" from the bear and had been on guard, not really comprehending what had made the sound. Following my shot, she walked slowly toward me until she saw the slumped animal lying on the leaves.

"Woohoo!" Hope yelled. "What did you just get? Wow, that's a bear! That's a really big bear!"

"You bet" was my retort. "He's a good size. I didn't expect to see one here today, let alone see one this big, but here he is."

As we both walked up to the bear, I made sure it was dead by poking at it with the barrel of my rifle. I didn't want to let my guard down if the bear was somehow still alive, especially when I would start gutting the bear with my knife. The bear never moved.

"Well, I don't know exactly how we are going to get this big boy out of here," I told Hope. "It's going to be a real challenge to get him back to the Jeep. Maybe it would be a good idea if you went back to the Jeep and see if you can find someone that could help. In fact, get a couple people if you can. In the meantime, I can gut him out and make him ready for his final trip down the mountain."

"Okay, I can do that," Hope said. "I will let you know when I find someone and be back as soon as possible. You do have a cell signal here, right?"

I checked my phone. My signal was good. I kissed Hope on the cheek, saying, "Be careful and watch out for strangers."

Hope knew what I meant.

I watched as Hope disappeared past the field's opening and into the woods. I began the task of removing the bear's entrails. It was a male. As I cut into its stomach, I could see a good layer of fat that had been put on in anticipation of the bear's impending hibernation. I looked at its mouth as well. It had a full set of impressive teeth in addition to massive feet complete with major claws. This had been a very healthy bear. I continued to work at gutting the bear, wishing Hope had been with me to help keep the stomach cavity open while

I pulled out the guts. Having to do it by myself, I finished looking like I had just taken a bloodbath, having my arms and chest as well as my head smeared with blood. I had taken off my hat as it just kept getting in my way, so my gray-streaked hair was now tinted red.

I sat back and waited for about ten minutes, after which I had the bright idea that I might be able to move the bear by myself. In fact, I could move the bear—about two inches every tug of the bear! After a minute of trying, I gave up. I would wait for help.

A half-hour later, my phone "*dinged*" me. I looked to find a text message from Hope saying she was headed back with help. She didn't say who or how many people she was bringing, but at least it would be help.

As I began to hear talking and heard crunchy footsteps, I saw Hope entering the field below me along with two men. As they grew closer, I recognized my boss, Chris, and a young man with him.

"Hey, Chris! Sure glad to see you," I said as they approached.

"Sure thing," Chris replied. "Hope here happened to cross our path as we were hauling out a nice little fork-horn that my son here shot."

"Congratulations," I offered. "Is this your first deer?"

"Yes, it is, sir," he answered as he smiled from ear to ear.

"Well, this is my first bear. And I'll bet getting this guy out of the woods is going to be a lot harder than you two experienced with your deer," I stated.

Chris answered, "I bet you're right! But we'll get it done one way or the other."

I had Hope carry my rifle while Chris, his strapping young son, and I pulled and lifted as we could. It was still a supreme effort to get the bear over deadfalls and a couple of stone walls. We were thankful when every now and then we hit an open downhill area. After almost an hour of sweat, the Jeep came into view. It was a welcome sight. Upon reaching the parked vehicles, we rested for a few minutes. As we did, we concluded that it would be easier to get the bear loaded into Chris's truck rather than try to stuff it into the back of my Jeep. Even doing that was a small miracle! As Chris and his son pulled the bear up the tailgate by the bear's front legs, Hope and I endeavored to get underneath the rear of the bear and lift up. I could feel my back straining and beginning to spasm when with a small groan from Hope, somehow, this little powerhouse was able to push just enough that we all got most of the bear over the tailgate and into the bed of the truck.

"Wow!" I gasped. "Dinner is on me! Couldn't have done it without you. I can't thank you enough!"

"Not sure about doing dinner tonight," Chris responded, "but how about sometime this week? We can celebrate two firsts—your first bear and my son's first deer! Mind if my wife comes to dinner?"

"Like I said, dinner is on me. I would love to have your wife join us. Hope will have an ally at the table," I joked.

"Do you think I need one?" asked Hope laughing.

"No, I really don't," I stated. "You seldom need anyone to stand by you."

"Oh, I don't know. I need you next to me," she responded.

We all climbed into our respective two vehicles and drove to the local weigh-in station. Chris's son's deer dressed out at 127 pounds. Sure to be a good eating deer. My bear weighed in at 268 pounds, a good indication of why we had so much trouble dragging the bear out of the woods. Chris drove the bear to my house, where we managed to hang it from a tree in my yard. After thanking Chris and his son once again, they drove to show Chris's wife their son's trophy. I was happier for the young man than I was for myself. But my nagging thought was still that Hope had yet to get her first deer.

To celebrate my good fortune of shooting a bear, Hope took me out to dinner after we had cleaned up. She decided on one of our favorite small restaurants serving really good Italian cuisine as well as exotic-type sandwiches. I chose a veal parmesan grinder with a side salad and glass of pinot gris while Hope went for a Caesar salad and wine. We toasted to a very successful hunt and then to an even more successful hunt for Hope in the near future.

Toward the end of our meal, my phone rang. It was Liz. We hadn't talked in some time; she was always on time with her rent money, and I had assumed all was good in Connecticut. I answered the phone with doubts.

"Hello," I began. "Liz, how are you doing?"

"Well, hello, stranger" was her reply. "I am fine, as are Dillon and my grandson! He is running around the house now, and we can hardly keep up! But what a joy! And Dillon is doing really well. He not only got himself a new job that pays well enough that he only has to work one job now, but he found himself a new girlfriend who is just lovely and who loves his boy as if he were her own. She is over a great deal, and we all get along wonderfully. And you—how are you doing?"

"I'm great! Hope and I are great! In fact, you caught us at the end of our meal out tonight in celebration of me shooting a nice black bear today. We have yet to get a deer but hopefully very soon. The signs are all good."

"That's great, congratulations!" Liz exclaimed. "Good to know you found someone that makes you happy and you spend time with doing what you love. That's why I called tonight. I knew that you would be out on opening day, and I wanted to touch base to see how you did. If you get down to Connecticut some time, please bring me some bear meat. I would love to make a stew with it."

"Will do, Liz. Hopefully sometime we can all get together for a nice dinner."

"That would be wonderful. I would love for you to meet my fiancé," Liz stated.

"Wow! There's the real reason for your call! Congratulations to you. When did that happen, and have you set a date yet?" I laughed while asking.

"We got engaged just two weeks ago, and we haven't set a date yet. But I wanted to let you know that I want to move out of your house in a month or two, but Dillon wants to rent the house from you if that is okay. He's making enough money now to afford it as long as you don't increase the rent on him, and we won't be far away to help him with his son and anything he needs help with here at the house."

"That would be great! You know I think Dillon is a great guy, and I would love to see him bring up his son in the house. It's a great spot for a young boy to grow up in. And no, I wouldn't think of going up on the rent. Dillon deserves to continue to live there."

"He will be thrilled with the news! Thank you! And that is for not only now but for everything you ever did for us, some of which I'm sure I don't even know about! I don't know what I or Dillon would have done without you. I will let you finish your celebratory dinner. Bye."

With the click of the phone, I turned to Hope and said, "The day just keeps getting better and better. There is nothing but good news from down in Connecticut, and we are having the time of our lives here in Vermont!"

"Yes, we are," toasted Hope as we raised our glasses and sipped our last drops of wine.

I filled Hope in on the conversation I had with Liz. All was good in the world.

The following morning brought snow. Four to six inches was predicted. Awesome for hunting. We set out for the woods at about ten in the morning, hoping we would be able to cross some good tracks on the way in. Twenty minutes up the mountain, we found one set of enormous tracks.

I was awestruck by their size. *This had to be the monster buck we had seen last year—or maybe an even bigger buck*, I thought to myself.

I didn't want to make Hope any more nervous than she might be by letting her know it was by far the biggest tracks I had ever seen. And I knew that she knew they were big tracks. But I don't think she knew exactly how big they were.

We continued on slowly up the mountain, following the tracks while keeping a watchful eye on the terrain in front of us. This deer had not gotten this large by being stupid. It was smart, knew every inch of the forest and fields, and knew every sound being made in the woods. Our advantage, at least for now, was that we could walk in silence yet follow the tracks easily.

We continued on progressing even more slowly as we were coming up to the first field near the top of the mountain. Hope was ten yards to my left when I saw movement ahead and stopped. Seeing me stop, Hope too came to a halt, looking at me and then to what was in front of both of us. We stood frozen for two full minutes. Nothing moved.

Then from behind a large pine tree that stood next to a gnarly old apple tree, I saw a flick of an ear—almost imperceptible. As I focused in on the slight movement, out of the corner of my eye, I could see Hope raise her .30-30. I had no shot, but that didn't mean that Hope didn't. I waited, almost not wanting to breath. Hope shouldered the gun and aimed, holding the gun up for what seemed forever. I knew she would start to waver and tire if she continued to hold like she was doing, yet I could do nothing about it. I had taught her all the right things to do and warned her of all the wrong things that could happen. She was on her own. I waited. She waited.

Another minute went by in the blink of a year! I was agonizing over the whole scene. Finally, the silence was broken by a loud snort! The big buck was on guard. He knew something was up but couldn't figure out what. The wind was not in his favor. We made no noise, and we hadn't moved a muscle in ages. Yet he sensed something wasn't right.

Finally I saw him take one step forward. I could now see his head, nothing else, just his head and his huge rack! I hoped he had stepped out far enough for Hope to have a decent shot, and I prayed that Hope had the stamina to hold her rifle steady for so long.

The lever action gun finally spoke as Hope squeezed the trigger. Then I heard her hurriedly lever another round into the chamber to await another shot. It never came. It didn't have to. Hope had dropped this huge animal in its tracks. It wasn't moving. Hope looked toward me. I looked at Hope and stifled a yell. I wasn't sure what had just happened until Hope lowered her gun and smiled.

"I think I got him," she whispered.

"Let's go see," I replied as we slowly walked up to the deer lying in the snow.

It was sixty paces from where Hope had shot. As we approached and got within a couple feet of the downed animal, Hope poked it with her gun. It only verified what we saw in the snow, a large pool of blood had turned the whiteness red. It was a clean one-shot kill.

— No Reason —

I spoke first. "Do you know how many points this animal has?" I asked with amazement.

"No, I haven't gotten that far" was the timid reply. "I'm counting. Am I right? I can't be right. How do you count the points? I count fourteen. Could that be right?"

"No, you're not exactly right," I corrected. "By my count there are fifteen points! What a monster!" I knelt down and pointed to each tip on the antler and counted with Hope.

I think it was then that Hope began breathing again! I laid my rifle against a nearby tree and threw my arms around her. We squeezed each other until our laughter finally stopped.

What a deer, I thought. "So now the real work begins," I stated. "You know what to do?"

Hope looked at me. "Well, sort of. I know what has to be done, but as far as doing it, I was kind of hoping that you would show me how. Will you?" she asked softly.

"No," I replied. "I'm not going to show you, but I will supervise and talk you through it. You will get greater satisfaction out of your experience if you do it yourself rather than have me do it for you."

"Okay then," Hope replied. "Let's get bloody. I know I have to start slicing down here, so we can get the entrails out. Right?"

"Exactly," I encouraged.

And for the next half hour, I tutored Hope in gutting out her first deer. She ended up arms deep in blood, and it wasn't easy, but when it was all done, she looked at what she had accomplished, and a huge smile crossed her face.

"Wow, that was an experience," she said. "It's actually easier shooting a rapist and criminal than shooting a deer—you don't have to mess with the criminals after they're shot," Hope said sarcastically. "Deer are actually something good that you want to bring home and be proud of, but people who are trying to hurt and kill you, I just want to leave in the woods to rot!"

I could tell this experience had brought out a bit of the past for Hope. She was still a little bitter, and rightfully so, about what had happened to her and what we had to do. At the same time, it was part of a healing process that Hope had stifled for a long time. She needed to get it out of her system.

"We have all had to do things in our past that weren't very nice at times, but nevertheless, they were things that needed to be done, either for our own good or for the good of others. As long as we are doing those things for the right reasons, we are doing good in the world," I emphasized. "When all is said and done today, Hope, you did good. You did real good! I can't tell you how proud I am and have been of you and what you have done. I love you."

"I love you too. Now let's see if we can drag this monster out of here," Hope added.

It took a while, but we managed to do it. We pulled together as much as we could, and at times, I took over and pulled by myself when Hope either couldn't or when I felt I could do it alone. Getting the deer into the Jeep was a chore too, but we finally managed inch by inch.

Arriving at the check station, a crowd soon gathered. Phones were out taking pictures and alerting hunters to the size of the animal Hope had bagged. There were many talking about a Boone and Crockett record. I hadn't said anything to Hope about it, but I was going to be sure to have the rack scored after the proper drying time to see what the rack measured at. I was sure I would never see another rack as big as this one anywhere in the northeast. Hope had once again turned into a celebrity in town. She seemed to have a knack for doing that. I made sure that I faded into the background. Hope deserved the fame, and I did not want it.

A couple of our friends followed us to my house after the weigh-in to help in hanging the deer. It was a struggle, even with four of us trying to handle the 230-pound deer!

I let Hope shower and clean up first after our escapade. I followed. Upon finishing in the bathroom, I found Hope asleep on the couch. She was exhausted. I was beat.

I nudged Hope awake. "How about I make a couple of grilled cheese sandwiches and we call it dinner?" I asked.

"Only if you slice some tomato on mine," she replied smiling.

"I think I can manage that."

It was like eating a gourmet meal. Comfort food. It was just all that we needed.

Sixty days later, I had arranged for an official Boone and Crockett scorer to measure Hope's deer. In order to be officially scored, the rack had to air-dry for that time. Without knowing exactly how racks are scored, I was sure this rack would at least get into the record books.

When the scorer first saw the rack, he stopped in his tracks. "This is one hell of a deer! I've never scored one this big. Wow!" he exclaimed.

Hope and I watched as the scorer methodically went about his chore. Many times, he obviously went back over his work to make sure he was being accurate. When all his measurements were completed, he took out his calculator and checked his work twice.

Looking up at us, he stated, "You, my dear, have the second largest rack ever taken in Vermont! The largest ever typical whitetail in Vermont scored 181. Your deer, I have scored at 179! Congratulations! You and your deer will go into the record books."

"My god!" exclaimed Hope. "I never would have even known to get this done if you hadn't done this for me," she said looking at me. She threw her arms around me and then we thanked the scorer for his process.

Two days after Hope shot her huge buck, I managed to down a nice six-pointer that had been feeding in a cornfield at the base of the mountain. It was an easy drag, and I needed no help, except I had Hope, who was now hunting for bear, carry my rifle for me. It would be excellent eating. We were both looking forward to a steady diet of venison for the next year.

Chapter 46

Over the course of the next few months, Hope and I made venison stew, venison meatballs, venison steaks and chops, venison burgers, and spaghetti with venison. Of course, we mixed in other foods, but we loved dining on the food we had hunted, including bear meat.

It was early May when Hope advised me that she had been picked to attend a conference on banking later that month. The bank manager should have been the one going, but she had a family wedding planned for that exact time, so she had asked Hope to go in her place. Hope was excited and agreed immediately. It was only after she had agreed that she found out where the conference was to be held—New York City!

Hope, like me, was not a city person. Rutland or Burlington was about as big as Hope or I ever wanted to go, but as she had already agreed with her manager, she felt obligated to attend on her behalf. After all, it would be only one day driving to the city, two days of conferences, and then driving back the following day.

I could tell there was some trepidation in Hope's voice as she told me about her trip. She was obviously nervous when she asked the next question. "Will you go with me to New York?" Hope almost whispered. "You could take a couple of your vacation days and go with me. I would feel so much better about being in the city if you were there too. You know I don't like cities, and I'm not accustomed to a city that large. I will be lost," Hope implored.

I looked at Hope.

She looked at me.

I really didn't want to go to New York City! Cities always confused me. They shouldn't have, but nevertheless, they did. I didn't like the chaos, the number of people, the garbage in the streets, the

— No Reason —

lousy air quality, the drunks and derelicts who walked the streets, and the always possible crime element. I was used to the country. Give me the woods, few people, clean air, and nature, and I was happy.

I caved and agreed to go with Hope. I had no idea what I was going to do there while she was attending conferences for two days, but if nothing else, I figured I could sit in our hotel room, relax, read, and scope out a good restaurant or two for Hope and me to eat at nights. And of course, I felt better about at least being in close proximity to her while she was there, not that I knew cities any better than she did.

Chris had had no problem with me taking a couple days off, so all was set for our trip to the city. The weather had warmed quite a bit, and the forecast was for sunny weather for our trip down and for nice weather the first day of Hope's conferences and for the day driving home. The third day had rain in the forecast, but there was nothing we could do about that.

We talked about the essentials we needed to bring and talked about how fancy we wanted to be when we were out for dinner. The first night of the conference also involved a reception that I could go to with Hope, so we had to dress up like bankers for that event. After we had pretty much decided what we both needed to pack, I brought up what I thought was going to be a somewhat controversial issue with Hope.

I began, "Hope, I know that carrying firearms in the city is prohibited, but I would feel a whole lot safer if I carried my 9 mm concealed while we were there. Like the old saying goes, better to be tried by twelve than carried by six! I would make sure I obey all the laws while driving or while in the city, but the fact that New York has these stupid laws against otherwise law-abiding citizens carrying a handgun is ridiculous. I would not feel safe there without my gun."

To my amazement, Hope answered with "I couldn't agree more! In fact, I was thinking about bringing my .380, and now you have just convinced me that I should. Thanks."

"Well, let's think about this," I hesitated as I spoke. "Me bringing my 9 mm is not a problem if I ever had to use it in New York as there aren't any prior ballistics on the gun anywhere, but the authorities have ballistics on your .380 as you had used it when you defended yourself from being attacked in the woods. It's the gun you used to shoot that asshole. Maybe we should find you another gun."

"That, my friend, is why I have you around! You think of all this stuff ahead of time. It would not have even crossed my mind. But I really hope I don't have to have a gun in the city to protect myself, but I didn't think I would need one in the woods either. Do you have another gun I could carry that I would be comfortable with?"

"Indeed I do," I answered with a grin. "As long as you wouldn't mind using a nice little revolver. I have a nice little Charter Arms .38 Special Undercover that I bought ages ago and hardly ever use. You could get used to that in a jiffy."

"Sounds good to me," replied Hope.

After work the following day, Hope and I met at my house and went out back to have her fire the revolver. She was a regular Annie Oakley. She would ruin anyone's day within about ten yards should they try to attack her. Beyond that distance was more of a guessing game, but beyond that distance, there is seldom need for self-defense. After picking up her target, we both walked away feeling happy and secure.

The following Thursday, Hope and I packed up her car for the trip down to New York. Hope wanted to drive from Vermont through Massachusetts, and she then wanted me to do the driving through Connecticut and into the city. I was good with all of that, except I had no yearning to be driving into the city itself. I would need a good navigator! That was going to be Hope's job.

After the fact, Hope did indeed do a good job of navigating us to our hotel aided by the navigation system in the car. Traffic had been lighter than expected all the way down as most of the traffic was headed north from whence we came. We checked in and got situated in our room. After looking at the menu in the hotel restaurant, we decided not to go out for the evening but to try dining in there. We were both a little tired from our trip, not that it was particularly long, but it was a little taxing on us both, especially the part where I had to drive with all of the taxis and confusion in the city.

Our dinner was lovely. We enjoyed a drink at the bar and then was escorted to our table, where we ordered another round and looked at the menu and listened to the waiter tell us about the night's specials. We decided to split a calamari appetizer followed by a small chef's salad. Hope's entrée was a beautifully presented pork tenderloin with garden vegetables while my dinner was a seafood dish featuring shrimp, scallops, and mussels over a bed of pasta and seasoned with just the right amount of garlic. We passed on dessert and took the elevator to our room.

The next morning, Hope was up at seven o'clock getting ready for her conference beginning at eight. Her day was scheduled to end at four, but then we had the bankers reception in the hotel starting at five and going until seven o'clock. After that, who knew? We had nothing planned.

Hope left for her conference downstairs a few minutes before eight. I tried reading but soon became bored. I began perusing magazines in the room for likely spots for us to eat in the evenings. While I had no idea where most of these restaurants were, I knew what I liked on their menu and came up with a selection for Hope and me on which to agree. For lunch, I decided on a simple burger with fries and a cranberry juice at the restaurant downstairs.

After lunch, I went for a walk, although not really keen on doing so. I decided to try to find a couple of the restaurants I thought might be interesting. Two of which were in fact fairly close to the hotel looked a bit ragtag from the outside and one matched the decor on the inside as well. The other would be acceptable. The third restaurant on my list was more blocks from my hotel than I realized, and I actually never did find it. New York had confused me again!

Upon turning around, I managed to take a few wrong turns but did realize my mistakes and made it back to the safety of the hotel. By four thirty, I was ready to accompany Hope to the reception, but as she had not yet come up to the room, I waited. A few minutes later, I heard the click of the door and she entered.

"Sorry I am late, but I had some great conversations with people after the conference and actually have hooked up with one of the gals with her husband in getting together for dinner after the reception tonight. If that is all right?" Hope asked.

"Of course, it is," I responded. "It is your deal here, and hopefully they know of a good restaurant nearby, rather than have me lead the way by brail."

Hope laughed. "Well, I hope so. The gal I met lives with her husband in Fairfield, Connecticut, and knows the city pretty well. I told her we would love to rely on their expertise."

Hope busily changed and got herself ready for the reception. I waited again. At five o'clock, we began our way down to the hall. After donning name tags and being greeted by who knows who in the banking world, we found an open bar and ordered a couple drinks. We then sampled the hors d'oeuvres. Pigs in a blanket, large bowls of shrimp with cocktail sauce, cheeses from all over the country, scallops wrapped in bacon, quiche, and more. It was quite a spread! But then again, these were bankers we were talking about.

After speaking with a few people Hope recognized from the conference during the day, she finally spied her new friend and her husband. Walking closer to them, they too saw us and met us halfway. Hope introduced me to her new acquaintance, Shelley, and then she introduced me to her husband, Richard. We began our conversation. They seemed nice, and I wanted to feel them out on their level of gourmet acuity as I have never trusted many people who recommend restaurants. After bantering back and forth a bit, I was somewhat satisfied as to their knowledge of food. We agreed to have them pick the restaurant and planned to meet up with them toward the end of the reception. We parted ways for the time being and wandered off to meet other people.

At seven o'clock, people began filtering out of the reception. We found Shelley and Richard and walked out together. They had made reservations at the restaurant they chose, so we were apparently on time for our table. It was going to be a fair walk, but we all agreed not to hail a taxi. Richard assured us it was a walk that goes through good neighborhoods, although I had to restrain myself from commenting on how I felt about the city on the whole. We took a twenty-minute walk.

It was a lovely dinner! Hope and I shared a stuffed mushroom appetizer and then she had veal piccata while I dined on a terrific pork shank with an al dente vegetable medley. Our conversation throughout dinner was enjoyable as well. They were fun people. Following dessert, Hope and I split a piece of red velvet cake. All four of us then walked back to our hotel. Thankfully, Richard and Shelley knew the way as Hope and I would have gotten lost in the darkened streets. Everything looked different than during daylight hours. I secretly yearned for the comfort of the woods.

The following day, Hope began her day as the one before had started. She got herself ready and took the elevator down to the conference. During the day, I amused myself reading and spent some time watching people in the lobby. I had picked out the restaurant I wanted to try that night, but again, I hadn't been there. I found it was in the opposite direction than where we had gone the previous night, and with us not knowing the city, we had no idea how bad or good the area was going to be. We were soon going to find out.

After finally getting bored watching people in the hotel lobby, I decided to ask the concierge for directions to the restaurant I wanted to go to on our last night in New York.

Upon telling him where we wanted to go, he looked enthused for us. "That's a very, very nice restaurant! I recommend it all the time. It is about six blocks from here and then down one of the side streets. You can certainly walk it or hail a cab if you prefer. Would you like for me to make a reservation for you?"

"That would be great," I responded. "And you don't suspect there is any problem walking in that direction or coming back later at night from there, right?"

"Oh, no, sir" was the firm answer from the concierge. "It's pretty safe around here all of the time. Very little crime. No, you are very safe."

Safe until you're not, I said to myself.

As I waited for him to confirm a seven o'clock reservation time, I thought how assured I was by having my gun on me in the city.

After being put on hold, the concierge looked up at me and said, "They are totally booked tonight until eight thirty. Will that be all right with you?"

Considering for just a second or two, I responded, "Yes, let's do that. We can have a drink in your bar before dinner."

Although later than I really wanted, it would allow Hope some time to unwind from her conference, give her time to tell me about her day, and allow me to tell her about some of the more interesting people I had watched during the day. I walked away from the concierge desk satisfied and encouraged that I had made a good choice for dinner. I also left what I thought was a well-deserved tip for the concierge.

Hope walked into our room at about five thirty, apologizing for being later than she had expected and asking how much time she had to get ready for dinner. She was pleasantly surprised that our reservation wasn't until eight thirty as I watched her "motor" downshift into a much slower drive.

"Oh, well, in that case, we can relax a bit, and I can take a shower and dress a little more leisurely than I thought I was going to have to," she said.

"Yes, we can" was my simple response as I smiled at her and gave her a kiss. "I love you, you know!"

"And I you!"

A few minutes after seven, we were on our way down to the hotel bar. We decided to grab two open chairs at the end of the bar, allowing us a good view of everyone coming in and leaving. It also allowed us to strike up a bit of a conversation with the lady bartender serving us. After a little banter back and forth, she asked what we were doing in New York and where we were eating later. Hope responded to her, telling her she was with the banker conference, and she allowed me to tell the bartender where we were going to eat.

"That's a fine restaurant," she said. "Good choice. When is your reservation for?"

"Eight thirty," I responded. "So I figure we should leave here five or ten minutes after eight. Sound right?"

"Yes, that should work for you. But let's see, I'm going to assume you will be dining for at least two hours, maybe close to three. That gets you out of there between ten thirty the earliest and eleven thirty.

— No Reason —

That's getting a bit late to be walking in that area of town. I would take a cab if I could—just to be safe."

Sounding a bit more ominous than did the concierge earlier, I took note of her advice and thanked her for her input and concern. Hope looked at me, and I looked at her.

"We'll call a cab," I assured Hope.

She smiled and we toasted to a safe return to Vermont. We were both of the mindset that Hope's conference had been beneficial to her, that the food we had found had overall been wonderful, but we agreed that neither of us ever wanted to be around this many people ever again. We had so much in common that we laughed at it all.

After getting our fill of watching the hotel staff deal with all kinds of people, some extremely nice and understanding about waiting times, lack of available seating—even in the bar area—we also observed contentious, self-righteous customers who came in demanding to be served and serviced faster and better than anyone else. There were just far too many obviously important people in the world! Sickening. We admired the flexibility the hotel staff had to bend and not break under such tension. And to think they did this day after day! What a way to live. The money wasn't worth it all in our humble opinions. But after all, who were we? We were the ones giving up our two choice bar seats to a nice young couple who had been pushed around in the bar area for the past ten minutes, trying not to spill their drinks all over themselves. They were not city folk either and both thanked us profusely. I left a generous tip for the bartender upon our departure from our places at the bar.

As we walked toward the restaurant, I made note of street signs and landmarks on the way. I also made sure to stop and look back from where we had come to be sure I could recognize landmarks on the way back from the restaurant should we need to, although the cab driver should make all that a moot point.

I felt like an owl. My head was continuously swiveling around, trying to watch in every direction as we walked. I didn't trust cities; not like I trusted the woods. Hope, too, I could see, was attempting to become more of an owl as well. She was cautiously looking around, and I could feel her becoming tenser as we passed closely by people and groups on the street. A minute before our reservation time, we spotted the sign for our restaurant. We had arrived. The small facade of the building gave way inside to a very large dining room with a couple more private dining areas off to one side. The long bar was nestled in on the opposite side of the room.

Shortly, we were greeted by a young hostess who looked up my name and followed up with an apology that they were running about ten minutes behind, but she assured us our table would be ready in that time. We understood. We waited. Ten minutes later, we followed the hostess to our table near a corner in one of the side rooms. It was a little quieter and nicer in this room than being in the large main dining area. Here we could actually converse in a normal tone rather than raise our voices or strain to hear in the main room.

Upon being served our drinks, two margaritas, one with salt and mine without, we both sipped and perused the menu and specials. I hadn't had escargot in a long time while Hope chose a simple shrimp cocktail for an appetizer. Both were served elegantly and done to perfection—the escargot having the proper garlic taste they should, and the shrimp being done just right so as not to be rubbery and complimented nicely with a tangy sauce.

Shortly after finishing the appetizers, a nice house salad was presented. We both chose the house dressing, which was a vinaigrette with chopped mushrooms and garlic. I had the waiter bring me a small side of bleu cheese dressing as well. The salads were awesome, crisp, and bright!

By this time, we changed over to a couple glasses of a lovely Grenache. We sipped, enjoyed our conversation, and digested while our main courses were being prepared. Our waiter soon served Hope. Her pork tenderloin, twice-baked potato, and asparagus looked fantastic. It was one of those things that people would take a picture of before they would start eating and then send it to all their friends and anyone else who would look at it all while the food was getting cold! We weren't like that! The presentation of my entrée was spectacular! Upon lifting the cover over the seafood and linguine plate, a small amount of Cognac was drizzled over the dish and lit on fire. The entire room watched. After just a few seconds, the flame died, and

— No Reason —

it was placed in front of me. The aroma was unforgettable. We both dug in. Just superb!

"You really hit a home run here," Hope said in between bites. "Sure glad this restaurant isn't near us in Vermont, otherwise we would be paupers, and both weigh about three hundred pounds!"

Of course, Hope had timed her comment to my taking a sip of wine, which I almost gagged on trying not to laugh. I thanked her for that.

Dessert was yet another matter. Every item on their menu looked great. Because we had indulged in everything else and been members of the clean plate club, we decided we would force ourselves to split something. The crème brûlée was much larger than expected but equally as awesome. It was a good decision to split dessert.

After refusing coffee or any more food or drink, we asked the waiter if they could call a cab for us. He assured us they would and offered us the check.

"Glad I'm not paying for this," I told Hope. "It's a mortgage payment," I joked.

"But we deserved it," she said.

Our waiter soon informed us that a cab should be arriving soon, so we could wait near the door. We got up and waited, watching for signs of a cab arriving. Ten minutes later, there was still no cab. Nor was there one ten minutes after that. We asked the hostess about getting us a cab again, and she promptly apologized and tried again.

Getting off of the phone, she began to explain what she had been told. "Apparently, two large conventions just ended, and cabs are all running very late tonight. They can't be sure when a cab might be here. It may be as much as another hour," she said sheepishly.

Hope and I looked at each other, and we knew what the other was thinking.

"I guess we will hoof it back to the hotel then," I said.

"Yep, that's how it looks," Hope chimed in.

Although we hadn't planned to, we felt we had little choice. We began walking. It was almost eleven thirty. We both agreed that we were headed in the right direction. In fact, after a block, I saw a landmark that I had remembered on the way to the restaurant. I was reassured.

As we were about to complete our next block, I stopped short to listen and held onto Hope's arm. Above the hissing of the vents and pipes of the buildings and in the streets, the occasional vehicular traffic and far-off sound of sirens, I heard what sounded like fighting. We moved forward slowly. Hope knew from our days and days of hunting together that we were both to be on guard and ready for anything. We approached a small side street. It was mostly dark. Hardly any light filtered down from anywhere.

We peered down the unlit street. Two people dressed in dark clothes were backed up against a wall. Three others appeared to be or were currently trying to beat them. They were forty yards away. Hope and I couldn't help it. We began walking toward them.

"Hope," I said. "Reach into your handbag and get a grasp on your gun and don't let it go no matter what happens. Don't show it unless I pull mine out."

She understood and acknowledged my instructions.

After a few more steps, we could see the fighting more clearly. The three men had the other two cornered. To my amazement, the two were New York City cops. Apparently, they had lost their weapons and were in deep trouble. In the faint light, a knife flashed in one of the assailants' hands. Then another. The third held what looked to be a bat. As they converged on the two policemen, the yelling got loud and the screams louder. No one noticed us until we were just ten yards away. By that time, the larger officer was down on one knee trying to defend himself but in obvious pain. He had been slashed across his arm and stomach. The other younger officer was trying to defend himself from the other two, holding up a garbage can lid in defense of another knife attack. It was no match for the bat, however. He soon lost that battle after receiving a blow to the shoulder, knocking him to the ground.

The first knife wielder turned to us. "Who the fuck are you? You want some of this?"

Hope and I separated. We had no reason to make an attack on us easier than it had to be. Then he noticed Hope was a woman.

No Reason

"Oh, man, this is going to be fun! Look who we have here. It's Batman and Catwoman! We're going to have fun with Catwoman. First let me take care of you motherfucker!"

As I drew my 9 mm, I thumbed off the safety. This attacker had to see it, even in the dark. The stainless gun was like a beacon in the dimly lit street. He kept coming toward me brandishing his knife, but when he was just three yards away, I fired.

He stopped, looking at me in disbelief. He uttered his last words, "Bat motherfucker!"

Now the other two had broken off and were charging toward us, yelling profanities. As the man with the baseball bat raised it to use on Hope, the little Undercover shot flames and stopped the assailant but only for a moment. The man was most likely high on something, and a .38 special isn't always going to stop someone like that with one shot. Hope pulled the trigger again and again. All were direct hits. The bat fell from the assailants hand, and he fell on top of it. In the chaos, the third man was trying to locate one of the officers' guns that had been stripped from them. When I saw him finally pick up the weapon, I let go with a barrage of three shots. He was but seven yards away. My first shot hit him in the shoulder. The second in the stomach, and the third hit him in the throat. I admit, he had made me angry!

The city grew quiet once more. Only the sounds of pipes hissing, traffic, and occasional talking could be heard, along with groaning coming from the two police officers. A few passersby on the main road never stopped, even when they heard gunfire. They didn't want to get involved and wanted to get away from any situation with which they might not be comfortable. Although it was a sad commentary on life, I was fine with it for the moment as hopefully it would allow Hope and I to flee the scene unnoticed.

The two officers were on the ground in pain. I ran to them and tied my handkerchief around the arm of the first wounded officer as a tourniquet. His arm was in worse shape than was his stomach. The second officer had a head wound that was bad but for which I could do nothing.

What I did do was click the officer's radio pinned to his shoulder and yelled into it, "Officer down! We need an ambulance. Two men down."

I figured they would have police there in a matter of minutes just homing in on where these two officers were on duty. We needed not to be there.

"Time to go, young lady," I said to Hope, making sure I didn't mention her name. "You okay?"

"Couldn't be better" was Hope's retort. "Sure wish we could do more for these two policemen."

"We already did," I assured her. "Now let's just walk, fast!"

We made it a block down the street when we heard NYPD cruisers screeching to a halt at the scene of the attack. The wailing of ambulance sirens soon followed. Our prayers were with the two men in blue. We didn't know what had brought on the attack, but we did know what had happened as a result.

The night hadn't turned out quite like we had planned, but then again, maybe it had turned out better. Hope and I had shared a great meal. We had saved two policemen's lives. We had eliminated three criminals of some kind or another. They would never harm anyone again. And we had walked away unscathed and undetected. Hope and I hated cities more than ever!

A few minutes later, we strolled into the hotel.

"How about an after-dinner drink?" I asked Hope.

"I think we deserve one," she responded.

I really loved Hope's attitude!

As we walked into the bar, there were our new friends, Shelley and Richard. We sat with them and enjoyed our drinks, telling them about the lovely dinner we had just enjoyed. We skipped the part about the walk back to the hotel.

The following morning, we were up and on the road. The New York radio station we had on in the car was reporting on the previous night's attack on two of New York's finest. Over the course of the following week, we followed updates on the officers' conditions as well as found out more about what had happened to precipitate the

— No Reason —

attack. Apparently, the three men found dead at the scene were drug dealers aligned with a Mexican cartel. Not so much anymore.

Online, we found interviews with the two police officers as they gave their accounts of what happened that evening. Both policemen agreed that while walking their beat, they heard suspicious sounds coming from down the darkened side street, prompting them to investigate. As they slowly walked down the street surrounded by dumpsters and garbage cans, they remember getting blindsided by someone with a baseball bat. As the younger officer went down, he tried taking out his pistol but lost it as he fell. He then found a garbage can lid with which he used to try to defend himself. Meanwhile, the bigger officer began drawing his gun but was slashed in the stomach and arm and could not complete extracting his gun from his holster. When he went to his knees, he too lost the gun he carried.

The following quote by the second officer was for Hope and me, somewhat amusing yet sad at the same time: "Two people came out of nowhere to save me and my partner. I don't remember it all that well, but I do remember one of our assailants saying that it was Batman and Catwoman coming onto the scene. It was too dark, and I was in a haze from my wounds. I do know that if it was indeed Batman and Catwoman, that they both saved our lives. I hope they stick around the city for a long time!"

The other officer added, "Without their help, both of us would be dead. Their use of deadly force with a gun, or guns, saved our lives. We all know that carrying a gun in the city is against the law for the most part, but maybe that law should be revisited after what just happened to us. We are both so grateful, and we would like to thank both people for their saving our lives. Whether they were just regular civilians doing the right thing or they were Batman and Catwoman, they made the city a safer place."

Hope and I smiled at each other. It was a good feeling to know that we had saved two of New York's finest. Of course, we both wondered how the New York mayor and other politicians would take the fact that the two officers were saved by two people using handguns in their city and talking about it! In the city, guns of all kinds are supposed to be bad and have been villainized for years. However, I have never known a gun to go off by itself nor with proper training has one been used by a law-abiding citizen for ill purpose. Had Hope and I not been carrying, I'm not sure we would have ventured down that side street, and we would be reading two obituaries instead of reading about three drug-dealing would-be murderers who were taken off the streets by possibly two superheroes! Maybe just that thought might keep a few more of the city's criminals at bay and cautious for a bit longer. Probably not—but a nice thought anyway.

Hope and I settled back into our normal routines. Both went to work each day. We spent as much time together as we could. We enjoyed cooking and eating together, and we enjoyed the shooting sports. Hope regularly carried her .380 once again, and I still had my 9 mm hidden from sight yet quickly accessible. We once again began practicing with our rifles for deer season, and I also purchased a nice little trap for throwing clay targets, so we could enjoy more shotgun time. It was all for a reason: life, freedom, and the pursuit of happiness.

As hunting season grew closer, Hope and I continued to hone our shooting skills. We met others in the area who enjoyed shooting as well, and we had friendly competitions every so often. Toward the end of October, we were invited by one of our shooting friends to attend a Halloween party they were throwing. We accepted. Batman and Catwoman showed up at the party! No one suspected our reason.

The end

About the Author

Laurence Ference is a native New Englander. Raised in Connecticut, he attended Cornell University, graduating with a BS in hotel and restaurant administration. He later moved to mid-state Vermont and now to Down East Maine. Having worked in all phases of the hospitality industry, he transitioned into a world-class cheese maker while living in Vermont. Prior to making cheese, Laurence worked in the firearms industry for twenty-three years in Connecticut. He enjoys most all sports, but hunting and cooking are his passions. Together with his wife, Joann, he enjoys the coastline of Maine, where they hunt and fish and spar over kitchen sovereignty.

Printed in the USA
CPSIA information can be obtained
at www.ICGtesting.com
LVHW041409271223
767436LV00060B/1272